ALSO BY MARY BRYAN STAFFORD

A Wasp in the Fig Tree

"Every so often, a great book comes along—one with an exciting story, full of twists and turns, one that pulls you into another world that you'd like to stay in for a while, one with carefully polished writing and real world dialogue. *A Wasp in the Fig Tree* by Mary Bryan Stafford is such a book."—*Story Circle* Reviewer Denise McAlister

The Last Whippoorwill

"A captivating family saga at the turn of the last century…gritty and sensual and poignant."—Cynthia Bowen author of *Proud Flesh*

THE
MUSIC
BOX

Mary Bryan Stafford

In collaboration with Jerrilyn Burrer McLerran

Happy Birthday, Sue!

Mary Bryan Stafford

Jerrilyn Burrer McLerran

High River Ranch Publishing

The Music Box

First edition 2022

978-1-7321682-5-1 Hardback
978-1-7321682-3-7 Paperback
978-1-7321682-4-4 ebook Kindle

Dedicated to the memory of the early settlers of Gillespie County, Texas, especially to the women, who were left at home to persevere despite difficulties and dangers. This story was inspired by Katarina Zammert Burrer and her sister Minna Zammert Langhennig, who lived and worked together on Katarina's farm while their husbands fought in the Civil War, Heinrich Langhennig for the Union and Gottlieb Burrer for the Confederacy.

ACKNOWLEDGEMENTS

Nobody ever writes a novel alone, and this book is no exception.

My writers' group and authors in their own right: Myra McIlvain, David Wilde, Elizabeth Crowder (my daughter) and Bob Holt happily nitpicked twice through the novel and found ways to improve it every step of the way. Regarding bees, Jodi McCumber, a local beekeeper, let me suit up and visit her bees. Ms. McCumber told me of her experiences, and I confess I borrowed her words, "I never felt closer to God." Evelyn Weinheimer, Archivist for the Gillespie County Historical Society, provided information essential to the story's outline.

Jerrilyn Burrer McLerran deserves a whole paragraph to herself. A resident of Fredericksburg, Texas and a descendant of the German families who immigrated to the Texas frontier, Jerrilyn dramatically influenced the development of this story. She read drafts of the novel many times over. She researched the quotes at the beginning of each chapter and held my feet to the fire regarding historical accuracy. Her suggestions changed the direction of the novel and made it better.

FREDERICKSBURG, TEXAS
1910

Dependent on a cane where once I skipped down the limestone bed of Wolf Creek, I shuffle along its banks turning up creek detritus—fossilized rock, arrowheads, remnants of Comanche wars. Graves, too, lie nearby. Still, it is a fond diversion, full of memories.

Beneath the drift from a recent storm, a glimmer catches my eye. Using my cane, I unearth a small metal box. My hands tremble as I whisk away muck from its floral design, its once gold-colored filigree.

It cannot be after all these years.

The small lever has to be prodded, but at last, it slips sideways, releasing a tiny mechanical bird. Its beak of bone is splintered, its metal quills tattered and dull, but I can still discern the painted-on feathers that had once been brilliant hues.

A hushed, heat-dazed afternoon half a century ago is upon me. What I hold is only a trinket, but it paid for our lives once. Now, there is no melody. The music is gone, but the story lingers—bittersweet, bittersweet.

CHAPTER 1

There are scattered forests, and in the midst of these, the sun-light shows up a village. That is Fredericksburg, the most prosperous settlement in Texas.
– Wm. Paul Burrier, Sr., Ed., *August Siemering's The Germans in Texas during the Civil War*

Near Fredericksburg, Texas
October 1861

Katarina

A rno's ears perked at the sound of the carriage's arrival, and he padded toward the entry. I held the door open as Günter's younger brother, Wilhelm, lighted down and offered his arms to his new bride.

Her auburn curls in only moderate disarray, she was a pretty little thing, fragile in her crinoline and bows. And young. Perhaps twenty years my junior. I guessed that annoyed me most—the smugness of youth. I tried to set my mouth right and not touch my own hair that was pulled back tightly revealing strands of gray streaking through the faded blond.

Realizing I was remiss, I stuttered, "*Willkommen.*"

The girl gasped at the sight of the dog but approached the porch with a nervous smile. With his resemblance to my husband and the same easy charm and swagger, Wilhelm smiled boldly as though he remembered me.

My husband closed the space behind me, and I felt his hand on my shoulder. "Well, move aside, Katarina, and allow them space to enter." Günter stepped past me to swing the door wide and embrace his brother. "Wilhelm! *Mein Gott*, you have become a man! And this lovely girl. Your wife, Eliza. No wonder you dallied so long in Galveston." He bent low over the child-like, dimpled hand she extended. With a sweeping gesture, he directed them into the parlor.

"*Ja, jawohl*," I murmured, at once inhibited by Günter's command of social graces. I envied his gift of generosity and ability to set his guests at ease. You could see how he affected Eliza. She fluttered and fawned with his attention. And she had yet to speak a word.

"May I take your bonnet, Fräulein…Frau Lange?" I asked before attempting a smile.

Günter slid the shawl from her shoulders. "I think we can dispense with formalities, my dear. After all, she is your sister by marriage. It is quite obvious to me that you must refer to her by her given name and she to yours, Katarina."

"Ma'am," Eliza said, looking directly at me. "Yes, please call me Eliza. I would be most charmed." She spoke with a butter-soft accent and offered both hands. For the first time, I saw an aptitude for seduction that might overtake the gentlemen.

I steeled myself against the charisma. "As you wish. Cup of tea?"

"After their long trek?" Günter said. "I think not! Bring out the schnapps. Sit! Sit! Tell us of your journey."

As my husband took it upon himself to pour the liqueur, I sat and folded my hands at my waist to wait for my next instruction. Arno stationed himself beside my knee.

Wilhelm began. "We are happy to arrive here. Of that you can be sure." He patted Eliza's small white hand before giving it a little squeeze. "It was a long, arduous trip despite our frequent stops. We spent the night in Fredericksburg to rest and repair, but my bride is unaccustomed to such hardship."

I watched his mouth, his lips full and soft. Sensuous. Like Günter's used to be when we were younger. I missed that last sign of a man's springtime. Now Günter's lips formed a harder line, firm and sure. He was a full man, and I loved the man, but sometimes, oh sometimes, I missed the youth.

"Oh, as I think of it, can you have your man take the horses around to be fed and curried?" Wilhelm asked, breaking me out of my reverie. "My wife is concerned that they be well cared for. She has made pets of them, I fear." He turned to smile indulgently at her. "And we have left them standing where we disembarked."

"I hold no laborers in bondage. Perhaps I did not make it clear in my letters." Günter's voice deepened as his eyes bored into his brother's. "While I now might afford the convenience of a few slaves, I find it abhorrent." Günter threw a sharp glance at Eliza, knowing full well that being of the Galveston elite, she was probably quite comfortable with the practice. "The issue," he continued, "has become a source of contention even this far west."

Eliza, who had been ready to sip her drink, quickly placed it on the table and sat with her hands in her lap. Quite sure she lacked any understanding of the German we spoke, she must have sensed the nuances, nonetheless.

"Such agitation, Günter!" said Wilhelm. "Considering the quality of your property, I merely assumed you had hired help." And then he laughed. "Good Lord, man!"

"Our two hands, Wilhelm, our own two hands," Günter said. "While I employ men when harvest is upon us, I delegate chores with great discretion. But you need not be concerned. I will personally see to your animals. You both must be exhausted."

"*Ja ja*, of course. I will show you to your room," I said in English, "and we will have supper shortly. In preparing for you, I have worked very hard." I meant it as a generous statement, but the surprise on the young woman's face convinced me she had misinterpreted my words. I tried to recover. "I hope you like our home. Your home now, I suppose. The limestone is very thick and makes a fine barrier against the hot and cold. We built it only a few years ago, and it was very difficult. But we are used to hard labor. We—"

"Thank you, Katarina," Günter said. "You were going to escort Eliza upstairs. Wilhelm will be up in a moment." He turned back to his brother. "Forgive my abruptness. I have had a difficult morning with the townsfolk. You and I may speak of it after supper when the ladies have retired."

So, I thought, not even for the first night of their arrival could he let it rest about this war.

Eliza rose to follow me but paused to study Arno. "Why, I do believe he is the biggest dog I have ever seen. I adore animals, but Papa was always such a tyrant about them being in the home. Mamá begged for a little one, even cried, but Papa would not relent. How is it you manage with this great beast about the house?"

I chose my English words very carefully. "Arno was small when first we have him." I demonstrated his former size with my hand. "We read that President Lincoln welcomes pups into the White House. Our modest home should accept the same."

"I hate to agree with that old Mr. Lincoln, but I must on this topic. Although Papa would *never* be dissuaded." She immediately bent eye to eye with Arno and ruffled his beard—rather daring considering his serious countenance, but he happily accepted her enthusiasm.

She followed me out the front door and up the stairs leading to sleeping quarters. "How very unusual to have your stairs outside of the house. Do you find it inconvenient? Perhaps not. Quite extraordinary."

I opened my mouth to respond, but without the slightest pause, she continued. "I thought we'd never get here," she said. "The roads are no more than trails. Just awful. Why, in Galveston, the streets are kept graveled, and did you know, we never have to put up with much mud? Well, except when we've had a little storm off the Gulf. I imagine you don't have tropical storms around here at all." She took a deep breath at the top of the stairs. "Do you?"

I wondered if she could keep up this banter indefinitely. I was to find out that she could. But remembering how hard life was when we first came here, I wanted to be kind to this young girl. Yet kindness might only make her more vulnerable to hardship.

Becoming tougher than I ever thought possible was the only way I managed not to be defeated by the losses. *Mein Gott*, the losses. It would be up to me to teach her what it took to survive. She must learn the price of following her heart.

Once like her, I was naïve and enamored, accompanying my lover to a promised land and freedom. She believed as I had—that love would conquer all. I saw it in her eyes. In truth, love could only dull the blade.

Eliza

Papa had warned me against going off half-cocked with a man I had known only a few months. He had reminded me of the inheritance I shunned, never mind the Germans being resistant to our own phi-losophy of states' rights. *But, shoo, who cares about ol' politics?*

And there we were, at last, alone in our room. Our trunks were brought up, but there was no one to unpack and hang my gowns, never mind the space to do so. It would be left to me, but I could think of nothing more inviting than to shed my petticoats, collapse onto the bed, and call for supper. I suspected that would never do. As I stood before the looking glass to remove my hat, Will's arms came around me.

"Are you happy to see your brother, darling?" I asked. "You look very much alike."

"He seems a stranger to me now. I hardly knew him before

he left to come here nearly ten years ago. We will become accustomed to each other." His voice softened. "You are my only concern at the moment." His lips brushed my cheek as his fingers fumbled with the buttons of my frock and the pins for my hair. He lifted me onto the bed where he slipped off my shoes and my stockings before kissing the arch of my foot, the dimple above my elbow, the heartbeat at my throat. And I was his.

~

Light from the late afternoon filtered through the live oak outside our window. I woke from my nap to moist breath against my cheek and thought to suggest Will have a refreshing mint. But when I opened my eyes, the black beard and steady stare of the mutt met me face on. I squealed, but he merely woofed in quiet reciprocation and continued to watch me as though I were the intruder.

The only evidence of Will's presence was his mussed side of the bed. He must have gone downstairs. I sat up but tucked my feet under me as a precaution. "You," I said. "Arno?"

The dog's tail began a slow wag.

"Short for Arnocer?" I snaked a hand from the cover and offered my knuckles for him to sniff. "I had a great-uncle named Arnocer. He had a beard too. Mamá found him abominable and often refused to allow him in the house. How do *you* manage such luxury?"

At this point, the dog stood, nosed the door open, and moseyed off without so much as a backward glance. Had I passed inspection? I could only hope. I intended to make this creature my friend. He had a solid, careful demeanor.

Propping the meager pillows behind me, I thought about Katarina. She appeared stiff. Stiff and suspicious. Taller than I, she was a strong, big-boned, stalwart kind of woman my family would have likened to the working class. Around her eyes were spider webs of fine lines, and between her brows was a crease from too much sun or grumpiness. I was not sure which. Oh, yes, I was.

I surveyed the room we'd been assigned. The rough stone walls were as thick as Katarina had boasted, but my goodness, had they never heard of wallpaper that could add some semblance of grace to a room? The chamber pot was hardly concealed. The curtains hung listlessly on the one small window that looked out on the heavy branches of the tree.

Unsure as to how to dress for supper, I changed into my chiné taffeta, although it had wrinkled badly. The bodice had a deep green sheen that tucked in at my waist. Will had once remarked how it suited me as it would no one else. He said it set off my auburn hair and dark eyes that I'd inherited from my mamá. He always said the most flattering things. Even if his accent was rather guttural, the passion in his voice convinced me of his admiration. Oh, if only my Chloë were with me to make this dress suitable and weave my hair into the elaborate braids I could never achieve on my own. I'd just have to apologize and go on.

Trekking down the outdoor stairway made my entrance to the parlor less than elegant, but I was determined to make a nice impression for Will's sake. When I opened the front door to inside, the men stood as I expected, but instead of jackets and ascots, both wore plain shirts. Katarina remained seated in the rather simple gray homespun dress that she'd worn when we arrived. Perhaps I had not understood how casual the dress was for supper, but my goodness gracious, I intended to maintain the rules of etiquette of my upbringing.

I had yet to see Katarina without a harried expression on her face. She spoke several times of the difficulty in preparing the meal along with sighs and repeated massaging of her hands, which did appear somewhat roughened. I smiled and complimented her efforts, but heavenly days!

Katarina

Günter carved and passed the plates around, smiling as he did so. I, out of courtesy and curiosity, began supper with the simple question as to how Wilhelm and Eliza met. I directed my query toward Wilhelm, but the young bride was too excited to leave the story to her husband's telling.

Eliza set down her fork. "Well," she said, her eyes luminous, "my mamá always said, 'Never be fooled by a good-looking man,' but she never met anyone like my Will." She simpered and fluttered her lashes as she reached for his hand. "I always wondered what handsome suitor did her wrong. Broke her heart. Made her distrust every strong-jawed, broad-smiling, dark-eyed man." She grinned and gazed at her groom. "Maybe that was why she married Papa. He certainly wasn't good-looking, but he was good at business. At least, he had no misgivings about beautiful women. Or wealthy ones. Because he claimed Mamá. She was a Pitot—a petite mademoiselle of *the* New Orleans Pitots. You may know of them." Her eyebrows raised in question, Eliza paused in apparent expectation that we acknowledge the name.

Günter and I exchanged glances.

"Of course, that meant Papa had to become Catholic."

Günter cleared his throat and said, "We are Lutheran here."

Eliza's mouth dropped a little in obvious confusion of what to say next, but taking a sip of wine, she sprang back into her story. "Well, Mamá and Papa only allowed me to stroll about the park under our Chloë's vigilance. That's where I saw Will, you see, and I could not take my eyes from his. He was beautiful in the way some men can be beautiful, his eyes so clear and blue that you could almost see his secrets through them." She blushed then, glancing between the two brothers, no doubt noting the resemblance. Wilhelm beamed, pleased with the effect he had had on his bride.

Eliza hardly took a breath before continuing. Her speech was so rapid and high-pitched that Arno whined and sat beside her. "I sent Chloë on a false errand and then just happened to drop my parasol as I strolled past Will." She pursed her lips in what I thought a conspiratorial expression and cut her eyes over to Wilhelm. "Of course, he bent to pick it up for me, but a gust of wind lifted and tumbled it toward the folks gathered at the Tremont House. 'Fräulein,' he yelled, 'do not worry! I will retrieve it.' And off he sprinted. Isn't he the most gallant?"

Again, I glanced toward Günter for a private joke, but he could hardly take his eyes off her, his smile fixed in the benevolence one would assign a favored pet. Not waiting for our confirmation of Wilhelm's heroic deeds, Eliza launched back into her tale.

"I tried to control my skirt and galloped after him, my hoops reeling and my curls coming undone. It must have been a silly image, and I broke out in giggles." She paused to do just that—giggle. "Just as I reached the edge of the crowd, I stumbled and collapsed on the walk, my skirt ballooning, which made me laugh even harder despite my embarrassment."

Wilhelm chuckled at this and gazed at her with adoration. Such infatuation between the two young lovers touched me. So intense. So fleeting.

"Well! By the time Will helped me to my feet, the crowd had swelled around us and pushed us forward. 'Governor Houston,' someone hissed. 'He's off on one of his tirades against the war.'

"Will didn't say a word, so I assumed him not in the least interested. I had noted his foreign accent, of course. The crowd booed and carried on so that my young man took me by the elbow and escorted me to a safe distance.

"So," she said, "you can see how it started." She tapped her lips prettily with her napkin. "Wilhelm later found a way to make proper introductions through a gentleman he'd met on the ship, and here we are now. Except for the few—shall we say, 'bumps' along the way. Oh, Papa did complain that Will was foreign, but how he could fuss about accents is beyond me when Mamá cannot control her French lilt. And she tells him that *he* sounds like a damn Yankee, even though he's from just north of the Mason-Dixon Line. I don't think damn Yankee is a bad thing to say, do you? And anyway, Wilhelm has practically mastered our language since being here, and what little accent he has, I find charming. Besides I plan to learn German." She pressed her lips together in coy expectation of applause. When the pause elicited no such expression, she continued. "Oh, I do go on, don't I? But Will doesn't seem to mind." She reached for his hand again. "Do you? Awfully?"

Wilhelm lifted her fingers to his lips to kiss them. "How could I ever tire of your delightful voice?" To us, he said in our native German, "My sweet wife has failed to mention that when I asked for her hand, her father broke an excellent whiskey glass on the fireplace and went off on a rant about her being overly familiar with a Bavarian who barely spoke English and wanted to lure her off to the hinterlands." Wilhelm grinned, squeezed his bride's hand, and slung the swath of hair away from his forehead where it kept relapsing. Some might have thought it a rakish gesture, but Eliza reached over and brushed the lock away, softly grazing his skin with her fingertips.

"I have carried on far too much," she went on. "Just chattered away."

Indeed, you have, I thought to myself and fought to suppress the sarcasm on my tongue.

Eliza steepled her fingertips at her chin. "Now you must tell us how you came to Texas and how you tempted Will to join you." She lifted her dessert spoon and gazed over it expectantly at Günter.

"Another time, perhaps," he said. So, he, too, had wearied of her prattle. "We will have opportunity. Wilhelm, join me for schnapps. We may leave the ladies to their pleasantries." He stood, dismissing us.

Eliza managed one more bite of pudding and jumped to her feet. "Why, of course, whatever you—" She looked from Günter to me, opened her mouth, and then sealed her lips as I stepped away from the table.

I lifted the platter to begin clearing. "It will be good to have help now that you are here," I said, nodding toward the dishes to be collected. "There is much to do." I meant it as encouragement to assist with the evening dishes.

Perhaps the translation into English was not what I hoped as Eliza stifled a yawn and said, "Please excuse me. The trip has left me too tired to think, much less capable of further conversation. I cannot hold my eyes open another minute. I must retire for the evening, but I'm sure we'll have time to visit more in the morning over coffee. Hopefully, you have some, although I hear it's in ever shorter supply. And you know very well it's the Yankee's intention."

Coffee *was* like gold dust. But likely not as hard to come by as the help I had so looked forward to having.

Time to visit over coffee, indeed.

Eliza

Retreating to our room, I reviewed the evening. I did detect the woman's disappointment that I was too weary to even think about doing the dishes. For a moment, I feared she would have had me scrub the copper-bottomed pots before I folded my napkin.

But heavens, it had been a long trip. Longer than I'd imagined even with the nice carriage and matched bay geldings. And in truth, I minded not one whit that Will was detained downstairs. Marriage was a delight, but solitude was a luxury—though I would never admit it to another soul.

The night air seemed dry for October. Cooler. Not the warm, mildew odors with the peepers tuning up in Galveston. My gown did not stick to me, but I missed that breeze, full of brine and seaweed. And the shimmy of the palm fronds like someone whispering me to sleep. Here the windows stayed open, too, but the coyotes called. They seemed night phantoms directed to the kill. It was thrilling. And terrifying.

A scratch at the door. That Arno again. Did he suspect me of ill intent? Is that why he lurked about?

"Shhh. Come in and be quiet," I said. "Watch me all you want. You'll find me a boring subject. Goodnight, sweet prince. Hairy one that you are. I am clasped in the arms of Morpheus."

I lay back, crushed the sheet to my throat, and closed my eyes.

CHAPTER 2

*It is a fair generalization to say that Hill Country Germans were
opposed to slavery and in favor of a strong Union, though, as we
will see, the equation was not quite that simple.*
– Jefferson Morgenthaler, *The German Settlement of the
Texas Hill Country*

Katarina

The brothers' voices sounded amicable enough. I could just
hear them over the clink of dishes. That Eliza. I hoped she
could reconcile herself to helping around the place. She seemed
quite privileged, so we might have a difficult period of adjustment.
They *had* traveled a long distance though, so I could forgive her
hasty retreat to bed. Still, she needed to understand the value of
vigilant attention to the homeplace.

Not much later, Wilhelm excused himself to retire, and I took
advantage of his absence to join Günter. Picking up my darning, I
asked if he thought Wilhelm much changed.

"You know he was barely ten when I left home," he said. "A
rascal then, and I fear the tendency is firmly embedded. Daring of
him to set out with apparent disregard for rumors of hostiles in the
area. Nonetheless, he will be of help to us here. His horses, though
fine stock, were done in. I spent a good bit of effort on them."
Günter paused. "His little wife is quite lively."

I took a quick glance up from my work. "Yes, is she not? The
dog seems taken with her."

Günter smiled and looked at me. "Bothers you, does it?"

"Do not be absurd. I suspect he feels the need to keep an eye on her." A shred of jealousy tugged at my heart. "Whether it is mistrust or protectiveness we will not know for a while. I count on him to be discerning." But I heard the obvious relief in my own voice when I said, "*Ach*, look. Here he comes now." The dog nosed through the door and came to lie at my feet. "Wilhelm probably ran him off."

~

At dawn, no one had made the slightest move to come downstairs, though I had heard rustlings from above. Perhaps if I clanged the supper bell loudly enough, they would understand that breakfast, if it is not to be missed, would be served before first light. There was work to be contributed, and I hoped Günter was clear in informing Wilhelm that they would be expected to get down to it. He was already about the horses, readying for a trip to town and expecting Wilhelm to keep him company.

Ah, at last, footsteps on the stairs. "*Guten Morgen*, Wilhelm," I said. "Sit and eat. Your brother is preparing the wagon. It is sunrise, and he has been expecting you."

"Then I must hurry. Tell Eliza of my whereabouts."

With that, he grabbed a biscuit and rushed out the door. I watched out the window as the two men spurred the horses and headed off toward Fredericksburg. After waiting another fifteen minutes for his bride to advance down the stairs, I sent Arno up to provide a little encouragement. If she was expecting coffee served in bed, she would be mightily disappointed. The dog would do.

It was only moments till Eliza, a book in hand, stumbled down the stairs and through the kitchen door in her negligee and peignoir, the frills and lace rustling against her pink skin. Farm life would make short work of that pampered countenance.

"Good Lord, have mercy," she said. "Is that animal your alarm clock? I *had* hoped to be spared a rude awakening."

When she noticed the look on my face, she changed her tune.

"Well, I only meant I was surprised." With dainty precision, she sat herself at the table and opened her book. Arno collapsed at her feet with a groan.

I motioned toward the stove, indicating she could choose from what was cooked. "Chores begin at dawn. Do you have suitable clothing?"

Placing a finger between the pages, she closed the book. "I, well, I—"

"Look in *der Schrank*. You will find suitable wear."

"Der what?"

"The armoire. You must learn some German. I worked very hard to learn English. We put great effort into learning the language before we came."

Raising an eyebrow, Eliza sniffed and opened her mouth as though she were about to put forth argument, but our relationship was young yet, and she thought better of it.

I did not mention a bonnet. Surely, she had enough sense to cover up. "I will go tend the cow. You can find me in the barn." I let the door slam behind me, but regretting the abruptness, called back, "Our husbands go to town." Then I strode off with great purpose, hoping to impart the need for prompt attention to tasks.

The march to the milking shed lent itself to reflection. The lace of her nightgown, its fineness and fragility, struck at my heart and envy pricked my conscience. Soon, though, *soon* she would see how her beauty would wither in a Texas summer, and she had best keep that red hair bonneted. Comanches were rumored to be attracted.

Eliza

"Well, I never," I said to the dog who rose as if to encourage me to get going. Pouring myself a cup of coffee, I stood at the kitchen window and gazed at the sunrise. Spears of light cast across the open pasture and hued the land in pinks and oranges. "Ah, 'the rosy-fingered Dawn.' More like a fist, wouldn't you say, Arno?" I broke a biscuit in half and gave it to him. "It's really lovely though, isn't it?" I thought of my favorite poet, Coleridge.

At morning's break, at evening's close
Inhales the sweetness of the rose
And hovers over the uninjured bloom
Sighing back the sweet perfume.

"A pity Missus Katarina doesn't take time to appreciate it." I sat on the windowsill, buttering my biscuit and smothering it in peach preserves. A mockingbird began its song, clear and varied, but a summons to rise, nonetheless. "Let's take a look at the attire for the day, shall we?"

Arno followed me to the parlor where I had seen *der Schrank*. He watched me as though he thought I might misbehave. Had Katarina sent him to keep an eye on me?

For such a barbaric word, I found *der Schrank* a lovely piece of furniture—the doors patterned to resemble a tree cut across the grain. Running my fingertips over its façade, I felt it smooth as marble and wondered if Günter had made it himself.

The dress hung on a knob inside, stained though it was. Its fabric of yellow flowers amid blue plaids had faded like a child's watercolor left in the rain. At least it could be covered with an apron, thank goodness. Why, Chloë had better clothes.

Passing through the kitchen, I pocketed two small apples for the horses and found Katarina in the barn. "Milking is done," she said. "Take the bucket to the kitchen. Yesterday's milk is separated. Skim the cream. Churn is on the back stoop. I will come to check on you soon. You can do butter making, *ja*? It is the easy job." She stared at my shoes. A slow grin distorted her face. "And those dainties? You intend to work with those on your feet?"

Her accent could be strong on occasion if she did not attend to her pronunciation, and it was hard to decipher her exact instructions. "I'm afraid most of us only speak English here in the South, although I do understand French," I said. "Do you speak French? Perhaps we could find a common ground that would be more satisfactory to us both."

She smirked at me and said, "*Avec plaisir. Oui, madame. Je parle français, italien, et espagnole. L'anglais est plus difficile à apprendre. En anglaise*—choose brogans," she continued, "if you do not wish to spoil the shoes you wear. Garden must be done." Then Kat (as I imagined calling her to her face) nodded toward the nearly full container of milk. "Ask for more instruction if you cannot do the job."

"Well," I said, not bothering to keep the huffiness out of my voice, "I have my own chore to attend to first." I turned to the stalls and laughed as the horses nickered and gobbled the apples like piglets. "Next time, let's follow the men to town." I stroked their necks and whispered to them. "Shall we?" I sighed but dutifully lugged the bucket to the house knowing full well that the sloshed milk on my skirt would smell like baby spit-up before the hour was out.

~

I set to work, all the while trying to imagine strolling the beach at home with a soft breeze off the Gulf, seabirds calling, and the hint of fishes and salt in the air. Every so often, Kat marched in to check my progress, criticize my technique, and grumble at the lack of effort I put into the assignment. Never mind that my hands cramped and stung.

Butter churned and skirt dabbed clean as I could, I finally excused myself, claiming a headache. Well, heavens, my head *did* hurt. If my fingers could ever flex again, I was going to write a letter to my mamá. I did miss her but not more than my Chloë. I longed for her to come. Oh, that Mamá would send her. What a blessing. I would ask Will the moment he returned. How could he refuse? Why, I saw a nice little cabin down close to the creek. Chloë might be more than comfortable there and safer, too, I bet, considering all that ruckus going on in Galveston. I retrieved my paper from my reticule, inked my pen, and sat to write. I began to feel better already.

Katarina

It was readily apparent that Wilhelm's delicate bride was avoiding responsibility. I could see now that Günter was going to have to speak to the young couple. Lecture his brother perhaps, although I doubted Wilhelm was capable of straightening out his little wife.

Late one afternoon I sat on the porch to rest for a while. I lay my hand on Arno's head and thought about how to make this arrangement more palatable while keeping myself out of the line of fire. Günter had criticized the sharpness of my tongue, but I found it the most direct way of getting the job done. I had had my own travails and was off-put by the moaning of others when my difficulties were much harder.

Eliza had never had to suffer at the hands of a taskmaster. It would do her good. Make her *appreciate* the finer amenities of life, rather than take them for granted. Her shoes, her dress, her tiny, corseted person had never faced the challenges of adulthood. Obviously, she had been petted and doted on and spoiled. "*Zum Donnerwetter!*"

Arno whined at my outburst.

"Oh, I suppose you defend her now too." *Is it just that she is so pretty?*

He whined again.

~

It was not much later in the afternoon when the men returned. I watched from the kitchen window as Wilhelm leaped from the wagon, flung the bundles over his shoulder, and rushed into the house without wiping his feet or closing the door behind him. He dropped the packages on the table without speaking, went back out to the stairs, and by the sound of it, took two at a time. Surely, his mother had instructed him better. She had reared both men. I would have to clean behind him. Günter still sat behind the horse, the reins limp in his hands.

I wiped the kitchen floor with an old, wet towel and wringing it, stepped out to the wagon where Günter still sat. *"Was ist los?"*

"Verdammt nochmal! The boy understands nothing. He is bewitched by the newness of marriage and falls prey to her Confederate sympathies. It is all glory and states' rights and rattling of sabers. He should know how we fled the homeland to avoid this kind of conflict."

I found it surprising to see Günter critical of his brother. "Maybe they will return to Galveston before winter," I said. "I am sure Missus Eliza prefers her luxuries. She seems unable or unwilling to familiarize herself with the demands of a household." I had tried to delicately put how I spurned the lack of work ethic on Eliza's part, but a certain smugness had crept into my voice. Even I recognized it.

Once again, without assistance, I prepared our evening meal. Supper that night was tense. Wearing a red and gold bold plaid taffeta skirt with full petticoats, Eliza insisted on dressing once again beyond my ability to compete. She struggled to get through the doorway, but still managed to make the effort look beguiling.

The uneasiness at supper was palpable. Günter did little to smooth over the argument between Wilhelm and himself. I thought Eliza might speak of her dissatisfaction with the chores assigned her, but she kept her eyes lowered, only commenting in a diminished voice about the lovely patina of my silver and asking if I had brought it from Deutschland when we first came. Otherwise, she surveyed the scene through her eyelashes and made no comment regarding the difficulty of her tasks. The whole time, however— the *whole* time—she sat with one hand on Arno's head that lay conveniently in her lap.

Not having seen his bride all day and perhaps not as ignorant of his brother's irritation as he attempted to portray, Wilhelm declined the after-supper schnapps and offered his hand to his bride. Eliza smiled timidly and stood to cater to her young husband's wishes. But I detected a flash of passion in her eyes. She could hardly wait. Arno rose as she did, but my hand on his ruff detained him. Still, he followed her with his eyes. I did not know why it offended me so. Had I no ally left?

Eliza

"I'm so awfully glad you're home," I said to Will. "It's been a trying day, and I've been thinking. Wouldn't it be marvelous if Chloë were to come stay here with us?" I maneuvered myself to sit demurely on his lap. "I've already requested it from Mamá. All we must do is post the letter. Here, you can read it beforehand. It would make life so much more comfortable, and that little cabin down by the creek would be perfect for Chloë, even though she hasn't slept in a cabin since she was a baby. And I just know that she would—"

"My dear, we are fighting a war over this very issue. Surely, you do not think Günter would permit you a slave!"

"It is not his to permit! Look at my hands, Will! Just look at them!" I held out my palms for him to inspect. He took them and kissed each blister and suggested I wear gloves.

"Have *you* ever tried to wear gloves and churn butter?" I couldn't keep the irritation out of my voice. "Well, have you? They slide on the handle, and it takes twice the time to get the abominable chore done. Making the stuff thick enough to form butter takes hours." I lifted my arm for his inspection. "Oh, Will! I think I might be getting a muscle." I paced about the room. "Hook up our horses for me, please, before you leave in the morning. I'm taking the buggy into town myself first thing."

"No, Eliza, you will not. I am telling you, Günter will not allow it."

I jerked my hands away and crossed my arms. With my face turned away from him, I said, "I must say, Will, are you going to let these people determine your loyalties? We are Southerners by birth—Texans—and we—"

"You are Southern, but I am new to this land, *mein Schatz.* I promised loyalty to the United States of America. When I left my homeland, Texas belonged to the United States, not the Confederacy. And my brother says—"

"Your brother is not married to me. You took vows to be true to *me.* You don't want to be called a traitor to our new country! Why, Will! What would Papa say?"

"Your father would happily indict me on any stance I took. Must I fight you as well as my brother?" He jammed his hands in his pockets.

"You don't sleep with your brother last I took into account." I sank to the bed and offered my arms. "Come. Let's not fuss about this ol' war. The Yankees can have their country, but the Confederacy is ours.

I think the states ought to just let each other alone. Anyway, if I'm to tussle, I'd rather it be with you, right here on this old feather bed."

"I didn't bargain for this when I came here," he said, but his knee was already sinking into the mattress beside me.

"Oh, Will, you didn't bargain on me."

~

The next morning, I dressed, secreted the letter in my pocket, and slipped down the stairs for my journey to Fredericksburg. Quite sure that Kat was already working in the garden, as squash and pumpkins were ready to be harvested, I gathered my skirt and headed for the barn. Surely, despite his objections, Will had tacked up the horses for me.

But no! Dancer and Legend stood quietly in their stalls with not one bit of leather on their withers.

"Hell's bells!" I stamped my foot. Turning on my heel, I stalked back to the house, removed my petticoats, and slipped on my flannel chemise and riding trousers. The sun was gaining on me, and if I did not make a quick departure, I would be discovered and discouraged, perhaps even denied. Back at the barn, I chose Dancer. He was not my favorite horse, but he'd always seemed the calmer of the two. He accepted the halter nicely, and I led him from the stall. I found a saddle that looked like it might fit. When all was done, I felt quite accomplished and walked Dancer to the upping block. I only had one foot in the stirrup when Kat appeared.

"*Und was ist das?*"

"I beg your pardon?"

Puckering her lips carefully to make the *w* sound, she said, "Where are you going?" She disregarded the soil on her hands and stuck her knuckles on her hips.

"Into Fredericksburg if you must ask. I have business to

attend." I continued to mount, but the bay sidestepped. Ignoring Kat, I said, "Dancer, you must stay still. This is different from the traces, but you be a good boy now."

"Not a good idea." She cocked her eyebrow. "Comanches." She circled her hand over toward the hills. "Do you not know what they do to women? They like red hair. *Und* Dancer may be your horse, but that is *Günter's* saddle. You may not use it." With that, she pivoted and returned to the garden, brandishing her trowel.

"Oh, you!" I led the horse back to his stall. She didn't care one whit about my hair, which was *auburn*, not red, but the thought of savages did cause me pause, not to mention Günter. Worst of all, I would not have my own dear Chloë. I would be a servant to Frau Katarina Lange.

~

Will was gone the next day when I awoke. The sun crept up the hills to the east. Good Lord Almighty, I was late again, and there'd be the devil to pay. Kat would have a list of chores as long as my arm. Arno, who had been waiting at the base of the stairs, led the way.

In the kitchen, the coffeepot had been upended and bread put away as well as the preserves. My punishment. I tied the unwashed apron around me and was out the door in minutes, painfully aware of the blisters that had begun on my heels from the clodhoppers Kat had provided. I stumbled to the barn to bring in the pail of milk that I'm sure she'd got from the cow at the first crack of dawn. There were eggs to collect and butter to churn and a grumpy matron to manage my efforts.

Her head pressed against the Jersey's flank, Kat squatted on the milking stool. Her shoulders lifted and fell. Barely above the shuffling of the horses and clucking of the chickens came the sound of soft weeping. Old stone-face was *crying*.

"Oh my! Have you injured yourself? Are you hurt? Shall I call Günter?" I stood rooted to the ground never expecting to see such a passionless woman behave so.

Arno crept up next to Kat and dropped his great head to her shoulder. She threw her arm around him, blew her nose on her apron, and struggled to stand.

I knew what I would want if I were distraught and thought to take her hand and pull her into a hug but couldn't imagine her being the least responsive to an embrace. Patting her shoulder would have to do. "There, there," I said. "Perhaps it's not so bad and can be mended. Would you like for me to—"

"It is nothing." Kat's face toughened almost imperceptibly, although tears still lay on her eyelashes. "Perhaps, I am only tired. The work never ends. Here, take the bucket. Time lost is never regained."

"Well, then." I lifted the pail and immediately regretted not finding gloves to wear as Will had suggested. Already my hands were forming calluses and my nails were ragged. At least, the men were here to do the harder labor of harvesting corn and hay grasses. I intended to mention at supper how they must consider hiring new help before I or even Kat faints from exhaustion.

Katarina

Embarrassed for being discovered in a weak state, I hurried to the garden to finish my work there. At least my tears would water the carrots with no one the wiser. Having finally accepted the idea of Wilhelm bringing a wife, I had expected a helpmate. Instead, I got Eliza. The girl complained that she could not understand my English and that her hands were blistered and that she could not lounge about with her book of poetry until the noon hour. What did Günter expect me to do with that good-for-nothing female? Bring her breakfast in bed?

At supper that night, I would recommend a proper division of chores to eliminate the imbalance. But the men would need to support me. The little missus would be obliged to obey Günter as well as her husband. Two married women should have equal responsibilities, and it was time that Wilhelm's wife learned how to be a productive one.

That evening, I made supper alone while Eliza napped. I was more than willing to cook without her help. *For the last time.*

All seated at the table, we watched Günter carve the pork. I cleared my throat and said, "I have a suggestion for responsibilities. Some here do not understand the importance of vork...work." I ignored Eliza with her fork poised in mid-air and her mouth open. "In order to make fair the work, I say that—"

"Why, Katarina, at last, we agree!" Eliza said. "I am so pleased, for I, too, have a wonderful idea to ease the stress of all the work that needs to be done. I have thought long and hard about this, and I am sure Will can confirm the validity of my idea. Without further delay, we must arrange for Chloë to come—"

"We have discussed this, *Liebling*. I am afraid it will not be possible." Wilhelm reached across the table and laid his hand on hers.

Was this his first step in taking charge of his little despot? I could only hope.

"But Chloë belongs to me," Eliza wailed. "She should have come with us in the first place. She—"

Günter set his cup down. "Not another word, Eliza. Your husband has spoken, and you are to obey him."

Tears welled in Eliza's eyes. Her chin quivered. "Well, then, you'll excuse me. I have lost my appetite." Clutching the napkin to her mouth, she scooted her chair away from the table and hurried out the door and up the stairs to her room. To my annoyance, Arno followed at her hem.

Wilhelm half-stood.

"Sit down, Wilhelm," said Günter. He chuckled. "My, my,

your little bride does not take disappointment well, but let us not allow her little tantrum to overshadow the importance of our plans. At least, this gives us the opportunity to speak more candidly. I suggest—"

Wilhelm matched his brother's tone. "You may be assured I intend to participate in the planning of our resistance to the Confederacy, but now, as you may imagine, I have ruffled feathers to smooth." He smiled so charmingly that I could only sympathize with his position.

Except Günter. Günter smirked. "We have a name for your behavior in our language, do we not? I will not use it in the presence of my wife, but I believe you know very well what I am thinking."

"And in the presence of your wife—whom you have been married to far longer than I to mine—I understand your lack of fervidness in that regard." He disappeared around the corner of the room before Günter could react.

"Why, that insolent...."

I rose and collected the plates. It *had* been a long time since my husband had attempted to lure me into an embrace. He had grown older as had I, but I missed the warmth, the affection, the small thrill of the pursuit. Once again, I put from my mind that these two young ones had a liaison I had long past forsaken. Or was I the forsaken one?

~

Günter hated answering my queries, so I declined to question him further. But I watched him closely over the next few weeks. The previous month, he had bought all the corn and other produce he could with United States dollars. While I paid little attention to it at the time and while we could afford the expense, I began to wonder why of late he seemed so satisfied and full of purpose regarding the surplus. One evening as we sat together in the parlor, I asked for his reasoning.

"You are not to be concerned," he said. With a quick frown, he glanced away from his book as though I had disturbed him with the question. "I am doing my part to keep gains out of the hands of the secessionists. It is a simple effort that requires no loss of blood." His eyes went back to his reading, but he said, "And I expect you to support my decisions."

"When the authorities find out, they may confiscate it and punish you with your *life*."

His mouth formed a hard line. Immediately sorry I had criticized him so frankly, I stuck the knitting needles into the ball of twine and set it aside. Kneeling by his chair, I leaned on his knee. I understood that while husbands might never admit it, they needed their wives to believe in their masculine wisdom.

"I do appreciate your resistance," I said, "but the consequences prey on my mind. You are too bold in your convictions. I fear for your safety."

"And not for your own, my dear?"

"My safety depends on yours. But that is not why I asked."

He started to let his hand rest on my head, an endearing gesture I welcomed. Instead, he merely brushed his fingers across my hair and rose to retire.

I had lost the ability to reach him as I once had when we were young. I was no longer his Fräulein. Nor the mother of his children. While we began some years ago to avoid the act of love that only resulted in miscarriage, Günter now avoided any show of affection that might lead to intimacy.

I no longer had his ear the way Eliza had Wilhelm's.

CHAPTER 3

Van der Stucken's company was made up principally of Germans from Gillespie County, and their fond hope was that they would see service on the frontier near their homes. For a short time this wish was realized as the new cavalry company was ordered to guard Federal prisoners at Fort Mason in adjoining Mason County.
– Frank W. Heintzen, *Fredericksburg, Texas During the Civil War and Reconstruction*

May 1862

Katarina

Although the men abhorred including me in their discussion, I had no intention of being kept in the dark regarding their affairs. That night, they lingered in the parlor long past their usual hour.

At the kitchen table, I knitted a sweater I had never finished last winter, and between each knit and purl, I gleaned confirmation of what I had suspected.

"You must see how joining van der Stucken's defense company will provide the perfect answer." Wilhelm's voice held a pleading quality that would not be lost on Günter. "I will be officially assigned to a Confederate company to please my wife, but the likelihood of my ever firing upon a Union soldier is remote. My energies will most likely be directed toward warding off Comanches. It hardly satisfies my little wife's bloodlust, but the defense company is as close to neutral as can be found. It is my best effort in pleasing you and placating my wife. What say you? Do I have your blessing?"

The silence must have intimidated Wilhelm as it always had me as Günter took a long draw from his pipe and said nothing. At last, he said, "It is one approach to a war that will have no good solution. I could not in all good conscience wear the Confederate gray. Do what *you* must." He stood and stretched his back. "I am done with the argument." He turned and left.

I had never seen Günter so defeated.

Eliza

We had hardly been here six months, but under the influence of Günter's misguided loyalty to the Union, Will had gone off again to town with his brother. I collected the milk and headed for the kitchen to churn. As I plunged the dasher time after time, I became angrier. I would speak directly to Kat. My irritation sped up the butter-making, and I was done in record time. If the butter was not quite proper yet, I no longer cared.

I stalked off to the garden and found Kat on her knees in the dirt. "Look here," I said.

She stared at my feet a moment as if she had no idea who might be standing before her. Finally, shielding her eyes, she looked up.

"Wilhelm would be happy to fight for our Confederacy," I said, "if you would just let him alone. It's the only right thing to do! We are Texans. We are Southerners. You come here and try to dictate our allegiances!" I stamped my foot. "I won't have it!"

Kat stood very slowly, pushing off the ground with her hands and slapping them against each other. I took a step back.

"I am tired of you," Kat said in the quietest voice. "We took an oath of allegiance to the United States and have an obligation to this country that welcomed us when we came to escape from the revolutions in our homeland. We do not want our homes burned and trampled by armies. You do not know what war can do, little girl." She narrowed her eyes at me. "You see only flags waving and boys marching to glory." Her voice dropped to a whisper. "You do not know the blood and horror of war."

I turned and ran. Stumbling, I caught myself on the gatepost. I pushed away the image of destruction she'd painted.

But two days later, it appeared that Wilhelm, at least, had come to reason. That evening, he came to me and lifting my hand to his lips said, "I have joined the Confederacy."

"Oh, Will!" I threw my arms around him. "You will be my hero!" I smothered him with kisses. Until I remembered Günter. I sat back. "So, at last, you stand against your brother?"

There was irony in Will's smile as he shook his head—a sad expression I tried to ignore.

"It has been made mandatory now, you see. But as it stands, under Frank van der Stucken, we hope to remain nearby and protect our families from the Comanches since Federal troops have been withdrawn. Does it not make you feel better that I might stay on in Texas rather than on the battlefields of Virginia?"

"I hardly think the Indians pose much of a threat. Why, I haven't seen one single Comanche. They are primitives with weapons no more dangerous than bows and arrows."

He slapped the side table with the palm of his hand. "You cannot be happy, can you?"

I flinched at the animosity in his face. "The Yankees are our deadly enemies. Does this mean you're actually not going into battle?"

"As part of the 1st Texas Cavalry, I will report to Fort Mason, some two days ride from here. We will have to guard the Union prisoners there, but it seems nothing will please you except my marching off to the battlefield!"

I shook my head. "No, Will, it's just that—"

"Stop it, Eliza. It is done. Since I was bound to fight for one side or the other, I guess it might as well be yours." He shook his head sadly but kissed my shoulder, then the hollow of my throat. "Had you rather I die for you?"

"Oh Will, even I am starting to hate this war. It hardly makes sense anymore. But I will be proud. You don't know what this means for you to fight for my country."

He scoffed at that. "Your country? Should it not *all* be *our* country and not some broken land that may separate us for centuries?"

I knew in my heart he was right, but I couldn't admit it then. Not then.

Katarina

In the early morning before dawn, Eliza stood in the doorway. "It is only me." Arno leaned against her. She bent over him and stroked his back. "I heard you here and thought I should join you since I had already awakened."

"*Gut*," I said, clearing my throat. "Cut out the biscuits. The oven is hot."

"I am afraid I have made Will angry."

I had nothing to say to this. Much of the time she had made us all angry. Still, it was strange to hear the distress in her voice and even more so to anticipate her confiding in me. "Günter tells me Wilhelm has joined the Confederacy. It pleases you, does it not?"

Eliza turned the biscuit cutter with tight quick twists of her wrist. "He has joined the Confederacy but hopes to remain on the frontier to protect against the Indians." Eliza shuffled about the kitchen. "It is a ploy to avoid real soldiering. Why, Galveston boys were honored to fight. Honored! I hardly think Will a coward, but he is so unwilling."

"Can you not be satisfied that he has compromised his conscience for you?" I said with barely concealed anger. "Just go collect the eggs! At least you will be helpful."

"It's hardly light. I—"

I flicked my apron at her. "Go! Sunrise hangs on the horizon."

Arno stood and jostled through the door behind her, leaving me alone.

~

Eliza returned as the men were finishing their breakfast. We sat without speaking, carefully avoiding each other's eyes. Through the window, Wilhelm studied the hens that scratched and pecked in the yard. He finally broke the silence. "What are their names? The chickens?"

"I do not name what I might eat," I said.

Eliza cut in with false gaiety. "I did. I named them. Matilda, Josephine, and Harriet. The others are—"

"Never mind," Wilhelm said. "I was only making conversation."

Her smile faded, and she turned to bend over the dog, where she hid her face in his thick neck.

That morning would change our lives. We were being pushed toward a precipice.

Eliza

The dawn was too beautiful for regret, but there in the early hours, I sat on the bed and watched my husband prepare his knapsack. I followed him to the stable and twisted my hands as he tacked up Dancer.

He turned to me. "Even if I cannot satisfy my little wife's battle cry," he said with a mock salute, "I will be off now."

"Oh, Will, I didn't mean to sound so disappointed. It's just that—"

"Speak no more of this." He turned his back to me and tightened the girth. "It is out of our hands. The Confederacy itself demands my service even without your pretty little voice. Perhaps you will like the cut of the gray uniform. I understand the cavalry jacket is quite dashing—if we ever get one."

Then I couldn't quite bear it. What had I thought? It might be months before I saw Will again. I took his lapels in my hands and whispered against his cheek. "I'll write. I will send you anything you need. You just say. Playing cards? Gloves? I'll find a way to knit a scarf for you. Wait and see."

He caught my arms and pulled me to him before mounting. "Goodbye, girl of mine. *Auf Wiedersehen.*"

"Dancer is such a fine little horse. He will take care of you. Godspeed, my darling." I let go and stepped away.

The war was more than a year old. It would not, could not last much longer. *My husband will come back to me in no time. No time.*

CHAPTER 4

The morning after our arrival we marched out fifteen miles to the west of the town and pitched camp on a stream called the Pedernalio, [sic] with the intention of remaining there about six weeks. Here Captain Dunn [sic] issued his proclamation announcing his appointment as Provost-Marshal, and giving the inhabitants three days to come in and take the oath of allegiance to the Confederacy ...
– Robert Hamilton Williams, *With the Border Ruffians, Memories of the Far West, 1852-1868*

June 1862

Katarina

Late one morning a rough looking party of six men rode up. I waited just outside the gate to block their entry into the yard. Arno growled low and stepped between me and the men. I touched him and commanded, "*Sitz dich.*"

Dust swirled about the horses' hooves, and the riders made a great show of their rifles. A stout man removed his hat and set it to his chest. "James Duff, the newly appointed provost marshal, at your service." He spoke with a Scotsman's brogue. Then he smirked. "We're here to speak with *Herr* Lange." He snorted and glanced back at his comrades as if seeking appreciation of his mocking tone. Leaning back in the saddle, he jerked on the reins. His horse's mouth grimaced against the shank bit. The animal jogged back to avoid the pressure but was spurred forward. Its eyes widened, showing the white that ringed the brown iris.

"I am sorry," I said. "He is not here."

Duff's eyes scanned the property. He squinted over my head and shouted, "Günter Lange! Come out!"

Choosing English, I shielded my eyes from the sun and spoke quietly "He is in town on business."

"I bet he is." The man spurred his horse again and loomed over me. "Then maybe he seen the notice regardin' the conscript law. In any case, you tell him we ain't shilly-shallyin' about. He will report to me and take the Confederate oath of allegiance." He spit a wad of tobacco at my feet. "Understand, ma'am?"

Although I thought of it later as a foolhardy stance, I stood my ground. His horse tried to step back again, but Duff sent it forward until I could feel its hot breath, smell its sweat, and see the pink flesh of its nostrils.

"Repeat it to me!"

My heart raced at the change from quiet menace to full-blown ferocity.

"*Ja*," I said. "Ah, yes." I ran my hands along my skirt to dry the perspiration. "He must sign allegiance. I understand and will tell him."

"See that you do." He whipped the horse's head around and galloped off with his party.

I grabbed the fence post to keep from falling. Turning back to the house, I found Eliza at the front door, partially blocking herself from view. After they were well out of range, she shouted after them. "My husband has signed up! The Texas Cavalry!" Wide-eyed, she stepped back and covered her mouth with one hand. She gripped a derringer in the other.

"Who do you think you will scare with that toy?" I asked. My hands were still shaking.

"My papa insisted I take it with me. He guaranteed this gun would inflict serious damage."

"Pressed against a man's belly."

"It's large caliber and twin shot."

For such a silly girl, she seemed surprisingly competent with the weapon at hand.

"Who was that man?" she asked before finally pocketing the pistol. "I thought he might run his horse over you."

"Some of your Confederate friends, I believe—provost marshal. He demanded Günter sign an oath of loyalty to the Confederacy." I did not hide the scorn I put on my face, "Are you proud?"

"He didn't look or act like our Galveston men. Why, nothing like them. I don't believe you."

"Believing me is not necessary." I pushed past her into the parlor, took the Henry rifle from the mantle, and set it behind the door. "There," I said and hoped my voice did not tremble.

It was nearly seven o'clock in the evening when Günter returned. The pork I had cooked was overdone, the corn gone cold, but he made no comment. He slammed his mug on the table each time he set it down until I feared it might shatter. I hesitated to tell him of the provost marshal's demands.

"They came today!" Eliza cried, clearly unable to hold her tongue any longer. "Those men!" She found my eyes and seemed to regret blurting out the news. "Tell him, Katarina."

I had hoped to speak of it privately with Günter after supper, but now no other recourse lay open to me. "*Ja*, they came looking for you. He was a brute, that man, the provost marshal." I tried to keep my voice steady. "He said you have to sign."

Günter pounded the table with his fist. "They may search elsewhere. I will *not* conscript." He pushed back from the table and stood, knocking the chair onto the floor. With his hands on the table, his knuckles white with pressure, he leaned forward. "Well, Eliza, you see the quality of men the Confederacy offers up." There was a sneer in his voice, and for the first time, I felt pity for the girl.

Eliza stood and, despite her petite stature, drew in her breath and pulled back her shoulders. "I had my derringer. Arno and I both were prepared to defend Katarina."

Suppressing the tendency to roll my eyes, I hoped to portray a measure of appreciation. "*Ja*, you did, but it will take more to discourage the marshal. He seemed…what are the words? Maddened with power?"

Eliza

I couldn't believe I'd drawn my gun against a countryman, but he was no representative of the gentlemen who fought for our independence. Why, he was no better than the ruffians who lurked about the Galveston docks! Günter and Katarina were now more than ever convinced that the Confederacy was made up of hooligans. And I couldn't say I blamed them.

Perhaps it was the threat that hung over us the next few days, but summer's longer daylight hours fed Kat's compulsion to fill every moment with labor—the harvest of tomatoes and corn and squash, and oh, the list goes on. According to her, we had to take advantage of this productive year, especially since the war threatened our livelihood at every moment. My hands had become brown, my feet callused, and I had a spray of freckles across my nose. I worried that my skin would soon look like Kat's.

I had made up my mind not to fuss about the consequences of the war or that horrible man who had come to threaten Günter. But two days later, he came again, insistent on buying Günter's corn reserves. Kat and I ceased our work and stood by the parlor door. We dared not show our faces but overheard Günter speaking to Duff.

"I received your message that I am required to conscript," Günter said. "Nevertheless, I regret that we are unable to respond to your request for more corn. While I understand your difficulty, the community has placed the responsibility of storing

it with me. They have paid with Union dollars. I cannot dishon-
or their trust."

"I don't give a hoot in hell about your honor nor dishonor neither one." Duff managed a humorless laugh. "I got to feed my
horses. I can shoot you right here or pay you in Confederate dollars. Don't make me no never mind, but I'd mind my p's and q's if I
was you. Rumors is going 'round about you and your politickin'."

Kat's mockery aside, I promptly retrieved my derringer from the
table drawer and slipped it into my apron pocket. And despite the
brave face she put on, her eyes darted to the rifle standing in the corner.

That night, Günter sat at the supper table with his head in
his hands. "Fifty bushels! I sold it for that worthless paper. I will
dump the harvest in the Pedernales before I donate another ear of
corn to that scoundrel and his lackeys."

Even Kat begged Günter to sign the oath of allegiance. "It's
pointless," she said, "to get yourself jailed or worse when you can
secretly be more effective."

It was beyond me why he did not realize that joining the
Confederate effort might make all our lives easier. Will had made
that sacrifice. Oh, I did hope Papa wasn't completely right about
the provinciality of German immigrants. A little nostalgia for the
homeland was understandable, but Günter's outright defection
from our cause was treasonous.

When Günter returned from town the next day, he had heard
and confirmed news that relieved us. The horrid James Duff had
reportedly left Gillespie County to harass others in the surrounding counties of Kerr and Kendall.

Katarina

The summer heated up with disquiet. Our only relief was the
breeze, and even it came filled with rumors of sedition. Amid
the oak leaves, the cicadas clamored out a warning—harsh and

unrelenting. One night, late beyond reckoning, Günter stepped quietly up the stairs. He unstrapped the gun belt he now wore before sliding out of his clothes and into bed. His breathing was measured as though he was trying to keep me from sensing his unease, but against my ear, his heartbeat thundered.

Waiting, I lay there against him. Would he never go to sleep? Shortly before dawn, I rose, one muscle at a time, and located Günter's britches draped across the ladderback chair. I found a crumpled wad of paper. Smoothing it flat on the window seat, all I could perceive in the moonlight were charcoal lines that appeared to be a creek and surrounding hills. I checked again to see that he still slept. He turned and groaned in his dreams but soon lay still again. I stepped away and faced the wall to light a candle. It took only a moment to make out the words "Bear Creek" on the paper and the line indicating a path through the hills.

I blew out the candle and replaced it on the table. It was not until I tried to recrumple the paper that I felt Günter's arms about me and his whispers against my neck as he leaned over my shoulder.

"And what do we have here?" He took the paper from my hand and crushed it in his fist. "Do you find it necessary to pilfer through my pockets to determine my business?"

"You are gone so late and do not tell me a thing! How am I to understand the truth if you hide it from me?" I tried to study his face in the dark before dawn. Once those crystal blue eyes held no secrets, but now it was as though I gazed into murky depths of the ocean. "All I hear you say is that you must support the Union with your efforts for peace. I fear these endeavors will get you killed."

"Enough, Katarina! Quite enough! You will not concern yourself with the responsibilities of men. You are to keep to duties of the home. I have agreed to join the Union Loyal League. That is all you need to know."

How dared he! I would not so easily be pushed out of his affairs. I had a right to know.

CHAPTER 5

Leisure is gone–gone where the spinning-wheels are gone, and the pack-horses, and the slow wagons, and the peddlers, who brought bargains to the door on sunny afternoons.
– George Eliot, *Adam Bede*

Katarina

It was late July and the afternoon burned hot, beyond what even I could tolerate. At the risk of spoiling Eliza, I suggested respite from the heat at the creek that ran below the hillside. Our first cabin was there, but the occasional floods had forced us to rebuild higher. Our new home caught the breeze, and we saw long views from its height, although we had sacrificed the close convenience of the water.

Ah, but the walk down was worth the effort. Arno bolted happily ahead of us, splashed, and shook a spray that sparkled in the light. The creek ran cool and refreshing. We removed our shoes, sat on the bank, and thrust our feet into the water.

"Delightful." Her skirt at her thighs, Eliza sighed and sank up to her knees into the stream. "It's different from the beach in Galveston. The Gulf water can be soothing, but the salt and sand do stick to your skin. And there's *never* shade except for your own parasol."

"Hmmm," I said, wishing she would stop the chatter and let me enjoy the peace of the moment.

"Yes, lovely," she said, but then she opened her eyes wide.

"Do you think there are many fishes? What if the Comanches come here to fish? Or cool down? Do you think wildlife waits to attack us here? What if—"

"*Ja*! We are in great danger if we say a single word. We must be absolutely silent."

"But how can—"

"Shhh!" I leaned back against a boulder. "Even whispers can be heard."

Her eyes darted about, and at last, she clamped her lips shut.

I slid deeper and closed my eyes to concentrate on the trill of the stream over my knees and across my thighs, putting out of mind the fear that my husband's politics could endanger us all.

When I next opened my eyes, the sun had lost its zenith and found a path across my brow. *How could I have dozed?* Arno barked in the distance. "Eliza, we must go! We have dallied too long, and Arno appears to have found something of interest."

She jumped up and shoved her feet into her shoes. Grasping her skirt like a little girl, she scrambled up the bank. "What could it be? Not that awful man, do you think?" She pulled her derringer from her pocket.

"Oh, put that away." I nearly laughed. "I can tell from Arno's bark, it is no warning. More of a welcome. Perhaps a friend."

"You have friends?"

Impudent child.

Eliza

Not more than a buckboard, it was laden with merchandise. Arno stood wagging his tail as the old man lumbered down from his seat on the wagon.

"Howdy, howdy. Stoppin' by to give y'all the first opportunity at these fine wares. And to see how y'all was doin' given the trouble about." Sweeping off his top hat, he smiled a toothless grin and ran his hand through a greasy tangle of gray hair. "And who is this little lady?" He bowed deeply with one leg extended like some courtier he must have seen drawings of.

I stepped back, waiting for Kat to take the lead.

Kat grinned. "Ah! Old friend! Sit a while. I bring you apple cider." She led him to a bench under the big oak.

I had to shut my mouth. She was always so suspicious and intolerant of strangers. How did this old coot worm his way into her regard? I stood a safe distance away with my hand on Arno. But when Kat headed to the house, the old man turned a rheumy eye on me.

"New here, ain'tcha? Picked a right chancy time to put your foot in here 'bouts. With that red hair and dark eyes, ya ain't German. You and me neither. Aloysius Adair, at your service. But you can call me Olly. Kinda got a ring to it, don't it? Learned to speak the language some though. No help for it if you wanna keep up business. Mrs. Lange? She's tolerant. Of me, anyhow. I'm the one that give her that pup there you got by the neck. Kinda got me in good with her. Puts a lot of stock in that critter. Glad he still remembers me when I come driving up. Hate to get on his bad side."

"Yes, sir. Pleased to meet you." I made a quick dip of a curtsy.

"Go on and take a look at what I got. May be the last time I get around here, seein' how things is heatin' up. Find you something. A little girl like you needs a pretty."

I wanted to correct him. Tell him I was not "a little girl." I was a married lady, but the wagon was just full of interesting things. I had little to add to the conversation since he and Kat would probably lapse into German the minute she returned. Although I had acquired some understanding, I spoke very little and was at a decided disadvantage if expected to contribute.

Marveling at the pots and jugs, knives, syrups, and potions, I circled the wagon, touching the items and wondering at their costs. Although cooking had never been my passion, I inspected a large pot. In it sat a small gold music box, elegant in its floral design. I held the trinket in the palms of my hands and opened it.

"Slide that little lever to the right," called Mr. Adair.

A mechanical bird emerged from the top. It charmed me—the little beak of bone, its feathers vividly colored—red and blue and green, the intricate metalwork, and delicate filigree of the box. The sweetest melody issued forth. I held it to my ear and swayed to the tempo of its tune—a waltz as though played on a harpsichord. Like a butterfly flitting flower to flower. I wanted to play it over and over. "Oh, oh, I must have it! I hope it is not too dear."

"Hard to say. Heard tell it come from a rich old widow woman in Louisiana. Entertained her guests with it till she died. So guessin' it's worth a pretty penny. How much ya got?"

"Why, I've got a lot of money!"

"Confederate paper?"

Straightening my shoulders, I put on a confident smile and said, "Of course! The currency of our country."

"That ain't enough. I got to make a livin'. You come up with a piece I can bite into and put a dent in, we might could work somethin' out."

The possibilities ran through my mind—my grandmother's cameo brooch, the pearl ring I'd been given on my fifteenth birthday, the five double eagles sewn into the hem of the dress I'd been married in. Chloë had pressed her lips together. "Hmmm," she had said with as much derision as she could muster. "Your daddy told me to have them stitched in. In case someday you come to your senses and want to get back home."

"I have something. I'll be right back." I hiked my skirt and took to the house as fast as I could go, the music box clutched in my fist.

"Hey! Leave that here!"

"I told you," I shouted over my shoulder. "I have something!"

I flew up the stairs to my room. The trunk was jammed against the wall, but I pulled it away. With scissors in hand, I snipped the threads from the hem of my gown. I loosened a gold coin and briefly contrasted it to the music box. A pittance for the pleasure. The box would give me endless hours of delight. *And shoo!* I'd never change my mind about Will. I'd never need to pay my fare back to Galveston. Not in a hundred years.

When I ran back outside, Kat was serving Olly Adair a mug of apple cider. I rushed over to him and slapped the coin into his free hand.

"Well, looky here. The girl goes for what she wants." His mouth stretched wide, he bit the gold piece with the few back teeth he had left and stuffed it into his watch pocket.

Kat's mouth dropped open. "You have a gold double eagle?"

"I do indeed. A gift from my daddy to be spent on anything I choose." I lifted the lid to the music box and slid the lever over. "Have you ever seen anything so darling?" The melody tinkled out and sang to my heart. It seemed music a fairy might play.

Kat frowned. "I have never seen such reckless waste in all my life. This is only gold-plated." She faced the old man. "Olly, give the child her money back."

He put his palm over his pocket and turned his head back and forth much as an owl might.

"No need," I said, "I would not take it. It is my decision to make, and I have made it."

"Ladies, ladies, let's not bicker. There's rumors to be heard if you're interested." Without waiting for our response, he launched into what was clearly a well-practiced soliloquy. "That Scotsman's back. Been makin' threats."

Kat and I locked eyes.

"Lucky I am too old and ornery to conscript," he continued, "but hearsay is you Germans is in his sights. Three days to conscript or he'll round you up and lock you down or worse. Hangin's been noted. Properties ransacked." He took a long slug of his drink. "Fightin' for the Confederacy ain't so bad. Meanin' if ya got

to choose between principles and hangin', I'd let my high-mind-
edness drop a notch or two."

With that, he limped to the wagon and struggled to the seat.
"Good day to ya now. Much obliged for the apple cider." He tipped
his hat, clucked to the mule, and yelled back over his shoulder.
"You enjoy that music box, hear!" The wagon pulled away, deep-
ening the ruts in the road from recent rains.

I clutched the small box to my breast. Oh, how I would treasure its music. It would put a little joy back in my life.

~

A week later a letter came from Will. He would be coming home
for another horse. Dancer had foundered. His poor feet were ruined, and the cavalry had no use for him. They shot him. Shot my
beautiful pony. He was never meant to be a warhorse, and they
had killed him. The anticipation of seeing my husband diminished
the loss, but the thought of Dancer lying in the dust hurt my heart.

Riding another horse too lame for cavalry service, Will would
come home on short leave with the purpose of attaining another
mount. He might want Legend, but I would never part with him.
He could beg a horse off Günter.

Still, my husband was returning! My darling was coming home!

~

Almost before I had the chance to make repairs to my person, we
heard the hoofbeats coming off the path from Fredericksburg. Will
threw his reins on the ground and burst through the gate. I was in
his arms, feeling his strength, the sweat, his rough beard—the man
he had become. I wanted to pull him straight up the stairs and not
share him with another soul. I would never let him leave me again.
The war be damned. But, of course, it was too late.

Kat stood unsmiling at the door. "Wilhelm," she said, "*Willkommen zu Hause*. Günter will be home soon, but let me offer you some supper." She stepped away, expecting him to follow, and for the first time I could remember, Will chose pork roast and turnip greens over me. He took off his hat, dusted off his britches, and marched straight into the kitchen. I grabbed his hand and hurried along beside him. Buttering his biscuits and gazing into his eyes, I tried to send an alluring message. Over his plate, he looked up at me and winked. He taunted me as I had so often teased him. Well, I would soon turn the tables.

Less than an hour later, I led him up the stairs. I sponged his face and neck, his arms and body, which gave evidence of his arousal. While I lay across him, shaving his face, I had to continually rebuff his hands until at last, I stood and undid the buttons on my dress until it dropped to the floor. I unbraided my hair, and brushing it, leaned over the looking glass. Laughing at my seduction, Will stood, grabbed me around my middle and deposited me in the bed, his bed now for at least a few days. Kat did not lay eyes on us until late the next day. I would not wash the bedding for days afterward.

CHAPTER 6

In the 1860s, the "dogs of war" unleashed here a sanguinary par-
oxysm of terror and death, a calamity that fostered for decades
thereafter bitterness and distrust.
– Joe Baulch, *The Dogs of War Unleashed: the Devil Concealed in*
  Men Unchained, West Texas Historical Association

Katarina

It was late the following afternoon when the lovers emerged
from their room with Eliza playing her music box over and over
for Wilhelm. Though the light stayed with us well past supper, I
was impatient for Günter to return home from what he referred to
as "a meeting of like minds."

At last, dust rose in the distance as Günter thundered down
the road. Wilhelm and I rushed forward to meet him as the horse's
haunches slid to a stop, and he dismounted. He threw the reins at
Wilhelm. "It has come to the worst," he said. "Duff is back, and
his men follow me. Hide a fresh horse for me by the creek and
bring it up when it is safe, and then remain with our wives. Since
you have signed on with the Confederate forces, you should be
safe. I will never commit treason against the United States, but
you did not forge that loyalty. For now, I must flee or hang. I will
return for the horse tonight."

Günter was gone to the fields before I could gather my thoughts
or ask what to do, and Wilhelm had haltered one of Günter's mares
and sprinted toward Wolf Creek.

Eliza stumbled forward. "What?" Clutching her trinket to her breast, she stopped and stepped back when she saw my face. "What's wrong?" Though I failed to completely understand what had befallen us, Eliza seemed truly naïve of our reality. We could do nothing but wait for Wilhelm to return. We paced the porch until he finally rushed up from the creek.

"It is nothing we cannot deal with," Wilhelm said. "But you must do as I tell you. Go to our bedroom. Take Arno with you. Bolt the door. James Duff will be paying another visit. He will likely cause damage in the search for Günter, but you must be quiet. You have not seen Günter and do not know where he might be." When Wilhelm held Eliza by her shoulders and stared into her eyes, she shook her head, then nodded as if she was confused about the right response.

As Wilhelm returned to the barn to hide a saddle for Günter, Eliza and I hurried up the stairs, calling Arno with us. It was not long until we heard riders. I lifted the window enough to hear threats demanding to know who Wilhelm was. Wilhelm informed Duff that he, himself, had conscripted with the Texas 1st.

Duff forced his way into the barn shouting for Günter. "His horse still got foam between his haunches," he said to Wilhelm. "Lange on foot then? Couldn't have got too far."

Wilhelm stuttered that Günter had gone to Bear Creek, hoping to recruit men to join the Confederacy—a ridiculous lie anyone would see through, and there was no point in trying to fool Duff. He knew well of my husband's loyalties. He sent his men to search the fields.

When the men reported back saying they had no success in finding Günter, Duff said, "He'll show up. Can't stay gone forever. He'll get too hungry for his sausage and sauerkraut." Duff moved out to the gate, pushing Wilhelm ahead of him. He swirled his hand over his head. "Take a look around, fellows. Bring along anything you think we can use. Them horses will do." Duff took

Wilhelm by the elbow. "Mount up, boy. If you ain't said your goodbyes, too bad. Pony that pretty little bay behind you, and we'll see if the Texas 1st really has you on their rolls. If you ain't, I'll *recruit* you into the Partisan Rangers."

Stiff-legged and hackles raised, Arno faced the window. Eliza laid her hand on him, but when she heard Duff order Wilhelm to his horse, she was out the bedroom and down the stairs with Arno leading the way. I followed and tried to stop her, but she threw herself against her husband's mount. "Not this way! This is not the way it is supposed to be!" Out of pure foolhardiness, she turned on Duff. "It is an honor and a privilege to fight for the Confederate States of America! Not abducted and demeaned by scum such as you! I will have you know my husband has already conscripted with the Texas 1st." She held onto Arno's ruff. "And you may not have my horse either. Legend is *mine*. My papa gave him to *me*!" A hot breeze blew dust into her eyes, and she put a fist to her face like a child.

I thought she would be shot through. Duff's face colored and he leveled his gun at her. Then he began to laugh. He turned to Wilhelm. "Not every German's got a little girl to speak up for him— and such a pretty one." Duff leaned back and crossed his arms. "Go ahead, kiss her goodbye. Make it good. I'm gonna watch."

Wilhelm leaned down into Eliza's lifted arms. "I will write. It will not be so bad. The war cannot last long, and I will do the best I can for your Confederacy." He dropped his voice. "Remember, it is Company C. The cavalry. You and Katarina are to be safe." He threw a threatening glance at Duff. "We knew it would probably come to this." He choked once but said again, "I will write."

Wilhelm rode toward Fredericksburg with Eliza running alongside until he spurred his horse and moved into the ranks of the party. With her skirts puddled around her, she sat in the road, sobbing, her arms around Arno until I came to lift her up and walk her back to the house.

~

It was after midnight when Arno stood at my open door, his tail in a slow whisk back and forth. I had heard nothing, but he must have sensed Günter was home. Stepping out into the warm night, I found Günter saddling the horse Wilhelm had hidden for him.

"How did you escape them?" I whispered, looking about me in fear that someone could hear us.

"The corn sheaves," he said. "Too many to look through. Duff's men came close, but they missed me." He cinched the horse a second time. "We are leaving. It has been planned for weeks now. The governor proclaimed that men who had not taken the Oath of Allegiance must leave the state within the month, but Duff prefers his own interpretation—three days. Herr Tegener, who we have appointed as leader of the Unionists, has sent word that any man unwilling to conscript can meet him at Turtle Creek where we will head to Mexico and join the Federal Army. It is the right thing to do. Wilhelm's joining the Confederates should deflect danger from you and the farm."

How could Günter dictate my life as though I had no investment in it? I slammed my hand against a barn plank. "And yet I am left to carry on with this no-account child for my only help? Somewhere your loyalties have drifted off the mark!"

"Regardless of my choice, you would be left to fend for yourselves. With no alternatives, we are between the devil and the deep blue sea." His mouth twisted in a smirk. "To coin a phrase."

I could not drive the anger from my heart. With little concern for me, he was leaving to follow his principles. I hated it all. The war. Unionists. Secessionists. Comanches. Men were makers of war. We women were left to bury the dead, bandage the fallen, and sweep up the ashes.

"Go then," I screamed. "Take your pride and your morals and run!" I felt the hot track of tears down my face. "Go!"

He shushed me with his mouth hard on mine. Did fear stoke his passion—the excitement of peril? But it evoked a dormant fire in me. I matched him. It was as it had been in the early days of our marriage—a compulsion to be together, a passion that could not be quelled. Until our lovemaking resulted in heartbreak, and he could not stand to watch me become consumed with sorrow for the lost babies. I wanted him. I refused to think of consequence. In moments, I was ready for him, loosening garments, helping him, easing the way.

As we lay together in the brief moments afterward, I begged in desperate whispers, "Do not go. Do not leave our life. I may never see you again. I may—"

He kissed me again, gentler this time. "I must. You will see me again. I promise you."

A sweet lie, but there was no use in arguing. He was stepping into the stirrup and urging the horse on before he was completely in the saddle.

If I did see him again, he would not be the same. Things would never be the same. He would leave me, but I swept everything from my mind except our moment together. And the one belief that if he never returned, that memory would be enough.

Eliza

His nails clicking on the plank floor, Arno left the room. I called his name quietly, but he continued out the door and down the stairs. I sat up in the bed, the sheet hot where I had lain. Moonlight cast fractured shadows through the oak branches—fractured like our lives. I had brought this on us—sweet-talking and pestering Wilhelm until he felt his only choice was to do what I wanted. Now he was gone.

At the sound of hoofbeats, I stepped to the window. Günter rode into the night while Kat held onto the fence railing and then crumpled to the ground. Arno ambled over to her, waiting till her shoulders stopped shaking to nudge her. She stood finally and made her way to the house. I heard her footsteps on the stairs and the quiet click of her bedroom door.

I could not bear it and yet had no means to bring her solace. I thought of my music box. Possibly its little tune could make her smile, no matter how briefly. She called it a trinket and perhaps it was, but it was all I had. Stealing down the hall to her room, I tapped on the door. "Kat…Katarina." No answer. I opened the door and tiptoed to her bed where she lay, her face pressed into the covers.

She turned away even farther as I touched her arm.

"You may play this little music box as many times as you like. Just slide the lever over. It may be silly, but it is a sweet distraction. Listen to it until you are too sleepy to wind it even one more time. I leave it with you." I touched her shoulder and held my hand there a few moments before slipping back to my room and wishing I had that sweet music to ease my own pain.

~

I woke to silence just before dawn. No busy clanking in the kitchen. No husband in my bed. No moon or stars in the black sky. It felt deserted. There was no help for it. I must rise and dress. Face this awful day.

In the kitchen, the cooking fire was not lit. How strange it felt to be awake and down before the industrious mistress of the house. I stepped back out into the early light. Dawn crept over the hills, the morning still cool before the searing heat of the summer sun. The chickens fussed to be let out, and the cow moaned in anticipation. How different when you're all alone in this Hill Country. I unlatched the coop before returning to the kitchen to make coffee. We had saved some, and this was a morning Kat and I both needed consolation—some small luxury she might otherwise deny us. I didn't feel afraid yet. Not yet. Just odd. The whole world was waking, but I dream-walked.

Perhaps the aroma drifted to Kat's room because at last, stirring came from above. Preceded by the echoes of Arno's nails, her first steps seemed cautious, but by the time Kat reached the ground floor, they smacked of their usual decisive grit. She opened the door with an unguarded look on her face that I had never seen before—loss, indecision—before it quickly reverted to the mask, that serenely blank expression, she wore to cloak frailty.

I felt the impulse to rise and comfort her, to find some common ground, for I needed consolation as well. I wanted my mamá, my Chloë. I wanted Galveston, the city streets away from this stark isolation. Oh, if only I could go there to wait for Will. Not have to work every day with Kat monitoring my every move. She could do just as well without me. I surely did wish she could be sweet to me. We might get on better. She was afraid too, but she would never admit it, never give in. She thought me a ninny.

Katarina set the music box on the table. "*Danke schön.*"

"I've made coffee," I said. "Not acorn coffee—*real* coffee. I know you think it's a luxury to be deferred, but let's choose to make it consolation." Remembering that instant before—that lost expression, the cut-to-the-quick helplessness before she recovered, I softened my voice. "Günter is gone too then." I waited.

"To fight for his country." She spoke with her chin raised, her lips pressed as though Günter's departure was far more noble than Wilhelm's.

"And you think Will is fighting for the enemy?" I asked. "At least, he's keeping that man Duff away. While Günter follows his principles, we are left to submit to this bully who is no more the Confederate gentleman than any of those bluecoats."

"If Günter stayed, we would all suffer, regardless of Wilhelm's stance." Kat used the hem of her skirt as a potholder and sloshed coffee into her cup. "Coffee is appropriate. But it is *my* coffee, and I will decide in the future when it is to be meted out."

With an open mouth, I struggled for a clever retort, but she cut me off.

A flash of regret crossed her face. "Let us not discuss our different thinking. We will survive as best we can. Do not doubt my competence. I have lived here for over ten years. When our men return, there will be a home to come home to. I intend to sustain it."

If I showed weakness, she would mock my tears. I would match her game. At least until I could find a way home. And I'd be gratified to leave her here stewing in her counterfeit bravado.

CHAPTER 7

*Tegener announced that all unwilling to serve the Confederacy
would rendezvous August 1 on Turtle Creek, southwest of Kerrville,
from whence they would proceed to the border. At the scheduled
time and place, sixty-two men left the Hill Country under Tegener's
direction, moving slowly westward toward the Rio Grande, taking
few precautions since they were within the thirty day time period
assumed given by the Governor.... Informed by his Kerr County
spy of the Tegener party's departure, James Duff ordered troops to
pursue. On the morning of August 10, on the upper reaches of the
West Nueces River, Confederates under Lieutenant C. D. McRae
surprised the Tegener party, initiating an uneven hour-long battle.*
– Joe Baulch, *The Dogs of War Unleashed: the Devil Concealed in
Men Unchained,* West Texas Historical Association

Katarina

L imestone walls insulated us against the heat, so indoor work
was left for afternoons. Having done our morning chores
without a word spoken between us, Eliza marched into the kitch-
en, slapped a piece of ham between slices of bread, and walked
back out, patting her leg for Arno to follow.

I, too, retired to my bed with a wet cloth for my neck, turning
it from spot to spot as my skin heated it. Staring at the ceiling, I
wondered where Günter was now and if he had made it to Turtle
Creek. Had he and the other men already begun their journey
to the border? Did his thoughts still linger on our last moments

together, or were his eyes and heart strained toward a future that did not include me?

Eliza probably lay on her bed considering our plight as well. She would be reliant on me to direct her. The corn was harvested and only moderately diminished by the sale to Duff. We could plant a small winter crop and let the chickens propagate. The horses were gone, but we had our cow, a few pigs. There would be cheese and smoked ham and sausage if we could slaughter a pig. The thought of bleeding the hog addled my mind—the squeal, the blood. Günter had always hired help at hog butchering time. I had contributed to the rendering but was spared the man's job. Now, it was my job. *Our* job, even if I had to solicit help from town since Eliza might faint at the task. I would have to teach her the worth of a woman.

Pride filled me. I would demonstrate no fear, no weakness. I would make do without the help of a man. I scrambled to the side table and began to list the bare basics we would have to accomplish to maintain our living standards.

~

As the afternoon breeze stirred the trees, I sat in the kitchen waiting for Eliza to come downstairs from her nap. Finally, I banged the supper bell to wake her.

Rubbing her eyes, she came to the kitchen, coaxing Arno to sit beside her, as if he were her talisman. I, in turn, enticed him with a ham biscuit. Loyalty bought with hors d'oeuvre.

I unfolded the assignment sheet. "I wrote a plan." I cleared my throat and handed Eliza the notes I had written. "This is what we will do. Commit it to memory. Habit will embed it even if you choose to avoid it. It will be our life until this rebellion is contained. And mark my words—it will be. We must simply make the best of it. We have more resources than most. Not so much in cash. The Confederate dollar is worth little." I thought about the gold pieces she had confessed were sewn into her skirt hem. In that respect, we were well fitted.

Eliza's hand shook—a slight tremor that had not been there before. She frowned at the print I had carefully produced in English.

"And each chore?" she asked. "Yours to impose and mine to curry favor with?"

"I see you need more time." I snatched the paper and smoothed it out on the table before turning my back on her. "As long as you can commit before day's end. I will go ahead with the work, but there is little idle time. Look about you—the fields, the barn, the house, and yard. It all depends on you and me. And we must rise to the occasion."

Eliza

A week had gone by since our men departed. No one had come to threaten or harass us, and we began to breathe easier. Perhaps Will's sacrifice had appeased the provost marshal, and he had given up chasing down Günter.

As if work were a salve for loss and heartache, Kat drove us hard with chores. She could think of nothing else but enumerating what needed to be done. Or darning. Or writing letters to Günter, ones she would never mail for she had no idea where he was or if he was even alive. It seemed she felt kindlier to him now that he was gone. When he was at home, they tended to ignore each other, focusing instead on responsibilities, while Will and I—my breath caught at the memory of those nights in his arms.

The following day, I would go into Fredericksburg to check for news or posts from Will. I didn't expect there to be any. Not yet. But maybe from Mamá. Until then, I was to collect the sheaves of corn and weed the last of the summer garden. Then stand over the hot stove pickling okra, my hair stringing and sticking to my cheeks, sweat dripping into my eyes while Kat scrutinized my every move. Walking the eight miles into town would be a reprieve from this drudgery. If I started out at dawn, I could be there in little more than two hours, and if I waited to return until very late afternoon, the sun would be low and not burning the life out of me.

It would not do to leave before sunrise, so I would have to face Kat as I walked out the door. I expected dire warnings of Comanches and Confederate bushwhackers who raided the countryside, and wolves and panthers and on and on. But in broad daylight, I had nothing to fear. I would carry my derringer. And when all was said and done, getting away for the day would be worth every supposed danger and every step of the journey. Why, I might even encounter an acquaintance along the way who would offer me a carriage ride. Pleasant diversion and clever repartee were desperately lacking in this household. My heart sped so with excitement, I thought I might not sleep.

~

Before the rooster crowed, I was dressed. At the last minute, I ripped the double eagles from my hem and stitched them into my petticoat. It made the fabric hang below my hem, but I hoisted the waistline a little higher on that side and hoped no one would think I was shabby. What if there were a coach headed for the coast? Dare I step into it, hand the driver my fare and leave the Kat here with her beloved labor? Might I? Oh yes, I might.

I strode into the kitchen, grabbed a biscuit, and continued out the door.

Following me, Kat cautioned me every step to the gate and down the path to the road, "I hope you take your little gun. Do not walk in the middle. Keep to the trees."

I never stopped, waving my arm over my head, and calling, "Don't fret, I shall be back before dark."

The dawn sent diagonals of light through the oak trees, bright shafts of sunshine that promised serenity in timid birdsong and the lighthearted murmur of the creek. I glanced back just once. Arno followed me to the end of the path, stopped to look back at Kat, then sat and watched me. Turning, I marched down the road, swinging my arms. Let the men fight their war. For now, I refused to think about another thing besides the mockingbird and soft breeze that began the day.

Katarina

From the kitchen, I watched Eliza walk away. Part of her petticoat drooped lopsided beneath her skirt giving her a comically asymmetrical appearance. Beneath her bonnet, that red hair was already slipping loose from the chignon she so haphazardly twisted into shape. The wavering window glass distorted her figure, and she seemed to shimmer as she sashayed off into the rising light. *Little fool.*

If she thought I was going to spend the day fretting about her, she was mistaken. The thought of a day of solitude brought peace. Fearing her being a nosy parker, I had not been to the little graves since she arrived. But on this hot sunny afternoon, I would take my tea and talk to my babies and imagine what might have been. Perhaps I would sit in the shade of their tree and visit in the afternoon with no interruption or question. It had been too long.

Rushing through my chores became a pilgrimage—a way back to the days of hope and loss and so very few happy memories. Their resting place, a secluded green spot overlooking Wolf Creek, was a short distance from the house. The red oak, grown taller now, shaded the slope. The *chirr* of cicadas quieted as I spread my quilt and sat. Arno grunted and settled nearby, seeming to know this was a solemn place.

If you stayed very still, you could imagine what it was like before our time. Before the Comanches. Before the Spaniards. Before humanity. You might still hear the scream of a red-tailed hawk, the wind song through the fine grasses, the trill of a meadowlark. How many lives crossed these paths, pondered the same beauty and treachery as I did now? How many children were sacrificed to this land?

I leaned back against the tree, cradling my arms before me, pretending to hold my baby against me, imagining the warmth, the delicate skin against mine, the life-giving sustenance I had to offer. My breasts ached with the dreaming. My children. The children who never even looked into my eyes or learned to smile. Two girls and a boy, so very, very small. Still, they were mine. Mine and Günter's—to bloom on earth, but blossom in heaven.

With each loss, I put away the few baby things I had made— the gowns, the blankets, and diapers—until finally, I gathered them and took everything to a woman in town who was expecting her first child. Günter knew about each loss but could not find words of comfort. For that, I could not summon forgiveness. Not for that.

What would life have been like with children in it? Would I have laughed more? Cried more easily? I plodded through my days with clenched fists and work my reason for living. "Stop," I said aloud. Arno perked his ears. "Oh, not you." I stroked his head. "It is me. I must stop my complaining. I will tell my children a story from the old country and the Brothers Grimm. And Arno? You listen as well, for you must protect us from the wolf.

"Once upon a time…."

Bees droned about, the sun briefly hid behind a cloud, and the breeze kicked up to cool us. *I should come here more often.* It was a sad peace, but peace, nonetheless. I closed my eyes.

Arno prodded me, and I woke with a start. It was not near dusk, but I cried aloud. Eliza might have returned by now, and I would have to explain my whereabouts. A lie formed as I hurried toward the house—I had been hunting for honey, though I had not found any. Certainly not near the red oak if she had seen me come from that direction. Glancing down the road, I breathed a sigh of relief. Nowhere was the bedraggled traveler.

Too early for the lanterns to be lit in the house and supper started, I paced about the kitchen planning for the evening meal. Perhaps I would just cook for me and explain that she had missed the hour. *Pity.* Still, Greta had to be milked and the chickens housed. My afternoon of reverie was costly. I chided myself for the time spent away from chores. Arno sensed my irritation and followed me from place to place, making an annoyance of himself. I pointed at the front steps and with my sternest voice ordered, "*Platz!*" He stared at me a moment too long for complete compliance but then dropped to his belly with a groan of complaint.

I prepared one serving of ham and corn, made a dessert of bread and blackberry jelly, and stared out the window. My mind was made. I would give her until seven this evening and then I would start down the road to meet her. Until then, I intended to set to work sweeping the floor. Then the hand scrubbing could be accomplished. It wore out my knees, but it begged to be done. It helped to switch arms every so often, and I was careful not to wipe my face with my free hand. I preferred to move, to do something rather than sit and stew over her whereabouts.

Eliza

I was directed to the post office on San Saba Road to collect our mail. It was such a small building that even the five or six people there made it feel crowded. Behind the counter, rows of mailboxes lined the wall, and I wondered which might belong to the Langes. I struggled through the people to ask the postmaster if any letters had come for a Mme. Wilhelm Lange or Miss Eliza Grey, in case my married name had slipped Mamá's mind. And just because I knew Kat would beleaguer me if I did not ask— "Or anything for Mrs. Günter Lange?"

The postmaster frowned and corrected me. "*Frau* Lange?" His eyebrows, gray and shaggy, hung like a shelf over his eyes. "*Nein*, I do not think there will be any letters from him," he continued in German. "Not for a while. If ever. I mean, there has been some news, but it is no good, and I hate for you to hear it from me."

It took a moment for me to understand what he implied. Then it felt like a stone dropped into my stomach. Oh God, was I going to have to deliver some terrible news to Katarina? Likely as not, she would blame me as the messenger. "Let me interrupt you, sir. Forgive my clumsy German, but perhaps I am not the party to whom you should be speaking. Let me inform Mrs. Lange that there is news, and she can pursue it on her own. I really do not think I should—"

"It is not for sure news. Of course, it is well known that Lange was in that group that set out for Mexico. He could have been one of them that got away, but if secessionists were involved, it is likely that things did not go well."

I lost track of his meaning and asked around for someone who might translate to English. A man stepped forward. He held a bowler hat in his hand and spoke English so precisely, I thought I was listening to one of my papa's business friends. How had he happened upon this dismal outpost?

"I understand the Scotsman sent troops to bring down the Unionists who escaped with a man called Tegener," he said. "They were told by the governor they had sufficient time to get out of Texas, but apparently that was not the case. Duff's men followed and caught them down by the Nueces about twenty miles north of Fort Clark. Assailed them in the middle of the night. Killed many."

I must have paled considerably because someone called for a chair and took my elbow to lead me to it.

The Englishman didn't miss a beat. "I am hardly involved in this squabble between the states, but it appears many have cast their integrity to the wind. Alas, it is the way of war. If the governor allowed dissenters time to get out of the state, then they were within their rights. I am sorry to be the bearer of this news, ma'am. Are you family?"

"Yes, yes. Is there any way we can confirm the survivors? I cannot bear to alarm Frau Lange with rumor."

"Little more to be done, ma'am, except to wait."

"Oh, then look again, please, for any mail from *Wilhelm* Lange," I said to the postmaster. "He's fighting for the South." I couldn't deny the pride in my voice, even in this mixed crowd. I knew many around here fought for the South because that was the only way to protect their family from the secessionists.

Folks glanced at each other and then at the floor. They understood my English better than they let on.

The postmaster made a show of shuffling through the letters and then shook his head sadly. "*Nein,* Frau Lange. But you check back soon. There will be something along directly."

"Directly? Do you mean in the next few days, or do you mean weeks or months from now? Honestly, I cannot tolerate this uncertainty!"

The postmaster sniffed and nodded to the person behind me to step forward.

I realized that coming across as uppity would gain me no ground. "I apologize. Forgive me. I am distraught. Surely, he would have written by now. It just seems impossible that no letter has come through."

He studied for a moment before speaking. "The war, Frau Lange. The war has hindered us all."

I *was* sincere in my apology. Mamá frequently reminded me that disappointment was better expressed through tears than tantrums. Galveston was a city with luxuries unheard of on this frontier. Mail was delivered on a regular basis there. If I could just get back to Galveston, I could send and receive mail without begging the postmaster. I could find Will's commanding officer and send word through him of my new address. I had to escape this godforsaken place. "I'm a citizen of Galveston, sir, and I really should get back home until this awful war is won. When does the stagecoach make its stop?" I asked. "And where might I buy a ticket?

An elderly man spoke up. "Why, ma'am, we ain't got no stage. What we got is seventy-five miles of bad roads, steep hills, and water crossings. Takes a week or more for a freight wagon to make a run to San Antonio and back. And ofttimes they ain't got mail. You might find a freight wagon, but a little thing like you couldn't tolerate the hardship clear to Galveston."

"Then no train?"

The group who had become interested spectators mocked me with "What? No train? No stagecoach to Galveston?" Oh, they spoke in German and lowered their voices, but I understood enough to detect derision. Someone blurted out, "How did you get here? It is clear you are not of this community." There was nodding and clearing of throats.

"I came by carriage with my husband. I thank you kindly." Taking a deep breath, I remembered how my mamá dealt with the impertinent. I lifted my chin and strolled off down the walk, taking carc to hide the apprehension I felt. It might be weeks before Kat would have to learn of the attack on Günter's group. Maybe she would hear from Günter. Maybe he escaped if he wasn't one of the victims. I wouldn't think about it anymore. It was of no use. Still, a flash of imagination revealed a scene of carnage.

Maybe I could hire a driver and his buckboard and just keep going straight on to Galveston. It couldn't be much worse than our travel when we came here. *Damn James Duff for stealing our horses!* I could take one breath easier—Will was not with

Günter's bunch. He, at least, had made the right choice to fight for our cause. I bit my tongue to keep from thinking that he had no alternative at all.

All I could do was pray. And pray I would. *Vereins Kirche*, the society church, was just across the street. I had heard it was available to all faiths. Pope Pius would not mind. At least, I didn't think he would. And surely, God had a sense of humor if he resided in a building shaped like a coffee grinder. Still, when I entered, it offered a quiet enough area, and despite a few others who milled about, I knelt in a small space by the door and asked God to spare Will and Günter. They had not wanted to go to war. All they had asked for was a few acres of land to build a new life after leaving the old country. I asked for forgiveness for my selfishness with regards to states' rights and slavery. I would free Chloë if that would please God. *I couldn't have her anyway.* Then I had to ask forgiveness for thinking that.

I felt better. Perhaps God had saved Günter and perhaps He would put an angel on Will's shoulder. Surely, *surely*, He would. Why, He just had to.

I stepped outside into the blazing sun of August. If there was no escape by stagecoach or train, and God would not intervene on my behalf, the only thing that would set me free was a horse. I turned on my heel and marched right back to the post office.

"The nearest livery stable, please?"

All heads turned toward me, but the old fellow who understood me spoke up. "Ma'am, they ain't gonna let you rent no horse to ride to Galveston. They ain't got no horses to rent, period. Secesh has got 'em if they's worth a Confederate dollar."

"The livery stable, sir." I stamped my foot. "I will be the judge of what is worth a Confederate dollar." I felt the weight of the double eagles in my hem.

"Ah, well then. Certainly, in *that* case. The Nimitz Hotel can oblige you in that department. Down the street to the end and across the road." He clamped his lips to suppress a snicker. "Keep a-going down thataway, and you'll find it. Can't miss it. Be sure to let us know what fine horse you choose." Someone behind me guffawed.

I dipped my chin in a stiff nod and headed out the door and down the street toward the livery.

The travelers had not yet arrived to board their mounts, and the stable appeared deserted, except for one stall that held a horse. It was a bay, gaunt and restless. Leaning over the railing, I studied the poor thing. I gasped. *Legend!* It was Legend! "Oh, sweet boy, what have they done to you?"

He nickered and snuffed my hand for treats. He had lost at least a hundred pounds and held his right hock off the ground.

"*Kann ich Ihnen helfen?*" Broad as he was tall, a man in the heavy apron of a blacksmith, stood behind me.

"Oh, my! You startled me." I took a deep breath and tried to appear calm. "Why, no. Not really. I was merely admiring this animal. I'm sorry but, *Sprechen sie Englisch*? I do much better in English."

"*Ja*, a little." He pinched his fingers together.

"Who owns this horse?"

The man snorted. "No gentleman, for sure. Duff stays here at the Nimitz. The horse is gone lame. I do best I can, but still no good. Fine horse. Shame."

"What do you mean? He'll get well, won't he?"

He shrugged his shoulders. "Herr Duff go to San Antonio in three days. If horse cannot go, give morphine. Sell quick."

"How much money?" I asked.

"If good, maybe two hundred Union. I make him *look* good."

Two hundred! I had less than half that. "Surely, the horse will regain his strength."

"*Nein*. Not in two days." The blacksmith shuffled in a bashful manner. "Your name, Fräulein?"

"Oh, Heidelberg. Frau Heidelberg." *What a stupid thing to say.*

"Heidelberg?" He scratched his head.

"Visiting." I hurried from the livery as quickly as I could and hoped with all my heart that he would not remember me.

If Duff was staying at the Nimitz, I must deny myself its general store. But surely, there were other places of interest. I ambled around the town but could think of nothing but Legend. One way or the other I would get him. Even Kat would stoop to bending her rules if it meant saving him.

In the heat of the day not many were out, and those who were seemed to immediately recognize me as an outsider. Rarely was there even a curt nod of the head. It would have never been like that in Galveston. Why, everyone smiled and happily answered any questions a traveler might have. I looked presentable enough. My parasol was the height of fashion, as well as my bonnet. Perhaps that was the problem. Stopping in front of a window storefront, I could see in my reflection that I did not conform to the dress of the local folk—the men wore blue striped hickory shirts, heavy boots, and no socks. Most fabrics were Kentucky denim. Women looked like Kat with their drab cotton dresses and boot-like shoes. Who in the world would want to embrace that style of attire?

My hem did sag a bit, and I hitched it up.

Could it be that I had walked the length of the town on both sides of the street and not taken advantage of my double eagles? Time had slipped away from me, and I looked with horror at the setting sun. In trouble again. I set out back to the house at a fast pace despite the ache in my limbs.

CHAPTER 8

We were traversing the eastern watershed of the mountains bordering the Rio Grande and the Mexican frontier, in which all the streams of Western Texas, such as the Pecos, Medina, Nueces, and Frio take their rise. Most of these, high up near their sources, run dry except in the heavy rains, or at best give only a scanty supply of water in pools, and at long intervals. But fortunately the Nueces was an exception, for we found it running strongly, though only a few inches deep, between cliffs a hundred feet high, and over a bed of solid rock of about the same number of feet in width. On this the trail was easy enough to follow, for the Germans' horses were all shod, and had left white marks on the rocks.
– Robert Hamilton Williams, *With the Border Ruffians, Memories of the Far West, 1852-1868*

Katarina

I felt justified in my anger. Was Eliza amused knowing I would start to worry? How dared she dawdle along the way when she knew it was unsafe? A waning moon rose as the sun was setting. An interesting phenomenon to distract me—the sun and the moon in the sky at the same moment. Was there some special name for it? If there was, was it foreboding?

I took the Henry from over the mantle and checked for ammunition. Loaded, as it should be. The Henry was what Günter would recommend. He had bought it just this year from a Union man desperate to sell. A rare find here in the South, this one would do great damage. "One of the finest weapons available," Günter had said the day he brought it in. "Sixteen shot rifle! I want you to learn to use it in case of Comanches or a panther. My musket is slow to load, and this will keep you safe."

Although I could barely manage the old muzzle-loading musket, I had protested. He grabbed my hand and pulled me out behind the garden to practice.

"Learn quickly and shoot sparingly," he had said. "The copper casings are dear, and I have a limited number. It is quite simple. One shot should discourage anyone who witnesses its authority."

And it did. I loaded it under his instruction and fired only three times to understand the power and response of the weapon. I knew I would feel quite safe with this at my side or on my shoulders—though its weight would be a hardship.

Arno and I set out down the road. Certainly not foolish enough to try the distance with the heavy rifle, I would go only partway, but any activity would help distract me from my worries. I told myself Eliza lacked thought for anything but her own entertainment, but what if she *was* in danger? I shook the thought from my mind.

The breeze seemed barely enough to move the clouds. No whippoorwills called in the August twilight, and except for the tremolo of screech owls, it was quiet enough that I could hear my own footsteps. Arno's panting as he followed along beside me gave no indication that anything was amiss, and I took that as comfort. The three-quarter moon had overtaken sundown. The road lay pale and clear in the moonlight, and our shadows wavered ahead of us—Arno's, a bear-like shape with a rambling gait, and mine, a tall, stick-like silhouette in the dust.

Reaching the curve in the road, the point at which I had predetermined to return to the house, I sighed. I could not imagine what she was thinking. Had she no sense of time and safety? And there I was, catering to a spoiled girl who seemed unconcerned about the dangers in this country.

Just as I turned to head back, Arno let out a welcoming bark, his tail waving over his rump. I thought to jump behind a tree and produce a war cry to put the fear of God in her. But Arno had already given us away.

There she came, her skirt dragging the ground, her hair undone. Before I had a chance to berate her, she ran forward, crying, "Oh, Katarina, Katarina! I found Legend!"

I held her at arm's length. "What do you talk about? I have struck out to meet you, yet I get no apology, only babble. Make sense, foolish girl."

"I found him! Lame at the livery in town. Duff near ruined him. They will sell him if he is not sound by Thursday. This is our chance! Don't you see? Come, let us think as we walk although my feet ache like fury. Do you suppose I could soak them when we get home? Oh, we can do this together, I just know, and you must help me devise a clever plan." She hugged me and kept a steady discourse until we finally came through our front gate, at which point she threw off her shoes, and with her skirt askew above her knees, ran past me for a bucket. Before I could hang my hat, I heard water pumping.

I made one last check on the barn and chickens and headed for the kitchen to have a glass of buttermilk before retiring. There at the table sat the girl, head dropped on her arms, feet soaking in water, and sound asleep. *Doof Mädchen.* Shaking my head, I heated up more water and added Epsom salts to the bucket at her feet.

~

Late as usual to the breakfast table the next morning, she sat to be served. I lifted the skillet and set it down hard. "Was there no letter from Günter or Wilhelm? Surely, we have some word by now. Nothing?"

"No. I asked twice, which required a translator in the form of a pompous little Englishman. But I was assured there was no letter from either of our men. Now! We must plan to—"

"It is time enough for a letter to get here from Mexico. I hope nothing—"

"You overestimate the efficiency of the mail, Katarina. We'll check again in a week or two. We've only got two days to save Legend. Please interrupt with any additions to my ideas, but here's what I've thought—"

I was sure interruption would have had to come in the form of firing the Henry.

"We'll need a good knife," she continued. "Your job will be to put it to the whetstone. I'll carry my derringer. The Henry would alert the stable hand. Then there is need for apple cider vinegar and witch hazel. Mix that up, will you please. I'll take a wrap and soak it once we get there. We'll use soot to cover the star on Legend's forehead and his white socks. There's one halter left. We'll wear our husband's shirts and trousers. Scarves will hold the pants up. What do you think of that?"

"Think? Just when do you propose we accomplish this heroic deed? Many obstacles stand in our way. Do you consider consequences? *Seriously* consider what might happen to us? I am quite sure this will land us in the prison at Fort Martin Scott."

Eliza stood. With a maniacal expression on her face, she pulled her shoulders up and back. "Why, if I pondered each and every casualty that in all happenstances might transpire every morning, it would be a marvel for me to put my feet on the floor. Legend is mine, and no damn renegade Secesh is going to rob me of him again." She turned away, hesitated, and faced me again. "What if our men return and need that horse?"

"Why do you imagine they would come back? Günter is well on his way to Mexico on his own mount." I studied Eliza carefully. Was she hiding something?

"Well, isn't it possible that something may have gone wrong, and he may need a horse?" Eliza stuttered on the words. "Oh, I don't know. We must be prepared. Don't you see?" But then she leaned forward, both palms flat on the table. "He's *my* horse!" The irises of her eyes, as dark as they always were, glittered black and full, and for the first time, I dared not thwart her.

Eliza

I lay awake that night and plotted. The moon would still be bright. Legend was a bay, but his three white stockings and even the star on his forehead might gleam bright on a clear night. If the Lord did not answer our prayers for a cloud-filled sky, then we would be prepared. And we must consider dark clothes, perhaps bandanas for our faces. Oh, there was so much to plan. So much detail and care. I turned on my side and stared out the window. "Go away, bold moon. Now is the time for surreptitious affairs, and you must hide your face." It filtered through the leaves of the oak and promised me nothing.

~

I was late again for breakfast, and Kat had done as she promised—the coffee pot was overturned, and the thin biscuits had hardened on the plate. I smothered one in blackberry preserves, stuffed it in my mouth, and ran out to the yard.

"The hogs snort with hunger," Kat said without looking up from her egg gathering. "Remember, what we feed them now affects the quality of our ham in the winter. Oh, but you take your time now. You chose to delay till the morning heat, and heavy sweat will be your reward."

"I spent the night planning and do believe I have it all worked out. I'll tell you at dinner, and you may certainly contribute to the strategy." I grabbed a bucket and headed out to slop the hogs. Calling over my shoulder, I said, "It may be very daring, but I firmly believe God is on our side." But when the ten o'clock sun hit my face, I could barely breathe and had to pull my bonnet down over my forehead. "Oh, please, God. No freckles."

At noon, I presented my ideas.

Kat glanced at the paper. "You numbered them."

"My mamá always recommended sequencing the steps to an objective. So," I continued, "if we depart late tomorrow afternoon, it will be quite dark by the time we arrive in town. Surely, there is a back way to the livery so as not to attract attention. The stable hand will have completed his tasks by then, and we'll be free to slip into the stall. Then you guide Legend away while I create a little diversion of smoke and stampeding horses!"

"Have you lost your mind? Burn down the barn?"

"Not enough to burn down the barn, Katarina. For goodness sake! But the horses may not flee without a little smoke to scare them. Oh, and who cares if it *does* burn down? I'll run the horses out in time. The important part is that it will take all night to collect the horses and realize that one is missing. We have a cause that begs our boldness."

Kat began to tie her apron as she gazed out the window. I waited for some confirmation. Instead, she turned on me and slung her apron away.

"I will not!" she said. "This is an irresponsible act. Childish crowing."

I narrowed my eyes at her. She was going to be stubborn. "All right! All right then," I said. "There is a little more to the story that I heard in town. Just a disconcerting rumor. Well, maybe not exactly rumor." I stepped forward to take her arm. "Some of the men in Günter's party may not have made it all the way to Mexico. Some, and I repeat, *some* may have been thwarted by Duff's Partisan Rangers down by the Nueces."

"Thwarted? Speak clearly!"

"A few of the men were hurt, others were captured and some escaped. You cannot deny that Günter might possibly return. I think it one more reason to have a horse for him, just in case."

Kat sat down hard in the chair. "You knew this all along? And you did not tell me?"

"Well, it was not *confirmed*…precisely. I didn't want to worry you needlessly."

"But you tell me *now* to manipulate me." She put her hands to her face. "You! You leave me no choice."

I shrugged. "You have to think of all the possibilities. It's worth the chance, Katarina. We need a fresh horse should Günter—"

"You have said quite enough. You get your way. I hope you know how hard it is to trust you."

"Well, Katarina, it's hardly a matter of trusting me. You must believe in the cause!"

~

Late afternoon the next day, we set out, the hems of our trousers dragging in the dust, our hair tied and tucked into the brimmed hats with rounded crowns that our husbands had left behind. We carried knapsacks containing soot, apple cider vinegar, and witch hazel, the halter, and lead rope. And the derringer. Having made Arno stay against his wishes, we listened to him complain until we were out of earshot. We looked back only once, but he remained behind the gate.

Her brow furrowed, her mouth grim, Kat hardly responded to my conversation. I supposed I *had* influenced the situation to my advantage. She'd probably counted every doubt and fear she had. A brief flash of guilt entered my mind, but I shook it off. There was a goal to be met, and I would see it through.

As the afternoon progressed, the sky began to cloud ever so slightly, and I prayed the good Lord listened to my pleas for a shrouded moon.

Only once did Kat speak out. "I *do* think you have gone mad, Eliza. It is likely that we will be the first women to hang in Gillespie County."

"My papa will see that that never happens. He is an influential man, and even if he has to denounce us as deranged and commit us to be locked in the attic for a period, he'll see that we're not garroted at the whim of a madman such as Duff."

"That is a fine thread to dangle our fates on."

"*Extremis malis extrema remedia.*"

"I, too, was schooled in Latin," Kat said, "but folks around here can be dangerous when challenged."

Approaching town, we confirmed the streets were quiet. To avoid San Saba Road, Kat suggested that even though we'd get wet, we should walk in through Town Creek running behind the livery. Our cuffs hung heavy with water, and my ankle turned more than once on stones in the creek bed. "Wait, here," I whispered as we left the creek to climb the short rise to the back of the livery. "Let me check on the stable boy." I wrung out my pants legs, slid through the split rail of the corral, and peered around the corner of the building. I spied a lad of about sixteen. His chair propped back on two legs, he leaned against the barn wall. With his arms folded on his chest and his chin sagged to his collarbone, he seemed insensible enough for us to continue.

We unhooked the two rails that would allow us to make our escape with Legend and slipped through the corral to the inside of the livery. In the dark, with the comforting smell of hay and horse dung, horses chuffed and shuffled in their stalls. I signaled for Kat to follow me.

Eight stalls. Feeling along the rough planks of each until I reached the fourth one, I whispered, "Legend, we have come to save you." I wanted to cry, but there was no time for tears. Slipping through the boards, I leaned against him and ran my hands over his neck, feeling the knots in the fine hair of his mane. With a little grunt, Kat squeezed in behind me.

Letting my hand slide across his back down to his hocks, I said, "This one feels cool to the touch. Let me try the other." And sure enough, the other leg felt heated as though after a long run. "This is the one. Here, soak the rags in the witch hazel and vinegar." I could tell by the set of Kat's jaw that it annoyed her to no end to have to take instructions from me, a girl from Galveston, but this was one thing I had chosen to acquaint myself with—the care of my horses. To Papa's dismay, our stable boy taught me that and much more. I was ordered to stay away while the help was employed there, but I disobeyed him too many times to count.

Kneeling, I wrung out the wet cloth, wrapped it around Legend's leg to ease the inflammation, and tore a strip with my teeth to tie it off. I emptied the sack of soot and rubbed it into Legend's white stockings.

"That is a sloppy job." Kat knelt and tried to plaster the color smoother.

I ignored her and slid the halter over his head and dabbed the last bit of sludge onto the star on his forehead. "I'm sorry. Be a good boy."

When we started to step into the barn aisle, Legend danced about us and knocked against a sideboard with a powerful whack. We heard muttering from the stable boy and the sound of his chair leveling to four legs. "Get back!" I said as I grabbed the halter off Legend, and Kat and I plunged to our knees back into the murky corners of his stall.

Light from the boy's lantern threw shadows as he held it over his head and patrolled the length of the livery. My heart hammered against my chest as Legend shuffled about to keep from stepping on us. I prayed for him to accept us around his feet. The boy paused at each stall and as he passed slowly by, the glare from the lantern reflected in Legend's eyes. I held my breath. At last, the footsteps faded, and the boy's chair creaked as he settled down on it again. Within moments, it was quiet. We waited to come to our

feet until once more the night sounds took up—the rhythmic pulse of crickets and the soft blow of a horse.

I led Legend to the rear opening where we had come in. "Go on as planned," I said to Kat. "I'll meet you down the road. Stay to the creek bed."

"Oh, give you one measure of authority, and you—"

I turned back to the livery. In the corner of the barn where the hay was piled, I laid dry stalks and put a Lucifer match to them. It smoldered but refused to catch. By the third attempt, my eyes were watering, and I could not see clearly. At last, a flame. It fed on itself and bloomed into a worthy start.

The horses moved restlessly now. But the boy, apparently satisfied with his previous search, merely yelled back for them to quiet. My scarf over my nose, I waited until the smoke almost obscured the stable. I unbolted all the latches and slapped the horses' hindquarters. They surged past me as I heard the boy scream, "*Feuer!*"

Katarina

I had been instructed not to let the horse trot, but it was a task not easily accomplished. Young and restless from days of being stalled, Legend had little restraint and fought me at the creek. I jerked on the rope, but he circled me more than once. We had not yet gone half a mile down the road toward home when the church bells rang out. Smoke tainted the air. We walked on as slowly as I could manage until I finally saw Eliza, a dark shadow. She tripped once on her trouser legs and fell but was up again and running toward me. Her hair had come down and her face was smoke-smudged.

"We did it!" She grabbed me and hugged me hard.

Her happy hysteria stunned me. "*Ja,* we did it," I said. "But why Legend is not limping?"

"Horses forget pain sometimes when they get excited. And this is exciting!" She threw her arms around me again.

"Do not celebrate yet. This is only the beginning. You must contain yourself." Yet, for that one moment, her youthful delight piqued my own thrill. And the camaraderie jolted me with a quick burst of exhilaration.

"Here, I'll manage him," Eliza said. "He's such a high-spirited boy, it is no wonder the Scotsman fancied him. But even the flamboyant can be subdued."

I had to smile at that. Would I subdue *Eliza*? Tame her so she could become a productive helpmate? What would that take? She had certainly proved capable of attaining her own objectives even at great risk to herself and those around her.

"Where do you plan to hide him?" I asked. "How have you not thought of that? Duff will come straight to our home even if he does not know you took Legend. A horse wants to return to its home barn."

"What then? Where?" Her voice came in gasps. "I will shoot the man if he tries to take him. I will—"

"You will do nothing of the kind. It would mean the end of us. Duff has no compunction about killing a woman." I shook her arm. "Settle yourself."

"Well, *what* then?"

"There are caves in the hills. Large enough to stall a horse for the short time it will take Duff to search our property. You said he returns to San Antonio tomorrow?"

"If we are to believe the blacksmith."

"The place I have in mind is some miles from the house on the other side of Wolf Creek where it loops to the south. Far enough away to be troublesome to find. We will have to graze and water him on the way for there will be no food for him there."

"I'll stay with him. I won't leave him alone as prey to predators of the night." Eliza stopped and set her jaw.

"Keep walking. Now is no time to sit and ponder." I marched ahead. "And voice your objections quietly. There is more to fear on these roads than the Confederates."

Eliza hitched up her husband's britches and shut her mouth.

"First of all," I continued, "Duff will demand to see both of us. We must appear as though we have been awakened and surprised. If you are gone, he will be even more suspicious. We will take Legend to the cave, tie him there, and when Duff arrives and satisfies himself that we do not have the horse, you can return to stay with Legend until I advise you of our safety."

Eliza snorted. "My, your English is coming along. Perhaps it is the prospect of ordering people about that inspires you."

"You know very well how I have been studying. I can only pray that with you as my only example, I do not acquire your southern drawl."

"Why, Kat…Katarina, dear, you will find how devastatingly charmin' the use of a glidin' vowel can be."

I could see the white of her teeth as she grinned in the dark. "Oh, hush. I know a deer trail that might lead us there directly."

"I am right behind you."

Eliza

I followed Kat blindly. She knew the landscape. And the dangers. As infuriatingly rigid as she was, Kat inspired respect. And what alternative did I have? Much as I might hate to admit it, her knowledge protected Legend and me. Well, it *was* for her own good. She needed a horse as much as I did, despite the risk from the Confederacy and the Comanches. As I struggled through the brush, I resolved to think more kindly of her.

Uneven slabs of limestone hindered our progress as we stumbled downhill toward Wolf Creek. Unshod, Legend left little evidence of our passage on the rock. The creek below us glinted as the moonlight glanced off the ripples. As we neared the water, Legend's head went up. The whites of his eyes shone from his soot-caked head, and his breathing changed to halting huffs.

"What is the matter with him?" Kat hissed. "We must hurry."

"He never crossed water at night before. I guess it looks different." I stepped into the stream and pulled him toward me. He snorted and yanked back.

I tried again, whispering, "You're all right. Come along." I patted his shoulder.

Three tries later, he put a hoof forward and moved into the stream.

One halting step at a time, we made the crossing with Kat leading the way to what looked like a large pile of rocks. On a steep incline, we squeezed through a space that opened into a small chamber. Perhaps it was the traces that had once confined him that familiarized him to tight structures, but Legend didn't object as so many horses might have. Water trickled somewhere deeper in the smaller hollows. I breathed in the damp and moldy chill that conjured up echoes.

Slipping the halter from his head, I lectured him to stay quiet and promised we would return first thing in the morning.

"Tie him up," said Kat. "We cannot leave him unsecured."

"He's helpless if he's tied, and a halter could hang on anything and choke him. We can't."

She shrugged. Without speaking, we blocked the entrance with a stack of stones and broken cedar branches and prayed that would be enough to hold him for the night. Surely it would be safe to return by dawn.

It had taken finagling, but if deception inspired Kat to adventure, I was happy to supply it. We had done it. *Together.*

~

Duff came after midnight with three riders. He didn't approach the door but barged into the stable, his torch above his head. We watched from Kat's room, hoping to appear asleep and avoid being questioned. How we fooled ourselves. "He's not going to burn it down, is he?"

"The man is capable of anything."

He lowered his torch, searching the grounds looking for hoofprints, I supposed. The only ones he would find were those belonging to the barnyard animals.

Then he gazed up at our windows. We stepped away, but he strode up to the front door and tried the latch. And then he pounded.

Throwing her wrap around her shoulders, Kat opened the upstairs door and called down to him. She gripped my pistol behind her back. "What can you possibly want at this hour?" She spoke in English, and her words rang firm and indignant.

Duff stood with his hand on the stair rail. "I want the horse," he said. "*Someone* tried to burn down the livery in town. And you serve to gain. I've found horses likely to return to their home barn. Where is he?"

"You are saying you lost our horse? The one you stole from us?" Kat sniffed in disdain. "He is not here. You are free to search."

"You can bet I'm free to search. I will do as I damn well please. If he is here and you have hidden him, I will jail both you and your pretty little sister...or whatever she is." He took one step up the stairs.

Kat took one step down. "There is nothing here for you, but if you are insecure in the matter, look about the place. I can only wish our horse *would* have returned to us. We are severely disadvantaged without him."

Duff scowled and set his jaw. "He was lame anyway. Them fancy ones don't hold up." He kicked the stairway post but turned away and signaled the men to mount up.

Not until the sound of hoofbeats disappeared did Kat sit on the top step, her arm holding the derringer limp between her knees.

CHAPTER 9

The Comanches were diplomatically brilliant, too, making treaties of convenience when it suited them and always looking to guarantee themselves trade advantages...

– S.C. Gwynne, *Empire of the Summer Moon, Quanah Parker and the Rise and Fall of the Comanches, the Most Powerful Indian Tribe in American History*

Katarina

Sleep evaded me after Duff left. I lay thinking about Günter. If he had been home, *he* would have stepped out and faced the Scotsman. And yet with Eliza's news, there was no confirmation that Günter was even alive. He could be lying shot between the eyes along the Nueces. He could be hiding in the hills, never able to return home until the war was over. He could be in Mexico, or in the ranks of the Union Army, or dead on the battlefield in Arkansas or Louisiana. *Stop!* I could not bear to imagine his fate. And neither could I sleep.

I decided to busy myself. I rose and tiptoed out the door down to the kitchen. At least there, I could put restlessness to work making Günter's favorite pie. As if he were coming home in the morning. Yes, maybe then he would come home. Perhaps I had dreamed this terrible war and when I woke next, Günter would be smiling at me for falling asleep at the table with Arno at my feet.

~

August went by. September was soon to become a memory. Legend healed after a few weeks of rest and cold compresses. We fed him well on corn and the hay Günter had put up. Determined to protect him from Comanches and bushwhackers, we gutted the corncrib beyond the hog pen and kept him hidden there except when Eliza hand-grazed him at sunup and exercised him on the longue line.

But one morning in late September while Eliza churned butter in the kitchen and I weeded the garden, the ground reverberated with hoofbeats. Arno, his hackles raised, his tail a rigid flag behind him, began a barrage of barking.

Eight Comanches, their eyes blackened with great tear-like streaks, rode boldly through the fence into the yard. As pickets splintered, I grabbed Arno and tried to pull him away. I wanted to run, scream for Eliza to hide, but I felt petrified as stone, my feet refusing to move, my arms heavy as though they carried water buckets.

Legend called out at the approach of other horses.

The leader, his long thick braids, the loops of silver dangling from his ears, smiled and stepped his black and white stallion forward. He jerked his chin toward the corncrib and bumped his animal even nearer to it.

"We have corn if you want." My voice took on a plaintive quality I hardly recognized. "We have some chickens and hogs." Never had I begged for anything. Oh, but I had. I had begged for the lives of my babies. I had bargained with far more than corn and chickens and hogs. I had beseeched God, offering my own life, but how could I bargain with a heathen? Prime for childbearing, they would take Eliza. Kill me and take her. And I would have been the fortunate one.

The front door opened, and Eliza stepped out onto the porch, the Henry nowhere to be seen. The Indian raised his eyes and stared at her with a brazenness I had never seen before. When I gasped, he looked down at me and laughed.

"The horse is sick," said Eliza. She held her hand to her throat and said, "Strangles." She coughed and looked down. "He will make your horses sick." She pointed at the Indian ponies and with a theatrical look of misery on her face, shook her head. "Sick," she repeated, stepping off the porch and walking toward me.

The Comanche's expression became unsettled, and he nudged his stallion back.

"I have brought you a gift." She offered it with both her hands outstretched in a gesture not unlike a playmate. "A music box."

He must have understood the word for gift. He turned and nodded at his fellow riders.

"It will play music for you." With her arms still extended, she offered her little treasure.

His eyes wide, the savage withdrew his horse a few more steps.

She will get us killed. I clasped my hands at my waist and closed my eyes. Then I heard the sound of laughter. A guttural chuckle, but one full of humor and surprise.

The Comanche dismounted and strode toward Eliza, coming within inches of her. She smiled with all the bravado I knew her capable of, even as her mouth quivered slightly, and her hands trembled as she offered up the music box.

The man's dark arm, muscled and tattooed, pressed against her sleeve. "Isatai," he said and thumped his chest. I will never forget the two of them, their heads touching, his black mane parted and smeared yellow against the prim crown of Eliza's own auburn braids. They looked into each other's eyes and grinned in mutual delight. Either Eliza was an actress par excellence, or she truly found joy in presenting this bauble to the savage.

"It's gold," Eliza whispered. She opened the box and brought forth a small brass key, itself in the shape of a bird. She wound it once and handed both the box and key to the man. His hands were small, not much larger than hers, and he had no trouble winding the mechanism. While he still held the box, she leaned forward and slid the lever over. The oval lid popped open, and the tiny bird emerged—its beak of bone, its feathers bright, colored red and blue and green. The delicate filigree of the box shimmered in the sunlight. And the bird sang.

He chuckled, a disarming laugh like one of our German youths delighted with a toy. I could have been charmed with the sound if I had not seen the man.

And then he reached up and pulled down her braid.

Eliza's red hair tumbled loose and fell about her shoulders.

Her hand flew to her mouth. I heard the gasp even as she tried to stifle it. He took her by the shoulders and turned her clear around and ran his fingers, the nails long and crusted with grime, through the soft, silken strands. Making humming noises, he stroked the sunlit locks. She covered her eyes with her hands, bowed her head, and let him molest her in this way.

Like a mural on a wall, I stood paralyzed, my hand still on Arno's ruff.

At last, the Indian stopped. Taking up the music box again, he began strolling about—strolling like he owned the farm, like he owned us—toward where we kept Legend.

Eliza cried out, "No!" She lifted her hair that had fallen across her shoulder. Lifted it as though proffering a gift, yet another, for the possibility of keeping her horse. "Isatai!" she called. Slipping a knife from her apron pocket, she made as if to cut the hair at her ear. She nodded and gave him a questioning proposal.

Did she not understand? He would take what he wanted, when he wanted, and that would include not just her hair but *her* in her entirety. "No, Eliza!" I cried, but she ignored me and took a step toward the man. The mounted Indians hooted and yipped. We were an amusing diversion, the stakes to be toyed with.

She directed him away from the stall and once again offered her hair. Isatai approached her with a sly grin on his face. Fingering the locks that she held out to him, he nodded. She cut through the strands. They fell limp in his fist like a bunch of wilted wildflowers. He grunted with what sounded like pleasure and walked to his horse. In one smooth leap, he mounted and turned away, waving his treasures above his head with his free hand. His fellows trotted behind, leaving only clouds of dust rising in the road.

Eliza

Kat said nothing but came to where I sat in the dirt yard and lifted me to my feet. Escorting me to the house, she poured two coffee cups of mustang grape wine and shoved one across the table to me. *"Drink!"*

I held the full cup with both hands and poured it down my throat. I tried hard not to cry. But when Kat stroked my hair, the lopped off remnants that hung about my chin, that had once been my vainglory, I dropped my face into my hands and sobbed.

"You saved us," Kat said.

I nodded, my head bobbing. *My music box! My hair!* At least, we still had Legend. We had plugged one hole in a sinking boat. A slight hiatus in the worry that plagued our days, but what would be the next thing sacrificed? This country was killing me. I ducked my head and let all my sorrow pour onto Katarina's boney shoulder.

That night a hog and a sack of corn disappeared. We never heard a sound.

CHAPTER 10

Black Haw was used extensively by the Native Americans, its berries as a food source and its root bark in many types of herbal remedies ...It was enthusiastically embraced by the early colonists to the United States, where its use was well documented. It was used as a uterine tonic, again to relieve menstrual cramps and afterbirth pains, and it was also taken to prevent miscarriage.
– https://www.indigo-herbs.co.uk/natural-health-guide/benefits/
   black-haw#field-benefits-description

Eliza

Despite the time during which she unabashedly shed tears as she tried to trim the ends of my hair to even lengths, Kat's tenderness waned. She began to exhibit unusual irritability over the smallest matters, often with herself.

"Let me see if this will fit," she had said, as she measured the back of my head with the span of her fingers and tried to fashion a yarn snood to cover my butchered locks. "*Nein*, I want it a little bigger." Her lips twisting into an angry pucker, she ripped out all her work and started again. "It should be measured precisely!" She set down the yarn and needles for a moment and leaned back as if to ponder the technique and then corrected herself in whispers. "Just right. It should be *just right*."

That there were no telltale signs of Kat's monthlies made me wonder. Surely, she could not be…. No, not after all these years that they'd had no children. Or was it what my mother complained of as she approached the age of forty—the cessation of the menses? Although why that would make one miserable was confounding to me. It would be a Godsend—no fear of more babies nor the monthly bother that afflicted us.

All this to say—Kat was not herself. I set about to watch her more carefully.

She took to spending our afternoon rest hour away from the house. I supposed she deserved solitude if that's what she craved. Although Lord knew there was plenty solitude to be had.

I stood in her room one day and observed the direction she walked with Arno at her heels. She made her way toward a knoll where a large red oak burned crimson and fevered in its last display of October. Perhaps that is why she retreated there, although she never exhibited any sensitivity toward beauty. She seemed to disdain it as frivolous. But work? Production? Sublime.

Determined to find an explanation for these excursions, I waited until she had been gone a few minutes and slipped out the door to follow her. I kept along the edges of woodland even though the broomweed and goldenrod made progress slow.

Upon reaching the hill, Kat sat with a book and leaned against the massive tree trunk. Arno sprawled close by. A motte of scrub oak provided me with cover from where I could safely observe them. Although I could not hear the words she spoke—they were hushed, undecipherable mutterings—she appeared to be reading aloud. She wiped away a tear every so often.

The breeze picked up—a cool reminder of the season—and leaves sifted down around Kat. Like the subject of an impressionist's painting, she seemed fragile, indistinct.

At last, she rose to go, taking slow steps to different spots and bending to touch each place one after the other. The dog stood with her and waited patiently while she performed the ritual.

How very odd, I thought, sinking back into the undergrowth and watching them return home.

I waited until I was sure she'd had enough time to go back inside the house before I circled to the far side of the hill. *What intrigue.* The adventure rivaled my expeditions alone on the streets of Galveston. Exhilarating, really, to put together one more puzzle piece in the enigma that was Kat.

I gripped the hem of my dress and trudged to the spot where I had seen her sit. At first, there seemed nothing other than the tree and the shade and the peace of the afternoon. But along the crest was a series of small stones. Not limestone but honed rock of pink crystalline. *Graves. Three graves.* Tiny ones. Of babies or the smallest of children. Katarina's babies?

I had resented her. Thought her intolerant. In reality, she had barely been able to abide each succeeding day. Alone, but for a husband who appeared to be unconcerned with her pain, who managed to avoid the very thought of loss—a talent some men had that eluded women.

My own mother also suffered the distress of stillbirth, but Mamá had no capacity for stoicism. She expressed her pain as the French did. With tears and lamentations. What had it cost Katarina to carry that anguish bundled and buried in her heart where it could never be released? She had girded herself with dispassion that overran its boundaries and made herself cold to the touch.

I started for the house filled with generosity of spirit. She needed me. I would amuse her and distract her, and after a while, I would induce her to speak of her grief and alleviate the sorrow. Hurrying with conviction of purpose, I stumbled into the kitchen where she waited.

"You followed me," she said, her back still to me. "You take away my most private moments. Have I nothing left of my own?"

I thought for a moment she would cry. Relieve some of the black thoughts that kept her distant from me. She gathered herself and turned to face me. But she did not weep.

"You will desist from prying. You will—"

I took a step toward her. "Let me—"

She raised her hand. "Do not come near me." She began kneading some dough in a furious attack—grasping and pounding. "I do not need—"

Kat stopped. A surprised grimace crossed her face. She clutched at her belly. One drop of blood appeared on the wood floor.

Katarina

It was bound to happen. It always did. Although usually not so soon. I did not want to have to deal with Eliza regarding this. She had no experience or womanly intuition about these matters.

Her hand over her mouth, Eliza stared at the floor and then back up at me with round, dark eyes. "Oh, Katarina!"

"If you will excuse me." I collected some old cotton fabric and walked out the door with as much dignity as I could muster. When I reached my room, I folded the cotton into a firm roll and slipped it into place. I lay on my bed with more towels under my hips and waited. Though I must have groaned with the cramps, I refused to cry out. This would pass. As had all the others.

I stayed past supper time in my room, watching the shadows slide across the window. The evening cooled, and still I waited. I did not light the lantern but closed my eyes against the fading light.

It was sundown when I heard footsteps mounting the stairs. Holding the lantern high with one hand, Eliza stepped into my room, the shadows flickering and distorting the gloom. "I want you to drink this," she said.

"Is it hemlock?" I thought my humor appropriately dark.

"Maybe later…depending." She handed me a cup of muddy-looking tea. "It's black haw bark tea," she said. "My Chloë swears by it and has given it to me when I found my menses unbearable. It has a quieting effect upon the irritable womb. She said she gave it to my mamá, and I was the result after many failures. I spent the afternoon searching for it."

I scoffed and pushed her hand away. "This is not my month-lies, silly girl. It is—"

For a moment, Eliza stood perfectly still. I could not see her face plainly but imagined her mouth agape as she contemplated dates and times and opportunities. If that *was* what she thought, she recovered quickly.

"Black haw treats all manner of a woman's needs, even your condition. You have nothing to lose, Katarina. I know you think me imbecilic, but I am all you've got."

She was right—I *had* nothing to lose, and she *was* all I had. With a certain resignation and perhaps even as an invitation to that final sleep, I took the cup and raised it in the air. "*Prost!*" I drank it down.

Eliza

After supper, I carried a bowl of soup and bread up to Kat. She fussed and insisted she would come down when she chose to. I ignored her and closed the door behind me. I would be back before bedtime to force another dose of tea down her. What's the worst it could do? It never killed *me*. And I told her so. She wanted Arno, and although I wished him with me while I finished up the last of the chores, I could hardly object. What was it about that big old shaggy canine that calmed us and gave us comfort?

How would our situation change now that Kat must be re-strained? Would she defy rational thought and insist on working just as hard? Or lapse into martyrdom? Or would this child go the way of the others—under a small mound headed by a pink crystalline stone?

If only Chloë were here. How many times have I wished that? Chloë would take charge and relieve us of worry. She would boss us terribly, but that would be little to bear given the care she would afford us.

~

At the first crow of the rooster, I bolted from my bed and down the stairs to prepare a breakfast of biscuits and ham and black haw tea for Kat. My hands were full, and I stepped into her room without knocking to find her standing unclothed before the mirror. Her breasts swollen, the nipples dark, she rested her hand on the smallest rise above her thin hips. The skin of her body that had been protected by clothing looked alabaster and delicate, a remarkable difference between her face and neck and hands. She had been fragile once—young and protected. Now the parts of her exposed to sun, strong soap and farm work were coarsened into leather. Will this be what happens to me? I looked away.

"I beg your pardon!" She grabbed her nightgown and held it before her.

"I suppose a kick on the door would have warned you, but I didn't think. I'm sorry."

She sniffed and turned her head.

Fluffing and stacking the pillows against the headboard, I said, "You will rest today. All day. And tomorrow morning we will see how you are faring. For now, take your breakfast in bed. And drink the tea."

"I have never eaten any meal in the bed, and I do not intend to begin such a regime now. I am better. Remove that tray, and I will come down as soon as I am properly dressed."

I drew myself up the way I had seen Chloë do and stood my ground. "You will not! You are better because you have drunk the tea and rested. You must consider the consequences. You *must*, Katarina! Think of what you risk!" I set down the tray and led her to the bed even as she clutched the faded cotton gown against her. "Don't make me bolt the door from the outside."

"You would not!"

"Wouldn't I?" Smiling back at her, I closed the door, this time letting Arno escape down the steps and out into the brightening day. The morning held a different slant of light, the first breath of autumn coolness. Breathing deeply, I gazed out over the countryside. The hills wavered blue in the distance, holding mystery beyond them—all out of our dominion, wild things, innumerable and unfathomable. Still, here in this little domain, I felt in control. For once, Kat would have to do as I say. For once.

Katarina

Holding my breath, I gulped the tea and leaned back against the pillow. I did not know what to do with myself. The bleeding had ceased, after all. Of course, it may have stopped regardless, and the potion Eliza cooked up may or may not have been the remedy. So now was I supposed to stay propped up like a doll on a shelf and be doted on like an invalid?

Still, I had not rested before when I was with child. Not known to rest. Other women never slowed down until the day after the baby was born. I remembered that from the old country. There was work to be done as there is now, and I could not ensconce myself on pillows and command the world to go on without my contribution. How could we survive like that?

I paused a moment. Günter never asked if I needed to rest. It simply had not occurred to us that while carrying a child, I perhaps should not manage a full load of chores. I was young. I was strong. It was out of the question that I retire to my bed. He was a good man, but he knew nothing of childbearing. Nor did I. We worked together toward the dream of our new home. I admit I had isolated myself except for a few friends who rarely visited. Günter was far more involved in the town's affairs.

None of my women acquaintances knew I had been expecting. I had never told them. I should have. Maybe they would have known what to do, how to help. At least, known how to give consolation. After each failure, Günter became more withdrawn. He patted my hand. He had suggested that getting back to our daily routine of work might take my mind off the loss. And now here I was in the counsel of Eliza, a child herself, who presumed knowledge I could not believe she had. Well, I was resigned. I would not put every hope and dream on this. Not this time.

My breakfast would grow cold if I ignored it to spite the little tyrant, but I could not tolerate waste. I pulled it to me, determined not to enjoy one bite of it. It was demeaning, stripping me of self-worth. Better than I thought it would be, I finished breakfast, drank the rest of her potion, and lay back against the pillows. Unwanted tears sprang to my eyes. Was this what it was like to be cosseted? To be deemed special enough to be protected from one's duty of daily labor? I did not mean for it to, but somehow the care seemed bred of, I would not say it, but very briefly the word *kindness* flitted across my mind.

~

Brightness haloed the closed shutters leaving oblique light patterns across the bed cover. Late morning and I had drifted off. Seldom did I dream, but the extra hour of sleep must have lent itself to such. In it, I was a child and working under my mother's direction. *You have not sliced the potatoes evenly nor are they thin enough. You are not good enough. No man will ever want you to mother his children.* My mother was usually kind, but in this dream, she diminished me. I awoke crying. My own losses and fears built this dream, not my mother's criticism. I recognized that.

She was proud of me, I believe. Even though women could never be admitted to university back home in Wittenberg, my father, a professor, had the wisdom and foresight to school me in advanced studies. And like him, I embraced liberalism. Günter was among his students. And that is where it all began.

My few letters home never completely revealed the hardships, except perhaps for the first one I wrote after we arrived by ship to Galveston, and in another I sent after we finally came to Fredericksburg. But after each babe was born far too early to survive, I never once let my tears dilute the ink. I evaded her thinly disguised questions. Thousands of miles afforded ambiguity. Still, there was no way to conceal that there had been no children. So, she must know. Perhaps she struggled with the same malady, as I was her only child. Yet, she had never said. Just as I had not.

Restless, I slipped off the bed and opened the shutters and the window. Sunlight blinded me. Blinking, I turned away and then heard quick little footsteps tripping up the stairs. My captor.

"I see you standing in there! Get back in bed this minute!" Eliza pushed through the door and bumped it closed with her hip. "I have milady's supper." She set it on the dresser and busied about as though she were the upstairs maid and I were *die Prinzessin*. She did not fool me—she relished the power in her new position.

"I am perfectly capable of getting my meal," I said. "I am no princess to be doted upon."

"You are no princess. But I have grown fond of you, O Wicked Queen. Eat!" She spread a napkin out with great flourish and handed me a spoon for the potato soup.

I could think of nothing to say. Fond of me? Her words took me aback. I felt a knot in my throat. And so, I was silent.

Eliza

Three months since Günter ran for the border. Oh my, if we must endure six more months of this, then for what had I just volunteered? Keeping Kat off her feet would keep me on mine day and night.

The only thing I ever bargained for was Will. He was everything I ever wanted, although his understanding of his brother's life must have been vague indeed. Or maybe he presumed all women admired work the way the Germans did. Or maybe, he saw the girl in a pretty package and never looked beyond the gift wrap. Well, here we were, weren't we. Or here I was. Kat upstairs in the bedroom and me out in the barnyard slopping the pigs. I would never get Chloë. I knew that, but what a lovely daydream to pin my hopes on.

Was it also a delusion that a letter might come from Will? Surely, he had had time to arrive at whatever post the Confederacy directed him. I planned to make the trip to town again in the coming week. Maybe something had come, and maybe there would be news of Günter if he was not already dead. Somebody should assassinate that Scotsman and his group of thugs. I would have been happy to do the honors had I been assured those men would not return fire and leave me in the dust. And steal my horse again.

The pecan tree nearby rustled in the breeze. A few more weeks and the nuts would begin to fall, and then it would be me against the squirrels. I had arisen before the sun, and the afternoon was warm. I intended to sit in its shade without fear of being pelted, prop my feet up and pretend Chloë was serving me my supper. In my imagination, I'd ask her to bring me a glass of Rothschild Bordeaux and take a full hour for my meal. Instead, I served myself—cornbread, a chunk of cheese, and rather than buttermilk, I poured a cup of Mustang grape wine. It tended to be bitter, but the effect was the same—an artificial calm. Leaning back, I sipped the wine and gazed at the clouds. Arno grunted and sprawled near my chair. So very peaceful if one didn't consider the realities. A red hawk screamed above us, but even that did not break the unity. He was part of the infinite blue above us.

I finally understood that life was not at all like I thought it would be. Just a few months ago, it spread out before me in a seamless span. A carriage ride to an exciting new countryside with promise everywhere—in the grasses and the trees and the autumn rains. A breathtakingly handsome young man who adored me. There would be darling children in our future. The Confederacy would restore our lives and regardless, the war would never touch us here on the frontier.

Was it true for everyone, or was I the only one to be brought up short? We have no children. The Confederacy has restored nothing. And war comes at us from all sides.

I stared out at the garden. It needed tending. I planned to start on it in a few minutes. First, I needed to plan carefully what I might say in my letter to Will. It should be well thought out so as not to make our hardships alarming nor so inconsequential as to make him think we were without travail.

The warmth, the wine, the Hill Country breeze. I must have dozed. A shadow blocked the light across my eyelids. I opened one eye, and then they both flew open. Katarina stood over me.

"A siesta, as the Mexicans say?" Her hands were on her hips.

"A constructive one, if you must. I was planning a letter to Will. Even if I can't mail it right away, I will have pages and pages for him when I get the opportunity. And it requires forethought." I sat up straight and collected the dishes around me. "You were to rest completely for the entire day."

"But this little scene—" she waved her hand expansively—"is the reason I cannot."

"I'll tell you what. You sit right here where I have sat and write down every little chore you find essential. You may even write it in German. It will be good for me to practice. And, as a bonus, you may supervise my every move. *Ist das gut?*" I winked at her.

She snorted. "Then bring the sewing basket. I have repairs to make as well. Luckily, I have the ability to keep an eye on my stitches and you at the same time."

I pushed out of the chair with both hands and went to collect the basket. I tossed in two of my own stockings and a blouse with a torn sleeve.

Katarina

I sat under the grape arbor and twisted wool into yarn. Having no spinning wheel made this chore tedious but hardly tiring. Still, I found myself losing patience. I took a deep breath and began again. I seemed annoyed with many things, particularly my guardian. How old is the little tyrant? Perhaps eighteen? With all the pomp and attitude of a mistress in a great household. After years of being waited on hand and foot herself, she knew exactly how to mimic attentive behavior. I dared say her slave, Chloë, provided the example. If I could overcome my own fears, I would tell her to take her little bossy ways to a playhouse and set up an imaginary tea party with her dolls.

A memory overwhelmed me—one that had disappeared from thought for over a quarter of a century. Papa brought her from Munich to me. Her eyes blue as the Danube, her cheeks a feverish pink, her lips pursed in a pretty little pout. Porcelain featured but dear as any real creature could be. Beloved. *Hilde.*

I caught my breath. The picnics we shared. The stories I read to her. Oh, to have her with me again. "*Ach!*" With those days gone, it was best to remain stoic, prepared. Dreams vanished like pretty bubbles. Not good to dwell in fantasy. It broke your heart.

I put away the yarn, picked up the darning, and tried to ignore the trembling of my hands as I attempted to thread the needle. Knotting the thread, I mentally assessed the things that needed done. Though how we were going to manage was beyond imagination.

I looked for ways to contribute. We could take the yarn into town for cash, and if Eliza brought in the rest of the peas, I could sit and shell them and perhaps divide the onions. Pitiful little if I was to maintain a sedentary posture.

"Eliza!" I called. And then called again. Rushing from around the side of the house she came, at last, a kerchief tied around that red hair and her face nearly the same russet shade.

"What?" She ran her forearm across her brow and wiped her cheeks with her apron. "What?" Panting, she stood waiting. "Are you all right?"

"I am all right. But I wish the opportunity to amend your tasks. Bring my slate from the kitchen. I will write big, *ja*? So you can see it from the garden."

Eliza rolled her eyes as she nodded and stepped into the house to comply with my request, and I wondered how long she would persist in this nurturing role.

With the slate on my lap, I printed the seasonal planting: broccoli, cabbage, lettuce, spinach, and carrots. I would add more when Eliza had managed to get those in the ground. Of course, I added the daily weeding. I held up the list for her to see. "To begin with," I said.

Her eyes grew wide, but she rallied. "*Jawohl!*" Her salute, however, I felt was in irony.

~

As the season moved from autumn to winter, I knew I must quell my frustration. The work done was substandard in quality and quantity, but I expressed myself to no one but Arno. And I did so on the two walks a day Eliza allowed, even encouraged, me to take in suitable weather.

Eliza had written her mother and asked for advice about attending childbirth. As if I knew nothing about the subject. I had witnessed childbirth on the voyage to Galveston. I had seen the pain and the blood, saw the tears and heard the screams, but then the joy. *Joy.* Even if it took the form of a red, squalling creature whose very life depended on an exhausted mother. On our ship, at least, the babes always, always, survived the miraculous event. So, I walked and complained to Arno and flicked stones out of my way with the cane Eliza had thrust upon me to prevent falls. Such a fine line between care and control. And she frequently overstepped it. Still, here I was at the fourth month and except for a very few spots of blood, the child and I were one. I submitted to examinations of my ankles for swelling, preparation of my meals as well as frequent doses of black haw and chamomile tea.

~

With December days often cold now, we huddled at the hearth in the evening. Sometimes the wind gusted down the chimney and the flame wavered to throw shadows, eerie and wraithlike across the wall. Except for the wind and the pops and flickers of fire, we sat in silence—a still, protective silence. It was then I felt the butterfly. A soft flutter beneath my belly. Moments later, it came again. I could not bear to speak of it lest I dare the fates. Holding my breath, I rested my palm on the spot but could feel nothing more. Yet I would be still and wait for another chance to feel it— the quickening.

Eliza

Of an evening, Kat and I spoke little. Exhaustion did not lend itself to conversation, and so much of our discussion only reflected our fear. We chose to deny it. The baby was evident now, and let out the seams of the two dresses she had. I tried to er wellbeing from the corner of my eye, so as not to annoy her, but I watched as she moved her hand to her belly and pressed ever so slightly. I hoped there were no contractions. Her expression, the suggestion of a smile, only indicated wonder. Such secrets she kept.

We had not received news that Günter had been killed. Rumors were about that he was one of the few who made it across the river to Mexico. If it were true, we could not guess when he would be able to write. Kat, though, seemed to harbor hope that every day she did not hear of his death was a day he was safe across the border.

It was almost Christmas. And what a grim one it would be. I thought of our celebrations in Galveston with Mamá and Papa, and even Chloë. Warm and windy, the weather seldom kept us housebound. Papa put on an ostentatious show for his staff. Mamá said so anyway, but she was the flamboyant one in the festivities—her dress of brocade and velvet, the lace that rested against her bosom. Papa couldn't attend the guests properly for watching the curve of her waist, the glint of her hair, the supple rise of her breasts above the lace. I could see why he adored her. I wanted to be adored like that. And petted, yes. She had outshone me every Christmas until I was fifteen. It was then I came into my own. Young men vied for my attention as well as some of Papa's old stodgy associates. After that, Papa put Chloë on watch. I was not to be let out of her sight. My continual delight became outfoxing my mammy.

But now, Christmas would come about with dismal deprivation. No husband to present me with little gifts under my pillow on Christmas morning. No coffee in bed with sliced oranges and chocolates. No sprigs of holly and mistletoe. No magnolia strewn about the dining table. No lemons and limes, pomegranates and kumquats and pineapple. No eggnog. Why, if we were to have ham at all, it would have to be through our own labor. Kat was quite capable of shooting the poor thing, but then it would be up to me to slit the throat and hoist him up to drain. No, I would not do it. And I could not allow Kat. I intended to put my foot down. A baked chicken with peach preserves and some of that grape wine would suffice. Our only extravagance should be the last of the flour and sugar made into a little cake—my surprise for Kat. If we were going to be faced with damnable deprivation of even small delights, then by all that is holy, this would be our one gesture of defiance.

Katarina

I had caught up on the mending. Made the list of chores. Shelled the peas and scraped the sweet corn from the cob. Spun wool until my fingers ached, but none of it the physical labor the farm required. At her own insistence, Eliza assumed that work. It was not done as I would have liked it, but why would I expect it to be? Eliza had no discipline or experience in housekeeping nor animal husbandry nor farming, although she occasionally did make some effort. I bit my lip to keep from commenting on the shortcomings that would have never escaped my washcloth or spade. But I deemed any endeavor on her part remarkable.

The war would be over soon. It couldn't last. Those hotheads would see the futility and stupidity of such endeavor. And Günter would come home. So, I embraced the refuge of optimism where grief had not yet touched me. Not yet.

I called Arno to sit by me and let me stroke his head. He seemed content to do so although his eyes followed Eliza as she moved from the table to the stove and back. Perhaps like her, I should have indulged him with little treats and sweet talk to keep some degree of faithfulness.

Eliza must have known I was quite aware that she longed to run back to her doting parents and that Chloë. Back where the *Haengerbande* was unnecessary since the population seemed to be of the same opinion—war, at any cost—and where the countryside was not filled with rogue bands. It would not have surprised me to wake one morning to find her disguised as a man and gone on her horse. She was inexperienced enough to overestimate her strength and abilities and naïve enough to underestimate the evil that could await her.

If I prayed for the best outcome of these last few months, Günter was merely away at war. Not a victim of Duff's band or some illness that struck soldiers. How was it that Günter could not get a letter home? He knew I must be worried. And surely with his education and maturity, the Union had given Günter a high rank.

I intended to ask Eliza again to go check for mail. I hated to send her walking to town, but we dared not risk losing the horse either to Comanches or the Confederates. Legend—our one precious commodity. Perhaps Monday if it appeared to be a promising day.

Meanwhile, it would have to be enough to sit and watch shadows dance on the walls while I kept a journal of this time in my life. Before, there had been no space in the day for such indulgence. And since this was very likely the last chance I had for a child, I intended to keep a record despite the unproductive hours, the doubt, the fear.

CHAPTER 11

Meanwhile, the partisan troops despoiled the region. Farm houses were ransacked, movable property stolen, families imprisoned, and houses burned.
– Joe Baulch, *The Dogs of War Unleashed: the Devil Concealed in Men Unchained,* West Texas Historical Association

Eliza

My assignment: Go straight to the post office, and after mailing my letter to Will, ask for any correspondence for Frau Lange. Kat made me practice my German should there be any confusion over my intent. Again, my language skills would be put to the test when I took the wool she had spun to the merchants and bargained for what pitiful little coin they were willing to pay. It was our only source of cash. Even if it was sometimes no more than twenty-five cents, I was willing to walk if she was willing to spin. Walking offered a freedom that bending and squatting and lifting did not. Yes. I was willing.

The pecan trees, always the last to drop their leaves, stood bare, and a weak sun filtered through their branches. Brisk and dry, the weather held. A red cardinal added the only color other than sumac, which flamed in the brush alongside the path. My stamina had improved, and I picked up my pace. How fine to be turned loose.

It was short-lived.

The boy lingered at the crossroad just beyond our property. Not more than nine or ten, he stood shifting his weight side to side, keeping one eye on Arno who waited at our gate—watchful, tail straight out behind him.

"*Guten Tag.*" I smiled, puzzled as to why the youngster remained seemingly without purpose so near the house.

He snatched the hat from his head, exposing an orange stand of hair. "Ma'am." He spoke so quietly I had to move closer to be sure what he said.

To be polite, I asked if I could help him. "*Kann ich Ihnen irgendwie helfen?*"

Looking at the ground, he clutched his hat in his fist and turned it around and around. "*Ich spreche nicht.* That's all I know how to say, ma'am. Don't talk like the folks around here." An Irish lilt bothered his English.

"Well, that's fine with me. I've spent months practicing the language, and I find it most difficult." I waited for him to explain his being there, but he glanced between Arno and me.

"That dog mean?"

"Arno? Why no. He's just big. Would you like to meet him?"

"No, ma'am, not just yet."

"Well, what in the world can I help you with? You're not lost, are you?"

He shrugged.

"I'm on my way to town." I started to step around him, but he did not move aside. His chin quivered. Just once. His knuckles were white around the edge of the hat he kept clenched in front of his belly, turning and turning, the brim already frayed and dark with sweat.

I put my hand on his shoulder. He flinched. And stared at his hat.

I sighed. "All right. Come with me." I nodded toward the house and pressed him forward gently. Perhaps Kat knew the family and would know how to deal with this child who refused to divulge worthwhile information. I knew she was capable of coercion. "The woman inside is German, but she speaks good English." As an afterthought, I added, "She can be nice."

He pulled back, his eyes locked on Arno.

"Arno loves boys," I said, having no idea how Arno felt about boys. The dog's ears pricked forward, his eyes fixed on the youngster. "Let's go meet him. I'll go first."

The boy set his hat onto his head with a firm tug and drew his mouth in a hard line. His body at a backward tilt, he shuffled two steps behind me.

The gate creaked as I opened it slowly and stepped inside. Arno stood and began a slow wag of his tail—a suspicious wag but with a willingness to negotiate.

"You might better remove your hat for this first meeting," I said. "I've always heard it was a good idea when you are first introduced, even to a dog. Maybe especially to a dog."

He crushed his hat under his arm and tucked his hands into his armpits. His forehead crinkled, the freckles clustering in the creases. He stepped forward then to meet his fate. Even if he was doomed.

At that moment, he endeared himself to me. Despite my not knowing what in the world he wanted or needed or intentioned, he broke my heart a little. But oh my, how would Kat react?

Turning to Arno, I said, "*Sitz dich*," in stern imitation of Kat's command.

Arno sat.

Holding out my hand to the boy, I nodded for him to come into the yard. "Arno meet—" I offered my friendliest smile and said, "Why, I don't know your name. Would you like to introduce yourself to Arno and me? My name is Eliza."

"F…Finn, ma'am."

"Arno meet Finn." I put my hand on the dog's shoulder and urged him forward. He needed no encouragement. Sniffing, he started at the boy's knees, worked his way up to his crotch, moved to the back, around to where the boy kept his fingers tucked, and finally to the boy's chin and ears.

Finn froze in rigid posture, his eyes pinched against the onslaught of snuffs and snorts.

And then Arno's tongue swiped his cheek.

Katarina

I watched from the kitchen window. Now, what had Eliza managed to put upon us? The boy could not have been German. No self-respecting mother of our heritage would allow her child to appear tattered and half-starved even in these times. Why, there was always milk and cheese and smoked ham. I stopped myself. We wouldn't have ham this year. In fact, with no man in the house, we would do well to put any meat on the table. Surely, Eliza would send the boy on his way. *Oh, was ist das*? Is she bringing him into the house?

The door opened with Arno leading the way and Eliza with the boy in tow.

"Look who I found!" Eliza said with great cheerfulness.

"And just who would that be?" I avoided the boy's eyes by looking over his head. He wasn't looking at me but allowed his gaze to wander about the room as though he had never seen a parlor and kitchen and painted walls.

"Katarina, I'd like you to meet Finn. Finn?" She touched his shoulder to bring him back into focus. "This is Frau Lange."

His eyes flickered on me before going back to the table where biscuits and preserves still sat.

"Just what did you have in mind here?" I asked Eliza.

She stared at him and then back at me. "I thought maybe you knew his family. He seems rather…" Eliza turned her head away from him, raised her eyebrows, and mouthed the word "lost."

I cleared my voice twice before the boy focused on me. "And your surname, Finn?"

He frowned and opened his mouth but said nothing.

"Your last name." My hands went to my hips, but I relaxed them knowing it was a strong gesture. The boy might be too intimidated to answer.

His eyes went back to the table. "Bailey, ma'am." He bent at the hips in an awkward little bow.

Eliza smiled and stepped for the door. "Well, now that we have that established, I'd better get on my way. I'm sure y'all will work something out." She patted him on the arm and was gone before I could think of a way to discourage her. Still, there might be a letter from Günter. I would just have to deal with this visitor on my own.

"Go!" I called after her even though she was already through the gate. "*Sitz*," I said to the boy. I put two cornbread biscuits, the butter, and peach preserves in front of him and poured a glass of milk.

He set to eating without a *danke* or even an appreciative smile.

I sat down across from him and watched him. Milk ran down the sides of his mouth. Crumbs peppered the tabletop. Finally, halfway through the last biscuit, he looked up at me and offered a nod and a blink. Perhaps his culture's way of showing thanks.

Even in his little piggy ways, my heart went out to him. I recognized him. Knew of the family. They lived less than five miles to the southwest of us. Günter had met the boy's father, Tom Bailey, when we first came here to the frontier. In fact, Günter and Bailey had helped build each other's first cabins. Language was always a barrier given Bailey's brogue at the time. I never met his wife and had only seen the boy once when he sat behind his father on the back of a fine stallion. I had thought at the time that horse would be a sore temptation to the Indians.

Two years ago, Comanches raided the Bailey place when the boy and his father were in the fields. It had been in the middle of the day, an odd time for an attack, but it was the last of four raids in the community, the others being more profitable. Little to take at the Bailey household except for that stallion. Little to kill for. So they took the mother and her two-year-old baby girl. Dragged them off by their red hair, I imagined. Burned the log cabin.

Oh, there were attempts to find the wife and daughter, but the strongest efforts were spent on German families that had also been molested. We took care of our own, and those Irish were not our own. Despite all the attempts, nothing was recovered from any of the raids. Not the horses, not the coffee grinders or the corsets, not the bonnets. And not the Bailey woman or her little girl.

"Were you sent to town?" I asked, thinking if he were, he could catch up to Eliza and they could go together.

Finn shook his head and took a heaping spoonful of preserves and popped it into his mouth. He gave me an apologetic grin. "'Tis good and sweet," he said.

"*Ja*…'tis. Well, then, why did you come this far from home?"

"Ma'am?"

"Your reason. Why did you walk this way?"

"Why, I was hungry, ma'am." He gulped his milk and ran his tongue over the milk mustache that lined his lips and then swiped his shirtsleeve across his face from cheek to cheek.

"And your father? Is he all right?"

"I guess he is. He made a run for it up to the hills when the Secesh come last week. He ain't for fightin' against the Union. He hid me till he comes back, but I'm not supposed to tell where."

"It is understandable." I tried to stay calm. "So you have no food at home?" I knew it was an unnecessary question. He had already said he was hungry.

"Well, it's got slim. Secesh turned over the bee boxes, and now that it's coming winter, we'll likely lose 'em if they can't find a good tree to hole up in. Maybe if they did, I could coax 'em back to a box in the spring. The spinning wheel got tore up. Not that I can spin. They shot our hog and burnt the barn. Tore up the cabin we been workin' on but didn't burn it. Maybe saved it for the Comanche." He looked away, but his face held no emotion—a mask to hide the pain.

"And how old are you? Eight?"

"No, ma'am. I'm nigh on ten. Come May."

The boy essentially had no home, and I could see where this was going.

Eliza

On my way home from town, the letter burned a hole in my pocket. It had come at last—a letter for Kat from Günter. It would do me no good to slip a knife under the flap and peruse its contents. While I had learned to speak German well enough to get by, I was less competent with the written word. The words went on and on, and I found it difficult to decipher the convoluted phrasing. I would have to rely on Kat's generosity in sharing the news.

When I asked the postmaster in careful German how long he thought it would take for me to receive a letter from my husband in the 1st Cavalry, he stared at me like I was not in control of my senses and said, "Frau Lange, it is not possible to estimate how long a journey a letter might take. You must not rely on any mail schedule. Patience is your only recourse."

I reacted rather badly, slapping the flat of my hand on the counter. "And you, sir, are a negative man!" I spoke in English—loudly and emphasizing my southern drawl. I didn't care if I turned heads and elicited clucks from onlookers. I didn't care one little bit.

Hurrying, I neared home. What had become of the boy? He was a rough little thing. Not so little, really, just stringy. Had Kat sent him on his way? He seemed quite old enough to retrace his steps. If he needed help and didn't speak German, he was in dire straits, given his shyness and reluctance to mime.

~

It was sundown, and Arno did not come out to meet me, so I worried if Kat was all right. I hated to leave her alone knowing she'd find some work inappropriate for her condition. I called out as I came through the door. "Katarina? Are you here?"

"*Ja*, I am here." Her voice was hushed, and she rounded the corner in haste, her fingers at her lips. "I have just got him fed enough and down for the night. I made a pallet for him." She nodded toward the fireplace where Arno and the boy lay stretched out together, both their heads on one of her feather pillows and covered by the quilt she had told me she brought from the old country.

"I do declare, Katarina. This is not like you at all."

She gave me a withering look. "I suppose you think me heartless, but after our care tonight, I think he will manage. We are not so very far away, and he can call on us when need be. No doubt his father has prepared him for survival after the disaster that befell his mother and sister."

It was then Kat told me the boy's story.

I was so appalled and distracted that I was brought to tears. It was not until I recovered from the news that it dawned on me. "Oh my God! Your letter! You have a letter!" I retrieved it from my pocket and presented it to her. "From Günter!"

Her mouth fell open. She gaped at the envelope and sat down in near collapse. "Give it to me," she said. Her outstretched fingers fumbled in their attempt to grasp it. When she was finally able to take hold, she hugged it to her and sat staring beyond me. She didn't open it or study the address or turn it front to back in wonder. Quietly she rose and walked outside to the stairs. I heard her steps, slow and measured as she climbed to her room. I did not see her for the rest of the night and I was left to plan how we would rescue our new little charge. Despite Kat's resistance.

Katarina

Pulling the lantern close to the chair, I lifted Günter's reading spectacles to my eyes. *At last, a letter.*

He was alive. At least, long enough to write to me. He had made it to Mexico. Safe. How could I have doubted his survival? But I had. I had pictured his body lying somewhere along the Nueces or pierced with bullet holes as he rode for the border. After being in his hands and the hands of dozens of others, now finally, this envelope rested in mine.

I reached for Günter's letter opener of scrimshaw ox bone, a whaling schooner engraved on its handle, and eased the blade beneath the flap. It tore.

> *My dear wife,*
> *I am safe here in Louisiana near New Orleans.*
> *We are well received with clean uniforms.*
> *I believe our assignment will further the cause,*
> *but I fear for you and my brother....*

I hoped he did not know the dangers we were still in. He must face his own, and I would not add to his worries. At least, he was alive. This might be all I can have of him—these vague words on paper already fragile, even now having lost the warmth of his hand.

I took my Bible, opened it to Isaiah 2:4, and pressed the one-page letter into the protection of the words.

> *He shall judge between the nations and shall decide*
> *disputes for many peoples; and they shall beat their swords*
> *into plowshares, and their spears into pruning hooks;*

*nation shall not lift up sword against nation, neither shall
they learn war anymore.*

Pressing one hand against my belly and gripping the Bible in
the other, I eased into bed. That night of all the long nights I had
waited, I finally slept.

~

I awoke to the sound of industry below in the kitchen—the boy's
high-pitched voice above the soft roll of Eliza's drawl. Then an
untroubled scrap of laughter. How quickly he was at ease with
her—so near his contemporary with probably no more than eight
years distance in their ages.

This child, this boy, Finn. What would he do to complicate our
lives? We could barely take care of ourselves. As I descended the
stairs, I met him coming onto the porch lugging a pail.

"Miss Eliza said to fetch the water. She's heatin' it up. I told
her I oughta hold off till the end of the day lest I get mussed
up all over again by bedtime, but she said it couldn't wait." He
stumbled and dumped a good amount before he got to the door.
He spit out some Gaelic oath then glanced at me, "Beggin' your
pardon, ma'am."

I stepped into the kitchen where steam from the heating water clouded the windows. Eliza turned toward me with a look of
exasperation. She stuck out her lower lip and blew at the strands
from her hair that had gotten loose and pasted themselves to her
cheeks. Her face was rosy with the heat, but despite it all, she re-
tained that undeniable beauty of youth. No wonder the boy was so
anxious to please her.

"I rigged a curtain for him with the quilt. Think he's capable of doing a respectable job of bathing? It looks like it might
take supervision."

"*Nein.* Too old for that. If he cannot manage his bathing, he will have to wait until his father returns. It may take more than one or two tries, but the young man is on his own."

At that moment, he bumped through the door with the pail, sloshing more water onto the floor. "Here 'tis," he called, grinning and seemingly oblivious to the mess he caused.

"I will check the henhouse while you finish up in here." I took the egg basket and called back over my shoulder. "It is past sunup, and the cow will be complaining, Eliza. Leave the boy to his ablutions."

A question on his face, Finn looked up at Eliza.

"That must be German for taking a bath." She handed him a towel and a piece of soap. "Do a good job, hear?"

Eliza followed me to the barn. "You have not spoken of Günter's letter. How does he fare? Did he have news of Will? You cannot leave me in the dark like this."

"Günter is well enough." I kept walking. "He worries about us, of course. He is in Louisiana but knows nothing of Wilhelm. There was no pertinent news. All that matters to me is that he is safe."

"If only Will would write. There is so little to pin our hopes on."

"That boy seems enough to distract you from your fears." I do not know why I said that. In retrospect, it was unkind. The youngster was no substitute for a husband. But the words were out before I could quell them.

Eliza pressed my shoulder and turned me to face her. Tears flooded her eyes. "How uncharitable of you. How heartless after receiving a letter from the man you love when I have heard nothing." She started back to the house but pivoted and announced in a quiet voice. "This once I am going to forgive you, Katarina. This *once.* You are expecting a child and are perhaps not yourself." She paused as though reconsidering those last words. "Perhaps." She took a deep breath. "You must give me a moment to pretend it never happened, and then I will join you in the barn." Her voice broke, but she collected herself and returned to the house.

~

It seemed a long while until I heard her step through the barn aisle, and I had had sufficient time to consider my callous words. I reached for her hands. "Forgive me, Eliza."

"I'll go with Finn to his home," she said as she tied Greta to a post, "and see what he has to manage with. His father will be back any day now, don't you think?" She balanced on the stool and rinsed off the cow's udder.

I snorted. "You know as well as I do that if those men hiding in the hills try to return home, the *Haengerbande* will murder them. The man can only pray his son will be self-sufficient and resourceful."

"But he's no more than a child. How can he possibly care for himself?"

"I've heard of wild children who survived quite well." I lowered my voice as if I could be heard from the house. "My father told me a story he read about a boy found in France who was about the same age as this Finn and that apparently lived on his own for a very long time. Would not be washed or touched, nor did he speak. But my point is that he survived. With a little help, our boy is quite capable, I believe."

"Our boy?"

"You understand exactly what I mean—the boy who wandered up here."

"But his mother and sister! Imagine how that affected him. He knows what is said about the atrocities that befall women at the hands of those heathens." Eliza twisted to stare up at me. "He and his father have suffered too much already. What's the harm in a little motherly attention?"

Greta lifted her hind leg in warning. Eliza must have squeezed too hard. "Sorry, sorry," she said as she pressed her head against the animal's side and continued.

I shifted the egg basket to my other arm. "Greta has always been a sensitive cow."

"I've been milking her for months now. This is the first time she's been really grumpy." Eliza stopped milking. "Listen, why don't you see if Finn has come out of the bath? The water is bound to have gone cold by now. Then I'll ride over to his place with him and see what might be done."

"Just remember, we do well to provide for just the two of us. You may not make any decisions regarding him without first consulting me."

Eliza glanced up at me and then leaned her head against Greta again. Speaking into the flank of the cow, she said, "Oh, I wouldn't dream of it."

Eliza

The boy sidled sheepishly from the kitchen with a bundle of fabric under his armpits, a little satin bow poking out. He sat down by the fire with a quilt around his shoulders and his arm around Arno. He refused to look at me. "I ain't wearing these bloomers out of the house."

I had bribed him with more biscuits and preserves to get him to wear my undergarments, and he finally relented. My bloomers came closest to fitting him. The men's clothes were far too large.

Kat and I both had to turn away to keep from breaking into laughter. "Your clothes will be dry soon," I said. "I pressed them between towels to hurry them up before I hung them. Your secret is safe with us."

Finn sniffed and stared into the flames.

"We'll ride Legend over to your place. You know, to see how things are there."

He glanced up at me and then away.

"You'll like Legend. He's a fast horse." As an afterthought, I added, "Will you help me with him? I may need your advice." I raised my eyebrows hopefully.

Finn didn't look at me, but I saw a lift that gathering at the corners of his mouth.

"Would you like to see him now? He won't mind a bit about your wearing bloomers and Herr Lange's shirt. And there's no one else about."

He stood, hitched up the bloomers, and nodded. "Got a belt?"

~

With the undergarments cinched to the boy's chest and the shirttail tied into a knot, we brought Legend out. Eager to be free from the confines of his hidden stall, the horse danced in a circle around us and refused to stand to be saddled. "Better let me calm him down, ma'am. He'll be too rowdy for a lady like you."

Declining to mention the considerable experience I had with "rowdy" horses, I let Finn take over. It wouldn't be easy to get the kinks out of this horse, but I was willing to watch the boy give it a try. I offered the longue line and lunging whip and stood back.

The boy did have a way with Legend. He gave him the freedom of a dead run on the longue line till the horse finally let go of adrenaline with great blows. Speaking soothing phrases, Finn finally turned and walked away. Legend trotted in and stood resting his head against the boy's shoulder. So, it was true about the skill of the Irish with their horses.

"I believe he'll be calmer for ya, now," said Finn. "Somebody oughta work with that horse." He gave me a meaningful look.

Midday had come around, and we had yet to start out for Finn's home. Legend stood tacked up and fairly patient at the post. I had done the saddling myself while Finn watched making critical remarks about the sidesaddle.

"You'd never be catching me sittin' on that contraption."

"Apparently, you've not seen a lady riding in 'this contraption.' It takes skill, young man. You must try it sometime." Having months before eschewed petticoats, I tucked my skirt between my legs and swung myself into the saddle. It was not a graceful maneuver, but I had given up graceful maneuvers. Mamá would be appalled as would Chloë. Grace and beauty would come back to me when this awful war was over, when ladies could be ladies again with true gentlemen to escort us.

"Ma'am?"

I sat the horse and stared down the road. When this war was over there would be no cow milking or scrubbing floors for me. No siree. No egg gathering or butter churning, no sunburned skin or—

"Ma'am?"

"What?"

"Hand up?"

"Oh, yes, of course." I held the rein steady and reached down. Legend had never carried two at a time. He flinched but took the light weight of the boy.

"Head to the southwest. That-a-way." Finn pointed. "Shouldn't take us no time if you pick up a trot. Not sure what you expect to see there anyways. Weren't nothin' much to start with."

We stayed at a fast walk, the boy identifying thinning shrubs and bare-limbed trees. "Ain't been much so far, but I believe winter's a'comin'. You can feel it in the air, and it smells different, don't it? Smell it?"

I inhaled deeply and breathed in a whiff of wood smoke where we'd burned some brush. Yes, a change. The air seemed heavier and in it the promise of fog. The wind carried a subtle moan in the way of a roadrunner's cry or the whine of an old dog. "Yes. Yes, it's in the air, isn't it?"

"It's in everything, ma'am. A little sad, ain't it?"

I nodded and hoped for quiet with nothing more than the shuffle of the horse's hooves through fallen leaves, the rasp of branches against our clothing.

"You're gonna follow the creek from here on out. Good caves along here to hide in, but I'm not supposed to tell."

"I bet you're right." I thought about the one where we'd hidden Legend. "I imagine the Comanches know all about them, too."

"And that's why I've been a'thinkin'." He shifted his weight closer to me. "I'm handy with choppin' firewood and totin' buckets of nearly anything you need. I ain't big but I'm stronger than you think."

"I'm quite sure you are, but—"

"What I'm gettin' at, ma'am, is…well, y'all need a man around the place. I can shoot a gun and—"

Then it came to me. "Can you stick a pig?"

"Yes, ma'am. You shoot him, and I'm ready to cut the vein. I know right where it is. It'll take two of us to hoist him though. I saw the one you got in mind out there in the pen. He oughta make a fine ham. Why, yes indeed, ma'am, I can stick a pig."

The vision of a Christmas ham filled my mind. Smoked and salted, the meat would last a long time. This boy could be a great deal of help. He could also be considerable trouble. "It's something to think about, isn't it? Frau Lange will need to be consulted, of course."

Shortly, we came upon the small clearing where his cabin stood. A cave might have been preferable. The structure resembled a large outhouse. He jumped down, but I waited while he stepped inside and returned with a small sack of corn and a wool shawl that must have been his mother's.

"Ain't much," he said nodding at the shack, "but it blocks the wind some. Da will be back one day, and till then I can make it all right. I'll be right proud to see that day a'comin'. 'Less'n you need a man about to take care of the hard stuff. And her? She might need somebody to run for help like I done when my ma's time come." He tossed his head like he was flicking hair from his eyes, but it was to sling the tears away. Like Oliver Twist, he squinted up at me, those freckles bunching on his nose, his pride a thin veneer over his fear.

CHAPTER 12

In a scene described by one of Duff's troopers, first, the wife and children of a suspected Unionist were taken prisoner, then the crops were "trampled and destroyed," the bee-hives in front of the cabin overturned, the living room furniture wrecked, and the loom in the kitchen smashed.
– Joe Baulch, *The Dogs of War Unleashed: The Devil Concealed in Men Unchained,* in West Texas Historical Association Year Book

Katarina

I watched them as they rode up, Finn's legs swinging happily along the horse's flanks. Eliza had done it again. After I specifically *told* her that I would have to be consulted before promises were made. I understood the boy's plight, but he should be able to manage until his father's return and of course, he could always ask us for assistance in an emergency.

Finn slid off the horse and held the reins for Eliza's dismount. It was a practiced move on her part—gliding, effortless. He led Legend back to the hiding stall. Eliza looked up to see me at the window, shrugged a weak apology, and marched up to the house.

"Before you start," she said, "his situation was untenable. You would have been the first to suggest bringing him back here." She studied my face. "Well, you would have, Katarina!"

Eliza's face held a certain amount of pity, a degree of desperation, but most of all, a volume of kindness. I was defeated before she said another word. "Well, let it be done then. We are all victims of this war. I have prepared supper. Call him in." I tied my apron. "*Und*, for goodness' sake, remind the little urchin to wash up."

~

At the table that evening, the three of us sat across from each other venturing polite expressions. Finn put much effort into directing charm toward me, being the tough nut to crack. I spoke of the new arrangement first. "I see you will be staying with us for a while."

He glanced questioningly at Eliza and then at me before releasing a grand smile that spanned his cheeks. "I plan to be handy, ma'am. You just ask. Why I'm good at lots of things—choppin' wood, haulin' water, and somebody needs to work the kinks outta that horse out there."

"Well." I collected the plates without looking up.

"I'll take care of those," said Eliza. "I bet Finn will help me, won't you?" She stood waiting for him to follow.

It was then that I saw it—a delineation of tasks framed in the child's mind. This was women's work. The mental struggle went on a few seconds, but he recovered long enough to sputter, "Why sure, ma'am, of course, I will." The maneuverings of his mind could almost be heard as he picked up the dishes and figured out a future strategy to avoid that very thing.

Eliza looked at me and nodded toward the rocking chair. "I know you've done more than you should today. That's why I hate to leave you. You cannot be trusted. So, either go sit down over there or consider retiring to your room for the evening. You have a few books to reread, or I am more than happy to offer my poetry collections. 'Kubla Khan' is beautiful if somewhat disturbing."

The audacity of the girl knew no limits. "Please allow me some latitude in my own home. I assure you I have done only minimal chores today."

"Katarina, there's considerable yardage between your idea of minimal and mine. I can look about me and see the stove has been cleaned and the porches swept." Eliza waved her hand about her. "Leave this to Finn and me." She put her arm about my waist as if to direct me. It was not worth the effort to dissuade her.

I took Goethe's *Faust II* from the mantle. Although I once had both volumes of his masterpiece, *Faust I* disappeared on our voyage to Galveston—a loss I agonized over. I sat, the rocker a welcome relief from the day's chores. Even if Eliza and Finn distracted my reading, it would be worth observing what *schinäglens* the two had in mind.

In *der Schrank* Eliza discovered a checkerboard and pieces, the ones Günter had made by hand. I had all but forgotten it, but as I listened to the giggles and whispers over the game, I was reminded of the joy that Günter and I had shared. It was all I could do to keep the tears from blinding me to the printed page.

After a while, talk centered around Finn's sleeping quarters. While the porch would do plenty well in the warmer months, the pallet must serve for now. Finn wiggled down under the covers and called Arno to him. I studied his face from the corner of my eye. Within moments he fell asleep.

For future nights we might move the small cabinet out of the alcove near the fireplace and make him a little cot of some kind with fabric stretched across its frame. It would not be so hard to do. I remembered the soft down I accumulated from the chickens last summer. Scraps of cloth might suffice for a pillowcase. I could rationalize the hours of sitting with the simple task of sewing.

The hour was not late, but I stood, collected my book, and nodded goodnight to Eliza. Despite the mandatory nap I was to take during the day, I felt achy and more than a little tired. The bed would be a welcome respite. I glanced again at the sleeping boy, his fist clutching the blanket corner against his chin. Awake, he was a wiry little thing, tough and bulletproof, determined to erect a brittle façade he thought might protect us from what he had already witnessed. But asleep his face flushed with the guileless innocence seen only on the face of a child.

Eliza

Embellished with an occasional blasphemy that would blister the ears of all but the most calloused souls, the sound of the ax striking wood woke me. Wrapping my robe around me, I stepped out to the stairs and rushed down the steps calling, "Finn Bailey! You hush that talk this minute! What are you thinking?"

"Beggin' your pardon, ma'am. Just thought I'd get an early start on these chores. I know you ladies are countin' on me."

"We are counting on not being affronted as well. Why even the rooster hasn't crowed. What possesses you?"

"Earning my keep like I promised. Sometimes a man slips up with his words. 'Scuse me." He set the ax head on the ground and leaned on the handle, a posture he must have observed of his father's. With his smaller stature, though, his arm rested above his shoulder. Suppressing my smile became impossible. He saw it and produced a self-satisfied grin back. The little blackguard!

Katarina cleared her throat and stared bleary-eyed at us from the top of the stairs.

"Mornin' to ya, Mrs. Lange. Getting an early start to the day, I am. And I've got a few suggestions to make if you don't mind. I thought we could talk about them over breakfast."

Kat and I stared at each other. Our compliant, eager to please stray had evolved overnight into a headstrong lad with his own aspirations well in mind.

~

His mouth full of blackberry jelly, Finn delegated our assignments. Despite our signals to finish chewing before speaking, he carried on in blind enthusiasm. "'Fore the weather gets to where it ain't handy to get out and about, I want you, ma'am," he said, looking pointedly at me, "to teach that horse to pull a cart so's we can collect them two bee boxes I got at my place and get them ready for a swarm come spring."

"Legend has been trained to a carriage. And—" I thought to clarify Legend's abilities, but Finn marched right over my words.

"I'll teach y'all how to set up the boxes so's to be ready for the first swarm I can find. I'm real good at coaxing them into a box as soon as they start to swarm. And I can pick the queen out without hardly tryin'."

Katarina and I paused, our spoons in midair.

"And when we get back from that, we can talk about that hog you mentioned. I seen how it's done, and it ain't no job for a lady." He nodded at me. "Guess we'll have to make do." His eyes lingered on my arms as if sizing me up for the job. "Maybe you're stronger than you look."

"I can see you are industrious." I caught Kat's eye.

"Can't say as I know what dustrious is, but I'm a hard worker. Y'all are going to be mighty thankful I'm around to take care of these sorts of things."

"Indeed, indeed." I rose from the table, collected the dishes, and said, "Frau Lange and I will prioritize the chores and let you know what we deem to be our next step. However, I commend you on your choice of tasks to be undertaken this morning. Isn't that right, Katarina?"

Mentally, Kat seemed to have wandered away. "I have a letter to write," she said as she stood. "I am confident you can determine a satisfactory plan."

How unlike her—this disinterest in controlling the minutiae of daily living. I'd have to investigate this change of attitude later. "Well, there you have it," I said to Finn. "Let me take a look at those hands before you head back out to the woodpile."

I held his small hands and ran my fingers across the palms, callused, but reddened by the morning's work. He flinched but stared straight into my eyes as if to defy any sensitivity.

"Günter left a good pair of gloves." So, Kat had been listening all along. "Let me retrieve them."

"Absolutely not, Katarina. I'll go with you to bring them down." I turned to the boy. "Run to check on Legend for me. Please shovel out his stall and tote some water and corn for him." I patted his shoulder. "I'll be right back." I followed Kat up the stairs.

She took the last steps up the stairs, let herself in the door and turned to challenge me. "Why do you beleaguer me?" she said. "I am about to do what you have been nagging me to do for weeks. One trip up and down the stairs will not overextend my capabilities." She waited for my reply, but her face suggested she was plotting her next retort.

I was not going to fuss with her about it. "Hand me the gloves, Katarina, and I will be on my way." I waited by the door. In moments, she thrust the pair of leather gloves at me. They were of fine leather, not meant for labor. "These are much too—"

"They are not being used. They may never be used. Take them."

I knew I should have kept my word and walked away, but this was so out of character. As though she didn't care. "You seemed detached is all. I wondered if you were feeling ill." I reached for her hand.

"Sometimes I *am* detached, Eliza. It is how I get by." She shut the door.

Katarina

Though never having had a whimsical personality, I nonetheless thought of myself as one who appreciated a sense of humor. But today I felt despondent. The arrival of the boy should not have affected me so. He was amusing when not annoying and promised to be of some help. Perhaps I felt left out as I watched Eliza and Finn cooperate and tease each other. Even Arno seemed to be caught up with the entertainment the boy provided. I admitted I isolated myself at times—a preventive measure against heartache or frustration. Well, let them carry on. There was much to be said for peace and solitude. I would recline there a moment to rest my back and imagine what to put in my letter to Günter. My lying down will be sure to please little Missus Eliza.

But I daydreamed remembering that springtime in Wittenberg, Although Günter had come to study with Father, he stepped out to the garden the moment his meeting finished. The bower under which I placed myself lay in obvious sight of the hall windows. He would have had to be blind to miss me. I sat primly despite the dress that sloped off my shoulders and the dahlia in my hair. I had seen a drawing of Jenny Lind wearing a dress I desperately tried to have copied despite my mother's concerns. *"I will pull the sleeves up to my neck, Mutter. Fräulein Lind was no older than I when she sat for that portrait."* It was an abrupt deviation from my usual dress, I confess, but once, just once in my life, I wanted to feel beautiful.

And so, I perched on the bench shaded by the chestnut tree, wanting the young scholar to be aware that I was alone. No. More than aware, I wanted him to fall in love. When he stepped into the garden, I pretended not to notice at first and then feigned surprise that he stood so near.

"May I?" His words carried a different tenor than our conversations under Father's tutelage. It was husky, almost secretive. Had I not already been beguiled by his quiet intellect, his voice would have captivated me.

"Of course." I pulled my skirt in closer to me leaving just enough space for him to sit.

"I am departing soon," he said. "There is promised land and intellectual freedom in Texas. Our country, even here in Wittenberg, stifles me. Your father agrees that politics has created an impossible venue for the growth of intellectualism." Günter took my hand. "Texas is my destiny. And I would like it to be yours. For you to be my wife."

I gazed into those blue eyes full of adventure and desire. All the upheaval and hardship this quest might entail held no significance to me. He wanted *me* to go with him as his wife, and I thought of nothing else. When I gained composure enough to speak, I asked, "But why me?"

"I have watched you. And listened to you, your insights. Your intelligence. Your endeavor to become more than many women in our society. And other things—things I cannot speak of until we are wed." His eyes traveled to my shoulders that I had bared the minute Mother had turned her back. "Then I will tell you the thoughts that belong only between husband and wife." He reached for my fingertips I clutched at my breast and brought them to his lips. His eyes found mine. "Meet me here in the garden tonight. I need—" He looked away for a moment. "I need you to realize the depth of my—" He pressed his cheek to mine and whispered against my ear. "Just meet me. I want to make you understand." His kiss was brief. Urgent. My imagination took over all reason.

That dawn, lying in my bed alone in the chill of early winter, I conjured up that day—the morning sun, the roses, and rhododendrons. I closed my eyes to memorize the sensation. There was a hum in the air, warm and honeyed. I imagined his lips still at my fingertips, his mouth on mine again, brushing my throat, his skin against my skin. My answer was, "Yes, yes," before any rational thought could interfere.

When I wrote Günter, I would share those memories. Perhaps he would be reminded of that beautiful time. Perhaps the memory would console him when he lay on a cot or in a trench and anticipated the battle before him. Or distract him from the horror, even if only for a moment.

My dear husband,
I take this pen in hand to tell you how I have longed to
hear from you. At last, my prayers that you made it into
Mexico and on to Louisiana are answered. Now my new
pleas begin for you to come home safely to me. Do you
recall our time in Wittenberg when we were young? Tell
me you do. It is sometimes the only way I get through the
days—reminiscing. I send these thoughts to you through
the long miles between us—remember, remember—

In the rest of the letter, I only mentioned the boy as a helper, not a probable orphan. Nor did I dare hint at any possibility of a babe even though I had gone some beyond the usual three months. I mentioned the pecan tree produced well and our garden was bountiful. There was no complaint about Eliza, which was sure to surprise him. No doubt, he would see through the reserved nature of my words as I did his, but to dwell on the realities seemed too brutal. Since grandiose expressions of ardor had never been our way, I signed "With affection." Even though tears stung my eyes and my breath came near constricted.

Eliza

Finn's freckled arm buckled with the effort. As hard as he tried, he lacked the strength to chop and split enough firewood to get us through January. Even if my palms already chafed from labor and it deflated his ego, I needed to step up to the task myself, but as I made the first swing, I winced and dropped the ax.

Finn rushed to check my hands. Rubbing his finger across the torn calluses, he raised an eyebrow in a knowledgeable arch. "Know what? Honey fixes that. Bees is good for lots of things. Till then, just spit on 'em."

"When did you want to bring over your hive boxes?" I asked. "Something I'll look forward to."

Finn brushed his own raw hands against his pant legs. "I say we get right to it after dinner."

While I suspected he dodged the chore at hand, a jaunt through the countryside held a good bit of charm.

~

Kat had our meal waiting when we came through the door. "I have a letter for Günter," she said. "Perhaps you could deliver it to be mailed."

"Finn thought we might retrieve the bee boxes." I approached Kat by the stove. Under my breath, I asked, "Why don't we let him decide if today or tomorrow would be better to go to town?"

Kat set the bowls down more firmly than necessary and returned to the stove. "Why do we give way to a child?"

Finn appeared to be deaf to the difference of opinion and continued to gobble his cornbread spread heavy with butter.

With hands on my hips, I hissed, "If it doesn't matter to us, why not let him feel important. Encourage his sense of belonging."

"*Belonging*? I think you hurry in your thinking," but Kat turned to him and said, "Finn?"

His mouth still full and working, he gazed up at her. "Ma'am?"

"Which day do *you* prefer to go to town so Miss Eliza can deliver a letter?"

He ran his shirtsleeve across his mouth. "Why, ma'am, any day that pleases you best. I believe we can have that horse ready to pull right away. You just say the word." His eyes were round in his eagerness to please.

Gathering dishes, Kat turned abruptly from the table. "I am sure you will make the right decision." The crease between her eyes deepened, and when she tried to produce a smile, it fell short.

Finn sat straighter. "Miss Eliza, let's me and you head to town right away. We can stop at the little grove on the south side, and I'll wait for you there whilst you walk in and post that letter."

"A fine plan." Kat spoke with her back to us. "Do you not want to go into the town, Finn?"

"Why, it ain't wise to expose a good horse nowadays," he said. "And that fine animal sure can't be left tied somewheres. Lotta folks about can't be trusted, and it'll give me and Legend a chance to spend time together. That's an important thing when it comes to working with horses. Not everybody knows that, but it's true. Da said so."

I started to take Finn's plate, but he nudged it closer and reached for the last of the cornbread. He grinned up at me. "A bit of butter left. Might as well use it up," He swiped the bread across the plate leaving little reason for soap and water.

As we walked out to the buggy, Kat handed the letter to me and two pennies to Finn. "Ask Miss Eliza to pick you out some peppermints or lemon drops. I thank you for helping her deliver my letter."

For once, the boy was speechless. Amazement in his eyes, he clutched the pennies and finally was able to say, "Thank you, Mrs. Lange, thank you."

"You may call me, Miss Katarina," she said. "I believe it would be appropriate now."

"Since we're like family?" Finn pressed the pennies to his chest.

"Well, I suppose. If you like." Kat looked over his head toward the red oak in the distance where the little graves were. I thought she might break down, but an unfamiliar expression formed in her eyes. "Yes," she murmured, "family." She put her hand on his head. "At least until your father returns."

~

Legend settled to the traces more quickly than Finn or I expected, though I did take the precaution of blinders. Encouraged by our appreciation of his skills, Finn chattered away, pointing out flora and fauna of the countryside. "Certain plants is good for certain things. Ma was the one that knew about that kind of thing," he said. "She called it her specialty."

"I know about black haw," I said. "Even if I am a city girl."

"Yes, ma'am. Ma had me picking that for her regular like. I heard her tell Da I'd be getting a baby brother or sister come that summer." His jaw twitched as though he clenched his teeth. "Never come to pass. Or maybe it did, and we just never could find her. Her or Eileen, my baby sister. We tried awful hard."

What could I possibly say? That skinny little kid trying to be tough. I patted his arm.

He cleared his throat. "Think Mrs. Lange will do all right? Being in the family way used to make Ma aggravated some, too."

I found his perception surprising and resisted the urge to say *aggravated* was Kat's natural state.

"Then Ma would turn around and do something extra sweet," Finn continued, "like makin' a peach pie and squeezin' on me and the like. Kinda hard to tell what it was gonna be one day to the next."

I wanted to hug him and tell him everything would be all right, but we both knew it would be a lie. "My goodness, Finn," I said, making my voice cheery. "I'm sure Miss Katarina will do just fine. We'll have to be patient with her, though, won't we?"

"Oh, yes, ma'am. And take good care of Mrs. Lange…Miss Katarina, that is."

CHAPTER 13

Bushwhacker was a term used to describe those "who beat the bushes" to avoid conscription.
– Joe Baulch, *The Dogs of War Unleashed: the Devil Concealed in Men Unchained,* West Texas Historical Association

Katarina

I watched Eliza and Finn until they cleared the lane. They chatted, heads nodding as if agreeing on some plan. I wanted to be a part of their camaraderie, and I did not know why I threw pitfalls in my own path.

I remembered the down feathers for Finn's pillow. This might be a good time to stitch the casing for it. The afternoon was quiet and cool. Retreating upstairs to my room, I collected the lavender silk from one of the dresses I brought from Germany and sat to sew with the finest stitches I could make. Worn but finely woven, it would be soft against his cheek. There would be plenty left for a baby girl's dress, but I could not bring myself to sew for a baby. Not yet.

Arno lay sleeping beside my rocking chair, his feet scrambling after some squirrel in his dreams. So peaceful the afternoon that I caught myself nodding over the work before a low growl startled me. Arno stood at the window, stiff-legged, his ears at attention to the front of the house.

The gate scraped against the post. We always knew to lift it slightly to avoid scratching the wood. I checked the clock on the dresser. It was not yet two o'clock. Too soon for Eliza and Finn. I set my needlework to the side and stood beside Arno, my hand on his head.

A man had stepped inside the yard. Gaunt and bearded, tattered. My eyes searched for a horse nearby, but it appeared he was on foot. His hand rested on the gun tucked into his waistband. He called, "Halloo, anybody home?"

Arno snarled but did not move. Below, I heard the front door open, and the man called again. The Henry. I had left the rifle on the mantle. We had been unmolested for such a long while that I let my guard down. Now I would pay for such laxity. I thought about Eliza's derringer she kept in her nightstand. Slipping off my shoes so as to not make a sound, I eased down the hall to her room and slid through the door, which complained on its hinges.

The drawer held only her treasured copy of poetry. She had taken the gun with her. Of course. She should have. I returned to the hallway and stood with my ear against the door to the outside landing. From below came the sounds of pilfering through our shelves, drawers opening and closing. The lid to the pot on the stove clanked. And then silence for what seemed like a very long while.

I chose to face the man. He would find me regardless. I could not imagine he would not search the rest of the house. The only thing that would serve as a weapon was Günter's scrimshaw letter opener. With that in one hand and Arno's ruff gripped in the other, I descended the stairs. Still, I heard no other noise as I tiptoed to the window and peered around the frame.

Leaning hard on both elbows, the man sat hunched over the table shoveling stew into his mouth. He had found the milk jug and left it there on the table to refill his mug without missing a bite. Unmindful of anything but the spoon going from bowl to mouth, he never looked up or wiped his beard. I could have called aloud and doubted he would have been aware.

Moving to the front door, I held my breath and stepped to the mantle where I lifted the Henry off its rack. It seemed the sound of my own breathing would alert the intruder as I crept to the kitchen. I pointed the rifle at the back of his neck. "Trespasser! Down on your knees!" I spoke in German.

He startled and turned to see the barrel of the Henry pointed at him. He dropped the spoon in the stew and slid off the chair to his hands and knees. "*Es tut mir Leid.*" His pronunciation murdered the language.

Switching to English, I said, "I am afraid an apology will not do. You will crawl out the door and down to the gate. Should you return, I will shoot you on sight." I could not think of a way to get him to remove the gun at his belt. If his hand gripped the weapon, he might fire before I could react. As long as I could see his hands on the ground, I felt safer.

He did as he was told. As he clambered away, the soles of his mismatched shoes revealed one military brogan lace-up and the other a boot with its Napoleon buckle peeled away from the leather. A pitiful picture, but I could afford neither mercy nor kindness. Arno rumbled with a predator's intent and searched my face for permission to eliminate him.

The man reached beyond the gate, stood and threw his hands in the air. "Frau Lange? Do ya not remember me?"

I lowered the rifle from my shoulder but kept it pointed at him.

"It's Tom Bailey, ma'am. Helped Günter set up your first cabin, and he helped with mine. Remember, Mrs. Lange? Tom Bailey, your neighbor."

"Mr. Bailey?"

"Yes, ma'am. Tom. Beggin' your pardon, can I put my hands down?"

"Put your hands down."

"I come to check on my boy, Finn. Couldn't find him where I left him to hide. Nor about our place. He's not yet ten years, but he's wily. I hoped he could make it on his own when I had to hightail it to the hills to keep from gettin' strung up by the *Haengerbande*. You've not seen him, have you? Red-headed tyke about yea high?" Mr. Bailey's hand marked even with his elbow. "I've been awful worried."

I drew a sigh of relief. "Finn is here. Not now, not right this minute. Gone to town with my sister-in-law. They will be back soon. You may stay until they return."

"I'm obliged." He blushed and swept his hat to his belly. "And I'm beholden to you for the stew. I was right famished and lost control of me manners. Let me work to make up for it." Mr. Bailey rubbed his arm and stood waiting for me to say something.

"If you would like to wash up, you may use our well. I think it best if you wait on the porch, but you may sit in the chair."

"Why, thank you. *Danke schön.* You're mighty kind."

"*Bitte*. It is nothing." I turned and walked back into the house. Arno lay down on the porch, but his eyes never left the man. I doubted he would allow him on the porch chair.

Upstairs I set about looking for something—anything—for Mr. Bailey to wear. Günter had a few things that might do—a shirt I had repaired several times and a pair of overalls. The man could keep those, but the shaving brush and razor and the mirror and bowl needed to be returned immediately. I had saved fragments of used lye soap and could spare those. No help for the shoes. I could not bear to part with that last good pair Günter owned. I just could not. It would be the same as saying he would not make it home from the war. I thought about the gloves I had sacrificed to Finn. Was it too late to retrieve them?

I carried the bundle down, set it on the ground for him near the well, and hurried back to the house as he approached. Why should I be so distressed by a man with whom I was acquainted? Perhaps because I had not seen a trustworthy man since Günter had escaped, or perhaps because I was alone. Pulling a chair to the parlor window, I sat with the rifle across my lap and watched Mr. Bailey. It seemed prudent to keep an eye on him. In these times even good men could become desperate and forego honorable behavior. Unaware I watched him, he peeled away his jacket that had come apart at most seams. The shirt underneath showed tears of hard travel in the brush. Stripping the suspenders from his shoulders, he leaned over the washbowl to scrub his face. He propped the mirror on the well bucket and lathered.

I meant to turn away, to not spy on this private activity, but it reminded me of watching Günter shave. How the back muscles tensed down to the slender waist, the flex of the bicep as he brought the razor to his cheek. Such a masculine endeavor. I felt the heat rise. Appalling. Had I become some wanton? Still, I could not look away. Who was to know? I owed it to my own safety to keep an eye on him, did I not? He turned once as if he was aware of being watched, and I looked away quickly. When he swished the razor in the water and returned to his task, my eyes settled once again on his fair skin, unmarked except for a white scar shaped like a scythe just above his shoulder blade. I felt the urge to press my lips to it.

Eliza

We pulled off the road into the homeplace. Finn sat quietly beside me finishing off the last of the peppermints. Examining each stripe as he licked, he never noticed the man who slouched on the porch chair with Arno blocking any entrance to the house. I couldn't breathe for a moment. Had Günter returned? The shirt, the overalls—I knew them to be Günter's. Could it be, even as I had just posted Kat's letter to him?

The man stood and took a step forward, his hand held up in greeting. "Son?"

Finn jolted forward as I pulled up Legend. "Da!" He turned to me. "It's my da!" He jumped down, bolted through the gate, and up the porch to his father's arms. Then with a quick look back at me, he cleared his throat, stepped back, and shook his father's hand. "Proud to see ya, sir. 'Tis been a while."

Kat waited in the doorway. "Mr. Tom Bailey. The boy's father."

Grinning, Finn waved his arm toward me. "This here's another Mrs. Lange, but to me, she's Miss Eliza."

I climbed down, wiped my hands on my skirt, and came forward to meet the man. "You have a fine son, Mr. Bailey."

"My thanks, ma'am. I'm proud of him. I've put a lot on him this last year, and he's had to grow up fast, I reckon." He put his arm around the boy's shoulders. By Finn's expression, you'd have thought he'd just won a decoration for valor. "Just the same, I worry, you know." Mr. Bailey's voice cracked, but he recovered so quickly I wondered if I'd really heard it.

All I could think to say was, "It's a worrisome time."

The Irish, I thought, are a fervent lot. Something to be said for it, even with the hullabaloo that might accompany them. My papa's best friend was an Irishman. I had adored him. While Papa tended to be on the stuffy side, at least around the house, his friend Riley might go from blithesome to lugubrious at the slightest provocation. His nature wore no disguises. I could not help but warm to the man who stood before us. Despite how much I knew he and his family had suffered, I saw in his gray eyes the man he must have been in happier times. "I hope you have been all right, Mr. Bailey."

"If staying in the hills kept me alive, then I would say fair to middlin'. I've mostly feared for my boy, but it gladdens my heart to see him here with you ladies." He held his hand to his chest and bent forward in a bow. "Mrs. Lange has been kind enough to provide me with these garments. I'm afraid I helped myself to dinner when I thought you all gone. It is an embarrassment. Before I leave, I hope to make it up to you. I see there's a load of wood to be split for the hearth."

"Now that will not be necessary, Mr. Bailey." Kat put her voice firm and dignified. "I am sure we can manage on our own."

I tried to keep silent, but had she lost her mind? We needed a man's help if it were only for one day of hard labor. I looked for a way around Kat's pure obstinacy.

"Why, Mr. Bailey, how very kind of you to offer," I said. "As you can see, Finn has made an excellent start. He also agreed to settle my horse into dependability. I think he would enjoy your partnership with the heavy work he has insisted on." I glanced at Kat who pressed her lips together and turned back to the house.

"Frau Lange is self-reliant, perhaps to a fault," I said, "but even she must count on friends, particularly at this time. I fear she does too much as it is."

Mr. Bailey gave me a sidelong grin. "Ah, I'm familiar with the resistance of a proud woman. 'Tis sometimes a detriment to her wellbeing. I offer out of gratitude, not superiority."

Finn broke in. "She's gonna have a—"

"That'll be enough of ye." Mr. Bailey took his son by the shoulders and pivoted him to the horse and buggy. "Lend yourself to the care of that fine animal. We'll not be needing your observations regarding these lovely ladies." He turned to me, doffed his hat, and tossed the ax easily on his shoulder.

I didn't care what Kat thought. We needed the strength of a man. Even if he wasn't our husband. Even if he would be gone by the end of the next day.

At supper that night, we broke into a bottle of wine, which lifted all our spirits. Kat relaxed, and Tom Bailey was transparent in his efforts to charm her. She insisted he sleep by the hearth with Finn.

"The night is too cold for the barn, and I will not have it," she said. "Here's a quilt. Maybe Finn will be generous with the pillow I made for him. Perhaps there will be another the next time you come." She blushed at her presumption, but Tom said that when the Secesh were in the far reaches of the county, he'd make another foray hereabouts. He winked when he said it, and I thought he'd won Kat's approval thrice over. Next morning, she left Günter's good shoes at the door with a note I was sure insisted on Mr. Bailey's wearing them.

Katarina

I had embarrassed myself on a score of topics—first, denying the man good shoes and then relenting, a clear showing of ambiguity. And laughing far too much at supper. Mr. Bailey must think me disingenuous, indeed. Worse yet, I allowed Eliza to undermine my decision about the firewood. But when I looked out the window and saw the cord of wood split and stacked, relief swept over me. I set to preparing a hearty meal for Mr. Bailey. Or Tom, as he insisted we call him. I did not encourage the use of my own given name. In truth, I would have liked it. It would have reminded me of days when Günter was at home—as did watching the man work. But there I had gone again into a fantasy that would serve no good.

Though the day had begun brisk even for December, a frigid wind by afternoon had dropped the temperature dramatically. I dried my hands on my apron, stepped outside, and took Tom a mug of hot tea that steamed in the air. Arno went with me to the woodpile. He now considered Tom a friendly presence.

"I thank you." Tom put the maul down and reached for the cup, his fingers grazing mine as he accepted the tea. "And I am beholden to you for the use of the shoes. They fit well enough, though 'tis a kindness I don't deserve."

"Let me decide who is deserving." I hurried to change the subject lest I show too much emotion at the donation of my husband's good shoes. "Eliza and Finn left for chores and should be back any moment now." I looked around as though searching for their whereabouts. Not really caring how long they stayed gone, I felt a wave of disappointment when I heard their cheery voices coming up from the field.

"I hope the boy is of good help to ya." Speaking as if in confidence, Tom leaned toward me. "Life has not been easy for him, so he'll not be expecting a lot of pettin'. See that he does a good job, and I'll speak to him, too, before I leave."

"You have helped us, Tom," I said. "I would like you on your way before word gets out. Treachery drifts on the wind. I have packed your supper."

"There's no help for it, I fear," he said, "Maybe my only hope of gettin' by is to try a different way to face this. I'm walking into Fredericksburg proper to sign up with the Texas 3rd Infantry. Sure, they'll march us to the coast to keep the Union from invading from the Gulf of Mexico, but I hope to get back here soon. Some boys desert at planting time to come home and work the fields. Oh, they have to dress up in their wife's clothes, but they've not been caught yet. Then they hustle on back to their units until harvest when they sneak home again. So, save me an old dress and a rag for my head, and I'll be your farmhand come March or soon as I can get loose." He waved to his son to come say his goodbyes.

Finn walked to the gate with his father and watched while Tom faded into the brush, a fugitive in his own county. The boy glimpsed us waiting at the kitchen window but shuffled back to the barn. With a brief whine, Arno followed at Finn's heels, his head low as if he understood the loss of being left behind.

"Well, what do you make of that?" Eliza asked. She dashed at her eyes with her sleeve.

"Make of what?"

"Oh, nothing, I guess. Just a man named Tom who might not see the next light of dawn. Might leave that boy an orphan complete. Feels different now that we know him. What would we do if—"

I turned and began picking up the dishes. "I refuse to cross that bridge till we come to it." But I had crossed it, of course. I had come to it when that carrot-topped kid first turned his face up to us pretending to face the future unafraid.

~

With Eliza and Finn working in the garden, I felt alone in the quiet house. I retired to rest as instructed, and this time I welcomed it. I lay back on my pillow and closed my eyes, but all I could see was Tom Bailey lathering shaving brush, splitting the firewood. I wished I had not watched him shave. It felt like a breach of my wedding vows. But even so, it made me long for Günter. Although he was sometimes aloof and arrogant, there were times when he was not. I filled my mind with those times.

Eighteen hundred fifty-two—our finest moments—the year we paced off our property boundaries. From the long distance of memory, I saw my young husband, full of daring and optimism, believing in the freedom of self-determination and the beauty of our new country.

CHAPTER 14

Throughout the long winter months of 1862 and 1863, the Hill Country pioneers quietly grieved, rebuilt their cabins, and struggled to obtain the basic necessities for life.
– Joe Baulch, *The Dogs of War Unleashed: the Devil Concealed in Men Unchained,* West Texas Historical Association

Katarina

It was the twenty-first of December. Saint Nicholas Day had come and gone, but we could recreate it on Christmas Eve. Finn had no room of his own, but we would fill his shoes with something sweet while he slept.

I thought about my own childhood in Wittenberg—the advent wreaths, the Christmas tree, the month-long joy of the season. How different here. Although Günter and I had celebrated, it was a modest version by far compared to our upbringing. I had imagined how it would be here with our children grouped around us. Our first year together we exchanged small handmade gifts. Günter made the checker game set, and I knitted him a sweater in the bluest wool I could find to match his eyes. We were in the little cabin then and sat before our fireplace eating salted ham with peas and carrots, along with the cornbread and apple turnovers I had learned to make in the old country. Huddled together, we gazed at the flames and tried to discern our future in the embers, thinking that surely, we would have a child by the next advent. We had worked so very hard, and although we barely had a roof over our head and food to eat, we had the promise of everything to come. Such a future in this new country—its bounty and liberty. Of course, we reckoned the dangers of an untamed land, but youth is blindly confident. We were the first of the generations to come. Pioneers!

Had we lost our minds?

~

Morning came cold again, but it was fitting for the season. I planned to feed Finn and send him out with an ax in search of a tree. The fact that it had to be a small cedar did not matter to him since he had never known the lovely spruce we most often chose for our Christmas tree back home.

Morning chores were easy enough for me—the chickens, even milking Greta. The animals brought peace to me for they never imagined the distress the rest of us contemplated. Except for the pigs. I stood at the pen and eyed our most likely victim. We had to confirm the choice shortly.

Finn came and stood at my elbow. "You thinking what I'm thinking?" He nodded toward smallest of the pigs. "It's about the only size me and Miss Eliza can handle." He gazed up at the sky and shivered. "Good weather for it." We heard Eliza call for us as she came down the stairs. He jerked his chin at her. "She's gonna want me to do the dirty work, I reckon. I hope I didn't overshoot the mark about me knowing how to slaughter a pig when I was talking the other day." Turning to welcome her, he resumed his swagger of feigned confidence. "Morning, Miss Eliza! We got us a job."

She nodded mutely and escaped into the kitchen. I turned to follow, but Finn rushed up beside me to say, "See if she'll let me use that little derringer? It should do the trick at close range, it being a .22 caliber." He glanced off. "I done it before. Da let me, so I can do it. I mean, it'd save Miss Eliza, her being kinda delicate and all."

I knew that was likely a falsehood, but I did agree with him that for Eliza, the experience might be too much. "I will shoot."

"Then I'll stick it," he said. "Maybe we can wash it off before she has to do the work that you can't because—well, you know why." He searched the horizon, "Seems fair. Mama didn't mind the boiling and scraping so much, but you couldn't get her near when we started chasing the pig. Wanted us to wait till she was out of earshot, and when that pig got to squealin', that was a far piece. Best warn Miss Eliza to put her head under a pillow." He manufactured a smile, but it faltered. "My mama didn't like to hear things suffer. She—" He scraped his shoes in the dirt. "Oh well, days like this make me...."

I did not know what to say to him. Likely nothing would ease the heartache. Still, I wish there was something I could do for him. My mother would always offer me a sweet, but then my misery had been no more than a lost toy.

"Let us get to it then," I said, knowing I had spoken over loudly. "I will grab the gun and forewarn Miss Eliza."

~

Finn and I stood at the pen, the scalding water steaming in a tub behind us. "Best don't scare it, ma'am. Just walk up friendly and put the gun to his head."

Being instructed by a youngster was nettlesome, but I tried to do as directed. I thought to offer gentle words of comfort to the piglet as I pressed the small barrel against its head. I remembered stories about how Indians said prayers of thanks for the sacrifice of their victim's life. Now for the first time, I understood. Hardly a *gift* from the piglet, but at least I wanted to offer appreciation of the animal's life. Whispering a word of gratitude and deep apology, I pulled the trigger.

Finn shouldered past me. "I'll bleed him and wash him off. Then he won't look so bad when Miss Eliza helps me lift him to the boiling pot. You go on now and sit down. We'll do the rest."

It was not yet noon, but it seemed the end of a long, long day.

Eliza

Finn and I were sent out to find a suitable tree—with specific dimensions. The woods were filled with a pale green light and the clean, sharp fragrance of cedar. Even though the pollen made my eyes burn and water, we persisted until we found it—a crooked little tree. Probably not at all what Kat had in mind, but it had a certain charm that appealed to both Finn and me.

The air had gone still and damp, and we worked quickly to chop the tree down and drag it between us to the house. My hands itched and ached with the labor, but Finn seemed unaffected. Christmas was almost upon us. Seeing his bright eyes and pink cheeks lifted my own spirits. I thought of Will. His last letter months ago had described tolerable conditions, but local reports on the war had been disheartening. If only I had a letter from him telling me that he was alive and offering words of forgiveness for wanting—no, pushing—him into uniform. Even though there had been little alternative.

I thought of Mamá and Papa and Chloë and imagined them there in Galveston. Perhaps without the gaiety of a year or two ago, but a celebration despite the war. I was sure of it. They had no knowledge of my existence here but had they, I imagined their reactions—Papa would remind me that he had predicted the likelihood of such a life, Mamá would commence with the vapors, retiring to her room, and refusing to hear another word. So, I would never tell them. Pretending happiness was my best course of action. To think on it, invention must be foremost in all our minds.

~

Christmas Eve, we set candle remnants in the tin holders that Kat had brought from her homeland. She had only four, but they brightened the tree. She made walnut shortbread cookies, which were wonderful to taste but crumbled when she tried to fasten them to the cedar branches. I watched her face as she tried so hard to keep a stiff upper lip but had to excuse herself when the last attempt failed.

We livened up at the thought of Finn opening our gifts. Thank heaven for this boy. He had provided a diversion from our hardships and made our days happier. Despite his own heartbreak, he managed to find some delight in his life with us.

We sat before the tree, watched the candles burn down, and ate the last of the walnut cookies. Kat broke the silence. "I have something for you, Finn. It is your merry Christmas gift." Gauging his hand size and adjusting the pattern for growth, she had made him leather gloves lined in rabbit fur. "Would you like to open it?" she asked.

"Yes, ma'am, I surely would! And I thank you for it."

She reached behind her and offered her gift to him. "I made them a little large for I know you will grow quickly."

Finn stroked the leather, but his eyes grew round when he slipped his hand inside to the rabbit fur. "Oh, ma'am. These is the best gloves I have ever wore."

She offered only a slight smile and a nod, but I didn't recall ever having seen Kat look so satisfied.

"Well, I have a gift for you as well," I said. "It may not excite you at first, but I believe it will bring you much enjoyment as time goes by."

I had felt at a loss for a practical idea. The one possible gift I had in my possession was a copy of *Moby Dick*—a story full of reprisal and obsession, I admitted, but it had its heroes and a moral. Other than my books of poetry, it was my treasure. I planned to read it to Finn, and he could learn to follow the words and add to his vocabulary. I handed him the calico-wrapped book, tied with one of my ribbons.

"It's good and heavy!" he said as he unwrapped it in the typical frenzy of a boy with a surprise. "Is it a gun?" But then the smile faded. "A book?"

"Yes sir, a book! And I signed it to you. Look inside. See? To Finn from Eliza, with love."

"What's it called?"

"*Moby Dick*—an adventure story. We'll read it together, and then you can learn to read it and—"

"Well, there ain't nuthin' wrong with it, I guess. Thanks to you." He put the book down and mumbled, trying to think of something to say. "I don't have nuthin' for you all just yet, but come March, I'll rebuild the beehive and show you how to coax bees into it. Honey will be my gift. The bees are the ones that make the honey, but I can get it." He looked up, a shy smile playing at the corners of his mouth. "So, well, it's from me and the bees."

We murmured our appreciation, but I did not put too much faith into his offer. It was a sweet thought, nonetheless.

I gave Kat the small gift I had spent a week trying to perfect—a baby blanket from wool skeins of assorted colors I had found. Perhaps out of fear of jinxing a healthy birth, Kat had made nothing for the baby. I hoped she would see the blanket as my confidence on her behalf. I meant it as such.

She unwrapped it but did not lift it up to admire. Carefully refolding it, she tucked her chin to her chest and whispered so that I could barely hear, "*Danke*." Without looking up, she handed me a hanky embroidered with my monogram in soft gray thread.

Standing, I stepped to her chair and kissed her cheek. She

had understood how dear small, beautiful things were to me. Having so little of the necessary practicalities, this gift was a flower out of season.

Kat flushed and hurried to get supper on the table—the artfully disguised piglet, the vegetables, and dried apple pie. With Arno beneath our feet, deeply involved with a ham bone, we sat in candlelight, gripped each other's hands, and prayed that the coming new year would be better, folks would be kinder, and please God, let the war be over.

After supper, Kat produced a small music box of marquetry inlay with three brass bells that played "Silent Night." She sang along softly as it played, her eyes shimmering with tears.

"Stille Nacht, heilige Nacht
Alles schläft einsam wacht"

Finn started with his own Gallic, *"Oíche chiúin, oíche Mhic Dé,"* but stumbled. "I used to know it, but I have plumb forgot."

And I? I could not utter a sound.

Our only prayers that Christmas had been to receive a letter from our husbands. Mine was not realized until late the month after when Will's letter finally came. Pulling the candle close to me, I sat at the hearth and read it over and over, trying to feel him between the lines. The price of paper so dear, he filled up every space, sometimes adding a word on the fringes or above the line. The edges were frayed now, the ink smudged with my fingers. I refused to let my tears fall for fear of making the letter illegible.

My dearest wife,
    I avail myself of this first opportunity of writing

*and sending you a letter. My company was assigned to
escort union soldiers here for a prisoner exchange. We
are all in camp here at Baton Rouge where we can see
the Mississippi water as far west as our vision extends.
Word is out that we will be leaving soon back to Texas.
Let me hear of Günter if you can. He may have got down
to Matamoros with the Union cavalry there. My health is
good and I believe I have gained flesh since I came here
though I have been slightly affected by dysentery but by
living prudently and dieting I am just about well again.
I can stand it well unless it gets worse. I have got out of
all the scrapes I have ever got into and I will get out of
this one, God willing. You must not worry about me. I
will send letters when I can. My thoughts belong to you
when I have even a moments peace. I wish I had had time
to bring your likeness with me to wear against my heart.
I will press my hand against my chest and wish that it
was your sweet countenance there instead. I am trying
to save all my money to go home if I ever get to go. War
has been little but hard riding, but it may prove perilous
as time goes by. Receive the love from the one who loves
you best. Remember me—Wilhelm to Eliza Lange.
Your loving husband*

Except for a few lines, it seemed full of everyday pedantry.
There was little detail in regard to the war itself. Perhaps he knew
his commanding officer read and censored the letters. At least, he
was alive and loved me still. I pressed each line into my memory,
repeating the phrase—*I have got out of all the scrapes I have ever
got into. Your loving husband, Wilhelm.*

When I wrote him back, I recognized the same glossing
over of reality. I dared not mention that we'd got Legend back
for fear of someone intercepting the letter and betraying us. *Die*

Haengerbande roamed the county and threatened every gain we eked out. Nor did I mention Kat's condition. It was not mine to tell, and since there was every possibility that it would not come to fruition, I could only respect her caution.

CHAPTER 15

Military authorities responded quickly and firmly to suppress what they perceived as resistance to the Confederacy, but after January of 1863 this overt hostility to the new government faded away, only to be replaced by a passive resistance by many German Texans. Within this atmosphere, Major Hunter, a friend to many of the German population in the Fredericksburg area, sent out his first patrols to enforce conscription and arrest deserters.

– David Paul Smith, *Frontier Defense in the Civil War, Texas' Rangers and Rebels*

Eliza

That day in February, the dishes were cleared, the butter churned, and the fire banked. I dreaded the thought of pumping water from the well and lugging the heavy buckets to the newly planted broccoli, cabbage, and lettuce. But it would mean the difference between hunger and satisfaction come spring. The only winter coat I had was a velvet cape—ridiculous for frontier living. I laughed at myself and shrugged on Will's black wool jacket he brought from Germany. It would do far better, but I wondered what he would be wearing now. Even though his warmth had dissipated long ago, I pressed the coat against my cheek and breathed in deeply hoping to find the scent of him infused in the wool.

I sighed at my naiveté. The thrill of following Will to the frontier had become a bad dream—bitter and marked with discord. Oh, I had begged for it. Demanded it. Angered at my own accountability in the matter, I did not hear the horseman until he was upon me. I hoisted the bucket like a shield and glared up into the man's face. Though half-covered by his slouched hat, I could see the pockmarks that scarred his cheeks. With a careless fling of his reins, he ground-tied his mount, a spotted pony, and stepped forward with a limp. "Heered tell you been takin' in outliers. I come to get him." He pulled his gun and reached for my arm. I dumped the full bucket of water at the intruder's britches and ran for the house. He caught me in the kitchen as I opened the drawer where I kept the derringer now. I whirled, my hands behind me, groping for the gun.

Kat stepped into the open doorway. "Stop before I call my husband from the barn!"

"You ain't got no husband, Frau." He leered at her belly and grinned. "Well, you had *some* man around here, by the looks of things. Took a likin' to that Irishman, did ya? Maybe you'd like a little more of the same."

I found the derringer, felt its cool pearl handle. "You leave her alone!" I cocked the hammer. The man did not appear to hear the click.

"Well now, if you insist," he said, turning back to me. "Anyway, I bet you're a purer little piece, disregardin' that nasty attitude you got." He patted my cheek, his callused hands chafing my skin. His breath reeked of rotted teeth. "But now if you give me a itty bitty hint as to where I might could find that Bailey fellow, I might be right sweet with ya." He grunted against my ear. "Get you where you like it and all."

Katarina moved closer. "Let her be, and I will give you directions as to where you can find him."

"No, Katarina!"

Still facing me, he said to her, "I'll get to you in a minute. I got business with this little girl first." He nuzzled me, his beard matted with saliva and last night's whiskey. His hand gripped my skirt and began to claw it upward.

I brought the derringer between us and felt its barrel press into the fat of his soft belly. Knowing this would be something I would never be able to forget, I fired.

His mouth formed an O of surprise. He stepped back and slapped me hard across the face. And I cocked the gun and fired again.

Katarina

I thought Eliza was murdered. She made no sound as he fell against her, pinning her to the cabinet. For the first few moments, the room was quiet, completely quiet. "Eliza!" I screamed. "Eliza!"

Then it was Arno roaring, a blur of black that launched itself against the intruder. He lifted the man from the back of his jacket and flung him away from Eliza. He was at the man's throat.

A rasping, strangling plea—"Get him off! Get—" Silence followed except for the wolfish, unforgiving retaliation that Arno inflicted. It answered each damning curse I had visited upon the man who embodied every evil we witnessed in this war. And I wished it on him, wished for my dog to commit the crime I could not. Still, I had to try to intervene. "Arno, no! *Aus*!" But he would not. Perhaps my voice lacked conviction. Arno's muzzle was bright with blood now, and when I reached for him, he snarled at me as though I had asked him to surrender the spoils of his private war.

The growls ceased. He seemed to be freeing his mind, bringing himself back to the domestic animal he was bred to be. Aware of me at last, his eyes cleared, but possessive and proud, he straddled his kill like a wild thing.

The derringer still in her hand, Eliza had fallen backward to the floor, her heels digging into the planking as she scrambled away to the far wall. Her eyes wide in disbelief, she flung the gun from her and tried to stand.

I rushed to her and felt my knees buckle. I sank beside her.

"Ma'am! Ma'am!" Out of breath, Finn rushed into the room

and grabbed the door frame to steady himself. "Jesus, Mary, and Joseph!" He froze in place and surveyed the scene. "I heard shots, but I couldn't keep up with Arno. I see he done took care of the situation. That dog is a serious one, he is. Christ!"

"Christ will have nothing to do with this man." I tried to sweeten my voice to call my dog. "Arno, here to me. *Hier.*"

Still possessive of his claim, the dog looked down at his prey. At last, he whined and stepped off the corpse and slunk grudgingly toward me. A look of remorse settled on his face as if he feared retribution for his savagery.

"Good boy, it is all right," I said. "Come along now." I pulled myself to my feet and took Arno's ruff. "Take him out, Finn. See if you can clean him up. We must hurry for there might be others. And you must forget what you have seen here. Do you understand? You know nothing of this."

"'Tis much to forget, ma'am. It seems painted on my mind. But I'll not speak a word of it to another living soul." He reached for the dog and stroked his head. "Arno, come on with ye. 'Tis a fine animal ya are and a brave lad to help the ladies in their dire need."

I reached down to Eliza who still sat like a rag doll, her legs splayed before her, her face white and incredulous.

"You've got to help me," I said to her and touched her shoulder.

She flinched. "He doesn't look real anymore, does he?" she said. "Not like a man at all. Just like some slaughtered barnyard animal. Doesn't he?"

"Now! You have to get up."

At last, she pushed off the floor and grasped the table edge for balance. Still leaning on the tabletop, she maneuvered her way to the cabinet where we kept the schnapps. She poured two cups of the stuff, handed one to me, and tossed hers down like a German.

I stared at Eliza and bolted mine as well. "Use the quilt to get him out. Drag him." I tried to think. "We need Finn's help to pull him away, but I hate to subject him to more than he's already witnessed."

"He's a strong boy." Eliza took a deep breath and faced me with such grim determination, I hardly recognized the girl child she had been when she came here.

We spread the quilt that had been Finn's sleeping pallet. "I'll roll him face down," said Eliza, grasping the sleeve of his jacket. "I cannot gaze upon that whoreson's face again."

Each taking an arm and a leg, we hauled the body onto the quilt and lugged it across the floor. Snagging and tearing, the fabric made a slithering noise, catching on imperfections in the planks. We heaved until we managed to get him out the door. Our breathing came in gasps in the still afternoon. Pressing my hands to my back I stretched and arched my back. "Just give me a moment," I said.

"Oh, God, Katarina! You shouldn't be doing this at all. Let me call Finn. He can help, and now that the lout is covered, it won't seem so bad." She straightened to call the boy.

"No!" I tried to sound rational. "You cannot do this by yourself. I am all right. I promise to stop if it hurts. It is just a little twinge in my back. I will be fine. We must stop a moment at any rate. Where are we going? What are we going to do with this thing?"

Eliza pulled herself to standing. "Why, I don't know. I only thought to get rid of him. Bury him. Hide him. Away from here." She began to twist her hands. "Down by the creek? The ground will be softer there."

"You and I cannot bury him deep enough to keep the animals from him." And then it came to me. "Let the animals have him. Let the wolves and coyotes do the work." It would erase all traces of the dog's attack—one canine could not be distinguished from the other. No one would know. "There is a drop-off not far from here. If we can get him over the edge, the wolves will take care of the rest. Our greatest difficulty will be to get him there. Will that gelding of yours pull a dead body?"

"He will pull a buggy. But we'll never lift that body into the buggy." Eliza sighed in frustration.

"A travois then. Can he pull a travois?"

"And what, pray tell, is a travois?"

"A sling dragged behind a horse. Indians use it. What if we strapped the quilt to Legend's traces and let him pull to the drop-off?"

"God, Katarina. I don't know." She swiped at the bloodstains sprayed across her shirtwaist. "I've got to get clean of this. I cannot—"

I took her by the shoulders. "Then *what*?"

She pinched her lips together. "All right. All right. Let me get Legend. He hasn't been out since yesterday. I hope he'll settle quickly." She hurried away, and I listened for a moment to her calling for Finn to help.

I wanted to sit. Somewhere warm and quiet where none of this could reach me. Where our men would be here to handle this grue-some task. I walked back to the porch, sank on the steps with my face in my arms and tried to clear my thoughts. Grisly scenarios played through my mind. If we looped the ropes around his arm-pits and again around a barn plank, the horse could drag him up the slope. Please, just let this be over. It was yet early afternoon, and the day seemed forever ahead of us. Restless, my unborn child burrowed close to my heart.

Eliza

I have murdered a man. The surprise in his eyes—his shock that I was capable registering on his face, his mouth agape as if to ob-ject. But he was shot, the blood already seeping through the small hole in his gut. Fear for myself and for Kat prompted the first pull of the trigger, but the second—the second was rage. How dare he? How *dare* he?

I called for Finn. And called again, not giving him time to respond. I fought panic. I *had* to calm myself. Like drowned rats, both soaked and shivering, Finn and Arno appeared from down near the creek. "Get Legend for me! Warm him up!"

The boy huddled against the dog, staring up at me with wide eyes. He was traumatized, mortally traumatized, and I had added fear in my own frenzy. "Oh, child, I am so sorry. So sorry. You've done a good job with Arno, but now I need you to warm up Legend, settle him down good, and set him to the traces. Please?" I took off Will's jacket and wrapped Finn in it. "Can you do that for me?"

Finn fought tears. I could see it in his face. "Yes, ma'am, Miss Eliza. I can do that." He put his head down and trudged to the hiding stall.

Tears blurred my vision as I watched him comply with what I asked. *What have we done to you, sweet boy? How much more can you take?* I just wanted to get through the day, those next few hours. I refused to think beyond that. Not beyond watching the ruffian's carcass slide over the rim. Then I would strip it from my memory.

Returning to the house, I saw Kat bent over her knees. It could finish her, too. But I had no idea how to protect her until this was done. She lifted her head and spoke as if we were in the midst of an ugly charade that could not possibly exist in reality. "A door," she said. "There's an old one in the barn."

I waited for an explanation.

Her voice firmed unexpectedly. "We can slide the body onto the door. Hay hooks and rope ought to hold it onto the traces. I hope you can make that horse equal to the task."

"Finn's warming him up now." I thought about my pretty little bay gelding, bred to pull smart buggies or show off under a side-saddle. The thought of his hauling a dead body like a jack-ass laboring under a heavy load sickened me. We were not reared to this brutal existence among thugs and Comanche barbarians. All I said was, "How far away is this drop-off?" I sat down beside her, and probably like her, tried to clear my mind to address what lay ahead.

"Two miles, I think. Maybe less." Kat stared out at the quilt-wrapped bulk.

"Far enough to deflect blame?"

"I do not know, Eliza!" She turned on me, her voice pitched with exasperation. "It is all we have got!" She pushed off the steps with a groan and marched toward the barn. "I will get the hooks and rope. You find the door. It leans on the back wall."

Within half an hour, Kat and I had managed to pull the corpse onto the door, and Finn brought Legend around to fasten him in the traces. The horse shied at the smell, which repulsed us as well—the congealing blood, the bowels purged in the body's final convulsions.

Kat vomited. She wiped her mouth with her sleeve. "Pay me no mind. It is just the—" She began to sob. I had seen her cry, but not like that. Not when Günter left, not when she spoke of those lost babies. Not like the tortuous sobs that broke from her as we tried to put the horse into motion against the weight and the stench of its burden.

Finn handed the lead rope to me and went to stand by Kat. "You go on inside now, Miss Katarina. Me and Miss Eliza will finish this. I know the drop-off you got in mind. It's a good place. You take a rest. We'll be back before dark. You go on now." He took her arm like a little soldier and offered to escort her.

Without turning to me or objecting in any way, Kat pulled away from him and walked back to the house, her skirt clenched in white fists.

Finn circled around to Legend's head. "It's best I walk here next to him. He'll calm down after he starts goin'." He spoke quietly against the horse's neck. "Movin' always helps him."

I nodded. Once again directed by this spindly boy, I followed behind, careful to note if the body started to slip. Blood had soaked through the quilt, leaving rust-like images on the fabric. We would burn it when we got back. I would burn it. I had killed the man. Arno only finished what the bullet had already accomplished. It was up to me to try to obliterate every reminder for the rest.

The wind had come up. I hugged my velvet cape around me and struggled up the slope following Legend and the boy. Will's jacket hung to Finn's knees, the shoulders sagging to his elbows. Our Finn, being asked to become a man too long before his time.

It must have been hours. It seemed so. I put one foot in front of the other, allowing no thought but the measure of each step as I leaned into the uphill grade. The door gouged the dirt, so we had to stop along the way to clear the debris. The rest would be the work of tomorrow—sweeping away the evidence of conveyance. As we reached the cliff, the day had grown colder yet, and the wind came stiff across the small canyon. The blue of the hills beyond seemed to smoke in the sunset. From their heights, the valley stretched a mile wide, the cliffs on the far side slick with caliche rock.

"Turn Legend around and back him until I tell you to stop," I said. "Stay at his head. You don't need to see any more than you have already."

Legend refused to back. Not even Finn's sweet talk convinced him. But I could manage. I *had* to manage. Grasping handfuls of fabric, I yanked and jerked the cloth until I got the body to the ledge. The quilt stuck to the coagulated blood until its squares of appliqued lilies, its pinks and lavenders, and fine florals finally released its burden. The nameless degenerate tumbled loose. I lingered to hear the dull thuds as it plummeted and recoiled against outcroppings on its way down until there was no sound but the wind. No witness but the darkening blue of sky where the sun had disappeared over the rim of the faraway hills. Somewhere in the distance, a wolf howled.

Katarina

It could be worse, I told myself. I could be the one dragging that body to the drop-off. I had cleaned the floor on my hands and knees many times before. Soaked up water and toweled the wood dry.

Merely housework. Dirt, not blood. Working through my nausea, I blocked images from my mind until the awful chore was done.

Soiled. I felt soiled. I climbed the stairs, tearing at my blouse and skirt. "*Autsch.*" I could not rid myself of them soon enough. Pouring water from the pitcher into the bowl, I saturated a cloth and scrubbed my body with lye soap that stripped my skin but cleansed me of the blood and smell, but not the horror. I wrapped myself in my gown and hurried down the steps to the kitchen to let Arno in. Still damp from his bath in the creek, he shivered in the cold afternoon as did I.

My back throbbed, a gripping ache that radiated around my hips. I would not think of the implication. If it were what I feared, nothing would help. Then I remembered Eliza's black haw tea. Where had she put it? *Mein Gott*, not upstairs. I could not take the stairs again.

At last, I found the potion in a jar behind the laudanum. How prudent of her to keep it brewed and ready. I took it down, stoked the fire, and clasping a blanket, I curled into Günter's chair. Its upholstery gave more comfort than the rest. Bidding the dog to lie beside me, I kept my hand on his head. "We will think of nothing for a while, nothing but the snap of the firewood, and the wind as it assaults the windows." I closed my eyes and tried to match the rise and fall of my dog's breathing.

I had no notion of the time when Eliza returned. She sat across from me waiting for me to come out of deep sleep. Blinking stupidly, I could only stare at her.

"It's done." Her voice was more tired than I had ever heard it.

Finn came through the door. "I put the other horse, that man's spotted one, in the barn. Didn't know where else. Legend's in the hiding stall. He's glad to be quit." He sat at the table and cradled his head in his arms. "Glad to be quit myself."

"We are all glad to have this done." I wrapped the quilt around me tighter and brought my knees close to my body. "Yes, Finn. Thank you for helping."

"You all right, Miss Katarina?"

I nodded. I wanted to sit up tall or stand, but all I could seem to do was speak from the fetal position I had nestled into. "Eliza? The man's horse. What—"

"God knows. We'll talk later about what must be done. It will wait until the morrow. I'll prepare our supper. Soup and cornbread will get us through the night along with the help of laudanum if necessary." She stood. "This is a night for forgetting."

"Mightn't I stay here?" I asked. "It seems as though I have just got where I could rest a bit."

Eliza turned to stare at the floor and then at me. "You cleaned it. Oh, Katarina, you should have waited for me." Reaching for the black haw, she studied it and looked at me. "Are you well? You're not, are you?" She came and knelt beside me. "Don't let this be the thing that defeats you. Not this awful thing. I'll fix you a good stout soup, and when you feel like it, I'll help you to your bed."

I nodded in numb compliance, too tired to form opinions. Turning my fate over to this girl seemed the practical thing to do. God knew it was the easiest. Let whatever befall us transpire. I had no will to resist it.

Supper was taken for sustenance, for distraction. Afterward, Eliza supported me up the stairs. I asked for Arno.

"Will you be satisfied if I let him stay until you are asleep? He may be a better protector if left on the first floor."

She was right. She waited with me through my preparations, through another dose of black haw and a bitter drop or two of laudanum in honey. As she extinguished the lantern, I reached to touch her arm and whispered, "Eliza, you did what you had to, and it saved us. Thank you. You and I and Finn will put this behind us. It is our contribution to the war effort. We cannot agree on North or South, but we can confirm what is evil."

Eliza only nodded, but she patted my hand on her arm and gave me a tremulous smile as she left the room.

~

Dawn broke in wintery brightness, the sky a sharp blue that defied regret. The discomfort I felt the night before had subsided as it usually did if I rested. I dressed and hurried to start breakfast before Eliza awoke. I thought about Tom Bailey. Had he joined up with the Texas 3rd Infantry? Would he make it safely out of Gillespie County to risk his life again in the army? I stepped downstairs where Finn lay sleeping on the floor. Arno rose and stretched and moved past me to the outside. Let the boy sleep. Let him dream, for dreams may be the only place left where he could still be a child.

I started the biscuits and waited for the aroma to rouse Finn. He seemed to struggle against waking in hopes of denying what the day might hold. "Come sit with me," I said. "There is blackberry jelly to be had." His red hair a tousled mass, he stumbled to the table. I wanted to smooth it, but he would think it very unlike me to be so affectionate. That was better reserved for effusive creatures like Eliza.

It would be nice to talk about something happy. But to disregard our current predicament seemed irresponsible. More ends needed to be tied up if we were to conceal the signs of a murder.

Wo ist Eliza? She knows how to cast optimism about when pressed. But when she came into the kitchen to pour herself a cup of tea, I could see this would not be the case.

Eliza

Sleep came little. I stared out the window at the heavy live oak limbs heaving about in the north wind, their small leather-like leaves rattling. The moon shone bright through the trees, leaving shadows changing form and substance on the wall. I imagined the corpse sprawled at the bottom of the cliff, moonlight glaring down on him, the shadows of predators and the sounds they made. I wondered if this is what men at war felt—this remorse backed up with the niggling satisfaction of vengeance. I would nourish the sense of revenge until it became a conviction of justice. Maybe that is how the soldiers endured—a blind eye to anything but self-righteousness.

~

The next morning, Kat and Finn watched me as I drank my tea, as though it were up to me to solve the dilemma put before us. I resented them for it, but I took a deep breath and launched into describing the plan I had lain awake all night considering. "I have been thinking," I said and watched hope wash across their faces.

Kat placed her hands quietly on the table and looked prepared to do anything I suggested. Anything. How our roles had switched. She had dictated every move I made, as far as she was able, and she had been quite proficient at it. Was it because of a self-protective maternal instinct that she happily surrendered responsibility to me? Of course, it had to be up to me for the chance-taking. Damn this war! It had taken our protectors and lovers and left it for us women to work the fields and shoot intruders. Damn the fates that seized our life and wrung the joy from it.

"Here's my plan," I said. "I'll pony the man's horse behind Legend and deposit the creature as far west into Comancheria as I dare. If he won't stay, I'll have to tie him with a breakaway and leave him. He'll get loose, but I should be long gone by then. Maybe he'll run across a herd. Maybe the Comanches will find him. Maybe he'll get struck by lightning. But he'll not remain as evidence of our…shall we say, 'disposal.'"

Arguments flitted across their faces. I knew they'd find logical reasons for me not to ride out alone. And rightly so, but it was one risk traded for another.

"Finn, I'll ask you to stay here and help Miss Katarina. You and Arno must protect the place. If trouble does come, take to the hiding stall. But before anything, use a rake or a broom of branch-es and cover yesterday's tracks around the house. We'll do the rest tomorrow. Can you do that for us?"

Finn nodded silently. Kat pushed herself to stand. "Follow alongside the road to San Saba," she said. "Stay within the trees to avoid being seen but you won't get lost. Take the Henry."

~

Dressed as a man in Will's wool jacket and a slouch hat, I kept to the live oaks and cedars. I rode astride Legend, the other horse plodding along behind me. He wore his saddle, which I planned to dump along the way. Legend, always happy to be the lead horse, forged ahead, keeping the rope in a constant state of tension. The air was frigid, and the horses' breaths blew vapor clouds. Frost-killed grass crunched under their feet. Even the sky seemed a crys-tallized blue that could shatter in the cold.

When I had ridden as far as I could and still have enough day-light to get home, I saw a small herd of horses gathered by a rocky creek below us. Their heads snapped up as we stopped to watch them, and they called. Both horses answered. I dismounted and tied Legend to a thin oak. I threw the spotted horse's saddle into the weeds, released the rope, and smacked him on the haunches with my hat. He was off, adding his plaintive whinny to the herd's call. He stopped once to look back at us, but I waved the hat at him again and watched him move toward the others in a fast trot. Legend tugged against his rope, but it held. It was not until I put my foot in the stirrup that I noticed three Comanches intercept the horse and examine him before staring back at me over the backs of the ponies they guarded.

It seemed my heart ceased to beat. They had watched from the beginning when I threw the saddle to the ground and removed my hat to swing it at the horse. Despite having tied my hair, it had come loose in the wind and whipped about my face before I could contain it. They had seen it all. One of them on a black and white paint came forward at a slow trot. I retrieved the saddle from the high grass and threw it forward, like an offering, a plea for my life in exchange. The Comanche was within a quarter of a mile when I managed to mount Legend and dig my heels into his flanks.

My breath, resounding in my ears as though I were underwater, matched each lunge my horse made. I bent low, pressing my cheek to his neck, his mane lashing my face. Every moment expecting to feel the pierce of an arrow or the savage riding so close he could snake out his arm and drag me from the saddle, I did not look back until we cleared the next hill. The rolling pasture behind me lay empty except for that one horse and rider who had advanced within a short distance. His expression was impossible to read, but he sat quietly in his benevolence, his superiority.

Legend was fast, but the Comanche could have caught me if he'd wanted. His speed, his agility, and strength could have overcome me. He chose not to. Did he consider the horse and saddle fair enough trade? He seemed familiar. Could he have been the one who took my music box in exchange for our lives? Though he covered himself in deerskin, he was small as I remembered but so much a part of his horse that he assumed a greater presence. A wash of memories came over me—the smell of him, the bear grease he lavished on himself, the fetidness of his predatory life.

We stared at each other for a long moment. I put my hand on the butt of the Henry but left it in the scabbard. It might incite the warrior were I to draw it, and I'd have an arrow in my chest before I could heave the weapon to my shoulder. My hat had long been carried off, so I fumbled with my hair and tied it into a knot at the nape of my neck. I turned and rode off at a walk suppressing the need to cry out over every stumble Legend made.

No one followed. We'd be all right. We would put it behind us.

All that remained was the long ride home and the forgetting.

CHAPTER 16

I also saw several large swarms of bees as they flew over me. It seemed to me that bee keeping should be a very profitable business in Texas because the bees there were able to fly throughout the entire year and did not need to be fed.
– Friedrich Schlecht, *On to Texas! A Journey to Texas in 1848*

March 1863

Katarina

Live oak leaves rattled and dropped in warmer winds, and the first wildflowers, dandelions, and buttercups dotted the countryside. I had grown big with child and yet could still not believe. I had made no preparations, no knitted blankets, and had none other than the multi-colored one Eliza had given me. No hand-sewn gowns. Oh, I had saved scraps of cotton fabric that if not worn as diapers could be used for housework. The babe tumbled within me, delivering little kicks to my kidneys and jabs to my bladder, but I never allowed it to touch my heart.

And this was the time Finn came to us about the bees. He was giddy with excitement. "It's that time of year for a swarm! You ladies better get ready. I'm gonna find us some bees!"

He scouted daily. He had repaired the two hives from his father's home and retrieved the rope basket he called a skep that his father had used to entice and collect bees. It was two weeks before he found the swarm on a lower branch of an oak. He came running back to the house, calling for us to follow him back to the tree. "Get a hat. Get a scarf and c'mon!" He stopped and looked back. "Better keep Arno here at the house. He ain't used to bees."

I carried the rope basket, which Finn had lined with honey. He dragged a ladder behind him, and we headed out. Eliza, naturally faster than I, dashed after him with the tin bucket and soup ladle he had instructed her to bring. The air was humid and heavy, redolent with blossom. It felt about to rain, and we hurried to find the bees. They hung in a complex, dark mass, thick with agitation and ambition, I supposed, for a new home. Bees. Their hum lay on the air, a soothing background harmony to the sounds of spring. Busy and determined, they focused on survival of the hive. Such enigmatic creatures.

Eliza stood gripping the bucket, her eyes wide and not without trepidation. "My God," she said, "they're so, so *intense*."

"It's a big 'un," Finn whispered. "Nigh on four, five pounds, maybe 10,000 bees. Ain't they something?"

"They certainly are." I approached and squinted to take in the immense density of them. "That many, you think?"

"Likely, according to what Da used to say. I hoped he'd make it back before they swarmed. He knows bees. But he taught me some. I believe we can do it."

Eliza and I smiled at each other, knowing how cocky he had been at Christmas, promising us honey achieved through his expertise in the capture and maintenance of the creatures.

"Let's hope these is friendly bees," Finn said. "Some are and some ain't. Best step back, Miss Katarina. And you, Miss Eliza, stay steady when them bees start heading your way. Bees like calm."

Eliza, her head covered by her hat and scarf, stood by as instructed and began a rhythmic beat with the spoon on the bucket—some ancient method of coaxing the bees into a new hive that Finn called tanging.

Whispering words in Irish, Finn took a deep breath and climbed the ladder. He leaned over the branch and began to shake the bees down into the basket. Gently, at first and then more vigorously until dislodged and fussy, the insects stirred and fell.

Eliza, eyes closed and lips clenched, squealed, but held her ground until one landed on her ear. She let go of the bucket and began slapping at the air as she ran for the protection of the trees. Her whimper became a shriek. The agitation of the bucket hitting the ground and the sudden activity set the bees into motion. Unchecked and confused, perhaps, but not aggressive, they rose in the air about us.

I shut my eyes and froze in place. Their wings palpated the air, a hum filling the space around me. I opened my eyes. In the midst of the morning air, the sun had come out, splintering light about me, the rays reflecting off the transparency of a thousand wings, and the wings, in turn, refracting the light into imprecise oblique colors.

"Don't move, Miss Katarina! Don't move!" Finn's words seemed far away. I cared to hear no other sound except the voices of the bees.

Awestruck, I lifted my arms into this air belonging to the bees and gazed up through them to the light. The glancing radiance, the colors, and the thrum of their wings enveloped me. The air was aglitter with their attendance. For one brief moment, I was aloft among them.

I had never felt closer to God.

And then it was over. The bees followed their queen into the basket and were quietened.

Eliza stepped from behind the protection of the cedars and returned, pausing to listen for a change of heart from the insects. A few stragglers looking to join the queen flitted about but only seemed intent on finding a way to enter the basket. At last, Eliza collected the bucket and ladle and grinned shamefacedly at Finn.

"'Tis nothing to be mortified of, Miss Eliza. It happens to all of us," he said as he lifted the basket containing the swarm.

Eliza came to stand next to me for I had not moved from the spot where the bees had found me. "Are you all right, Katarina? You're not stung?" She searched my person with her eyes and then ran her hands over my shoulders. "Let's go on back."

I smiled at her, not really wanting to talk, not wanting to break the spell. "You two get started. I'll be along. Go on now."

"I hate to leave you here. I think—"

I put my finger to my lips and shook my head.

"Just for a while then," Eliza said. She and Finn headed back to the house but turned to stare at me before disappearing into the shrub.

"You know that Miss Katarina could be a bee charmer," I heard Finn say. "I never saw nothing like it."

I remained a while longer. Peace. It would last only moments, but it gave me a memory to fall back on when I thought I might collapse under the weight of all this strife. Once again, I believed in the benevolence of God, a promise that He would never take *everything* from me. There would always be a fulcrum of balance in the world.

I sat and leaned against the tree and thought about this child to come. I rested my hands on my belly. The child remained still now as though my own tranquility filtered through to him. I wondered if he would be born with a taste for honey. For the first time, I saw a scene of our future—one day we would go a'hunting bees.

Eliza

After I ran from the bees, I watched Kat from the protection of a cedar. How odd she was, never flinching, never shrinking from the horde that encircled her. Sure she would be killed, I cried out, but she seemed not to hear. She welcomed them, joined them. It was the strangest thing I had ever seen. I always thought her stoic to a fault, but this gave her an air of mysticism. I was in awe of her.

Finn and I sat on the front steps of the house waiting for Kat. She delayed well over half an hour. "We better go get her." Finn twisted his hands together. "Maybe she *was* stung and didn't tell us. What with the baby and all, she coulda lost her mind. I've heard tell of that happening to women when something shocking happens. They can go plumb…well, you know." He peered through the trees, looking for a sign of Katarina.

"She's fine. I am sure she's fine." But I wasn't. Not at all. "If she doesn't return in five minutes, I'll go get her." The basket vibrated with the hum of the bees. "Why don't you get busy transferring the bees to the hive?"

"I was thinking Miss Katarina might like to see me do it, is all. Or do you think she's had enough of bees for the day?"

"To tell you the truth, Finn, I am at a loss for what she might think. I would've thought she'd have smacked those bees dead. You know how she can be when she's provoked. But it seemed like they adored her and that she welcomed them. Wasn't that magical? Truly magical?"

"'Twas, Miss Eliza. 'Twas, indeed. Never heard of such. Well, I heard of it but didn't believe it."

"'There are more things in heaven and Earth, Horatio, than are dreamt of in your philosophy.'"

"My name ain't Horatio." He swelled up and frowned.

I hugged Finn, for he was still of huggable age. Laughing, I explained. "Oh, my goodness, I know that! That phrase is a quote from the famous playwright, William Shakespeare. You'll learn about him one day."

"Not if I can help it." He stood to add a little more honey to the box he had rebuilt for the hive. "Five minutes up yet? I think we ought to go find Miss Katarina."

I pushed off the porch step and smoothed out my skirt. "Let me go. You stay and make final preparations for the transfer. You have done a good thing, Finn. It took bravery to shake down those bees and collect them. It's a wonderful Christmas present, especially in March when we needed a little sweetness in our lives."

He blushed, that freckled skin flushing to the color of primroses.

"I'll be back," I called to him. "You carry on."

~

She sat under the oak tree, leaning her head against it. She was so very quiet I thought perhaps she had fallen asleep. "Katarina?"

"Yes?" She did not open her eyes.

"Are you all right? I mean, really? We waited and when you didn't come, we thought to see about you. Are you not stung at all?"

"Not at all."

"Will you come along with me now?" I stepped closer to her, careful not to be abrupt for she seemed as fragile as the bees. "Finn's waiting to move the bees into their new hive box, and before he completely depletes us of honey to feed the critters, we better get back to supervise him." I held out my hand to help her to her feet.

She looked up at me and smiled. It was a rather mysterious expression as though she knew a secret I would never possess. Perhaps she did.

It was the oddest feeling I had toward her—protective and sisterly. She let herself be lifted to standing, and I put my arm around her. "Let's go home now, shall we? Wouldn't you like to see Finn coax the new family into the hive?"

"I would love that," she said. "They have much to offer. I would like to be the one who cares for them. It seems only natural, don't you think?"

"Of course, if you like," I said, at the same time wondering if Finn had been right when he suggested she may have gone a bit moonstruck.

When we came into the clearing around the house, Finn jumped to his feet. "You had quite a visit with the bees, didn't ya, ma'am."

He glanced at me apparently looking for a clue as to her state of mind before continuing. "You doin' all right now, though?"

"Just fine, Finn," she answered in a rather disembodied voice. "Quite well, thank you."

He looked back again at me for reassurance but went on with his plan. "Got it all ready. I've loaded the box with honey to feed them till they can get started on their own doings."

I nodded my head and said, "Oh, he certainly has."

With the box propped open, Finn dumped the skep out on a board next to it. He gave the basket a hard, sharp shake to dump the bees near the entrance to the hive. And lo and behold, with little confusion, the bees began their entrance into their new home. Finn hovered over them searching for the queen. "There she is! See her?" he cried. "The big fat one. That's her all right. They'll stay for sure now. Long as she's kept happy."

Breathing a sigh of relief, I said, "Well, I'll see about supper. Katarina, go lie down now. It's been a long day for you, and I fear, worrisome."

"I believe I will stay and watch the bees a while longer. Do not fret. I am better than I have been in a long time."

I stared at her a moment longer. Yes, I believed she was.

Katarina

The evening breeze picked up as it is wont to do, and I slipped my scarf around my shoulders as I sat waiting for the straggler bees to find their way into the hive. How quiet except for the occasional buzz that lowered in tone as the insects moved into the box to be with their fellow workers and queen. The society of bees—they were intent on staying together, planning, and murmuring among themselves to make their lives better. A far cry from humanity, I thought, bent on its own destruction. I would content myself with the company of bees.

~

Warmer days were upon us with the nights still comfortably cool. The bees and I spent hours in the garden. I left the hard assignments to Finn and Eliza since I was much scolded and sent to my bed if I stood to stretch my back.

Indeed, my back did ache more these days. Sleep became fitful, and I felt like I carried a circus acrobat in my belly. At last, I had belief, confidence even, that my dearest hope was within reality. I began to sew and consider names and imagine the child at my breast—the color of his eyes, the texture of his hair, the line of his jaw, and his beginning steps. It was treacherous ground—this believing. It was beyond hoping. It was daring.

If only I could tell Günter. But not yet. Not till the dream was realized. And even then, how would I find him? There had been no real news except about battles raging in the eastern states. I had no idea where he might be or if he was injured or even alive.

There was so much work to be done. It was April now, and there were tomatoes to plant and corn and beans and the endless weeding. Eliza was solicitous to the point of aggravation with her ready black haw and admonitions. It became her ambition as much as mine to have this baby arrive as fat and healthy as any carefully tended child of a crown princess. Finn began to look above my head so that his eyes came nowhere near my belly, and he avoided being alone with me, his face flushing at any mention of my condition. Still, he worked harder than any ten-year-old boy I had ever heard of, and despite his propensity for braggadocio, he was willing to take on the most difficult assignment so that later he could boast about it.

The one interest we kept in common was our beehive, but we left them to their honeycomb and honey-making after feeding them from our own supply in the beginning.

"You like 'em, don't you? The bees," Finn said. "I expect them buzzing about you like that and not stinging caused you to be pretty friendly with 'em. And rightly so."

"Rightly so." I tousled his hair, which made him blush again and run off to find another chore to do.

CHAPTER 17

During war years a diphtheria epidemic...kept him riding from house to house over the county swabbing the throats of young patients.
– Esther L. Mueller, *Dr. Wilhelm Victor Keidel*, in *Pioneers in God's Hills, Volume One*

Katarina

Sometimes on late afternoons when I had been cautioned to rest, I searched the hills, hoping Tom Bailey was making his way back to us. We never spoke of him, but we all came to attention when the wind brought the sound of a traveler or Arno stood with ears perked at the road. Of course, Tom would not come by the road. He would appear from the cedar trees at dawn or twilight. I supposed I never really quite believed he could make it back to us, but somewhere, somehow in that angry wartime, a blessing might occur. And so, I studied the landscape, if for no other reason than foolish imagination. We needed him.

One early morning, I took my half cup of tea to the small arbor just beginning to host the grapevines. Except for the cooing of mourning doves, the dawn was silent as sunlight crept over the hills and streamed through the trees. I closed my eyes and breathed in the April air, the fading fragrance of peach blossoms.

Arno stood, a rumble in his throat. A man's voice came from the shadows. "Frau Lange?"

Although the voice was tentative and kind, my heart stopped. I threw my arm over Arno and pulled him to me.

"It's me, Tom Bailey. Do ya not remember me?"

"Tom?" And then "Tom Bailey! It *is* you. I feared we would never see you again." Calling over my shoulder, I cried out for Finn, and he came running.

"Da! You made it! We've been waiting for ya!" Finn barreled into his father's chest and then looked chagrined as though men should behave with more restraint. But his father grabbed him back into his arms with a rough hug.

I stretched out both hands and welcomed Tom. Thin and rough with the long travel, he came leading a worn-out horse. Nonetheless, his smile warmed my heart.

"Found this old nag for y'all to take into town," he said. "Maybe keep Legend outta public view. Led her most of the way."

"It is kind of you. *Danke, danke.* Come. Sit."

"Glad to see you're doing well," he said as his eyes drifted to my belly. He was still shaking my hand when he looked up and beyond me.

"Tom! You've come back!" Eliza had stepped out from her room above.

His face changed, a certain yearning came upon it as he said, "Why, Miss Eliza." He cleared his throat to speak. "*Frau* Eliza, good mornin' to ya." He glanced back at me, but it was too late. I had seen the longing in his eyes.

Thinking of it later, I wondered if I read too much in Tom's expression when he saw her. Perhaps it was the angle of the sunrise or the fragrant air. Or my own need for a man to look at me the way I saw Tom Bailey regard Eliza, the wife of another man.

Eliza seemed unaware of any innuendo in the softness of his voice when he said her name. Smiling and holding his gaze, she skipped down the stairs and looked as though she might embrace him before she thought better of it. "How very good to see you,

Tom! We've been waiting for you since March and had about given up hope."

He looked crestfallen, as though she had meant it as a criticism, but she finished by clutching her hands together and chirping, "But we are ever so glad you are here now. Aren't we, Katarina? Ever so!"

Relief cleared his brow, and he could smile again.

How good it was to see him and to see the look on Finn's face. Although he had not spoken much of his father these last few months, I knew he worried. We all did. But Tom was here now. More than having a strong working man around to assume the arduous planting, the lifting, and carrying, it was the comfort of being protected—his way of going, the sound of his voice.

We sat at supper that night listening to Tom. "Desertion is worse than it was before," he said. "Morale is maybe even poorer with the officers. Nobody seems to notice when soldiers disappear come spring and show back up after the plantin' season is done. I figure they don't care much. Not that they wouldn't shoot us dead if the mood struck 'em."

Finn spilled his milk and rushed to mop it up with a dishrag.

"Sorry, Miss Katarina," he said. "Sorry. I didn't see the edge of the plate. I—" He rinsed the cloth out in the kitchen bucket and then went to sit with Arno. He said almost nothing for the rest of the evening except to offer to share his pallet with his father.

"You must be truly tired, Tom. I will send Finn down with extra blankets for you, but after tonight, I want you to take over the little cabin down by the creek. Günter would not mind, and I can spare a few items. You might have some things of your own to furnish the place with, as well. I know you will appreciate the privacy." I shot Eliza a meaningful glance as I placed the last piece of cake before him. "I believe I will go on up to bed now. And you, Eliza?"

"Why, I thought I might—" Eliza's face blistered red. "Oh, of course, yes. Please excuse me. We'll see you in the morning then."

She followed me up the stairs, no doubt disappointed that she had not had the chance to visit longer with Tom. I understood. It had been a long time since she had enjoyed conversation with a man. We were both completely out of practice. *Well, she is too eager.*

The next morning, Eliza and I fussed over Tom's breakfast. Heavy now with child and often sleepless, I had been up for hours. I found an old, flowered bonnet and apron for Tom to wear as a disguise. He had shaved and pulled back his hair to rope it with a leather strip, so perhaps he could fool faraway observers.

Eliza grinned and poured him another glass of milk. "I do believe the forget-me-nots of the fabric bring out the color of your eyes, Tom."

At first, he looked abashed and then smiled broadly at her. "'Twould look a sight better on the likes of you, I suspect."

I swept his plate from the table and snapped at Finn. "Chores started first thing in the morning are more likely to be done by the end of day. Get along with you."

The pleasure evaporated from their faces. "True words. Let's skedaddle, my boy." Tom turned to me. "I'll send Finn back soon for a list of what you want done first," he said, "and we'll get to it." He threw an arm around the boy's shoulder as they hurried out the door.

"Well, Katarina, that was abrupt. Are you not feeling well?" Eliza failed to keep the irritation out of her voice.

"Quite well. There is too much to be done for hours of prattle." I took the egg basket and headed for the door.

"It was hardly hours—"

I clicked my fingers for Arno. "Minutes become hours."

Eliza

Old biddie. I finished the dishes and made my way to the garden. The routine work gave rise to reverie, and I wondered again where Will might be. Weeks had passed since a letter had come from him. Not much news of the war had leaked down to us except that we'd heard of the clash at Arkansas Post—a Union victory. Will could have been there. He'd said his company escorted Union prisoners to Louisiana and they could have gone to Arkansas from there. The struggle had been bitter, and by reports, the Confederates put up a good fight. That gave me hope that Will had fared well. Please God.

If he had just signed up with the 3rd regiment infantry like Tom, he could have sneaked home twice a year, too. He could have. He didn't have to be a martyr to please me. But I had laid the kindling and fed the flame. Would it have been an affront to *his* ego to dress in women's clothes for tending the fields and escaping to the hillside? Or was it the German blood that ran through his veins—that inflexible honor?

~

Her face white and strained, Kat stepped into the kitchen. She often looked stressed. It was her nature, and so I poured her a glass of water and told her to sit at the table. "You've done too much again. I can tell. Now you've worn yourself out. For just once I wish you'd—"

"I can hardly breathe." Looking up at me, she clutched the glass then set it down. "I do not think I can take another step," she said. Her face clouded, and she pressed her lips together in a low moan. "If this is not it, then I must be dying." She grinned as if trying to make a joke.

"Oh, Katarina. Do you think it could be?" I looked out the window to see if I could see Tom or Finn. "Surely, this is only your body practicing." The words tumbled from me. "The body does that sometimes I hear. You know, a rehearsal, but it goes away and it's another month or so before—"

"Hush! Just stop talking. I cannot bear it."

I clamped my lips together. Turning to the cupboard, I swept jars aside to look for the black haw. My hands shook but I poured a spoonful and pressed it against her mouth. "Take it—quickly!"

She placed her hand on mine to steady it and took down the medicine. "Now, help me to my room." She stood and started toward the door. A startled expression came on her face, and she pressed her hand against her skirt to stem the flow of fluid. "Oh, it's happening. Oh, Eliza!" She tried to straighten. "Günter!" she cried. And then she covered her face with both hands. "I mean to say—Tom. We better call Tom to get me up the stairs. I am not sturdy."

"They're in the cornfield. Can you wait?" I started for the door.

Her laugh became a gasp. "My other options?"

"Oh, God, I know. I'm going." I ran for the field, calling for Tom. I saw them ahead, bending over their work, deaf to my voice. Stumbling over the newly plowed furrows, I fell once but grabbed my skirt in one hand and kept running, waving, and calling.

They looked up at last and dropping their hoes, sprinted toward me. I stopped and waited, my hands on my knees, trying to find my breath.

"It's Katarina. The baby. It's time!"

Neither spoke but hurried on ahead of me toward the house. The sun had hardly reached its zenith, and the day stretched on forever ahead of us. When I reached the kitchen, Tom met me as he headed out the door to the stairs with Katarina in his arms. Kat held onto his neck in a mortal grip, her face buried against his chest. I ran ahead to open doors and pull back the covers to her bed.

"Should we go for a doctor?" I realized I knew nothing about childbirth other than the dreadful stories overheard from Mamá's friends.

Katarina pushed up to lean against the headboard. "Dr. Keidel used to be here, but he may be gone to war. They would want a man like him. He used to help me some when—" She stopped talking.

"Finn, you go. Take Legend. Go as fast as you can. Find Dr. Keidel and tell him we need him."

"But Miss Eliza, somebody will see that horse. Somebody will get him. They'll take him right from under me. We can't—"

"It is all right." Kat lay back on her pillow. "It is better now. It is not so bad."

"But your water broke, Katarina. I think that means you're going to have this baby today." I turned to Tom for confirmation. He looked stricken.

I grabbed Finn by the shoulders. "You go, you hear me. You out-ride anybody looks like they want Legend. You can! You don't have to come back here. Head for the caves if there's danger—*after* you tell the doctor. *Not* before. Don't you stop until you have delivered the message! You understand?"

Finn's eyes grew large. "Why, yes, ma'am." His head bobbed up and down. "Yes, I understand you. It's just that—"

"Maybe I should go." Tom moved between Finn and me. "I know the man. He might be quicker to come if I asked him."

"Your boy's been bragging about what a stellar rider he is for months. Let him prove it. Besides, they'll sure enough hang *you* high if they get their hands on you." I steered Finn out the door.

Finn turned and clomped down the stairs. "I'll do it! Me and that horse will!"

"Besides," I said to Tom, "I need you here. You've seen this, I imagine, and know something about what to do."

"The midwife came," he said. "Hard to remember exactly what did happen. I admit to breaking into our last bottle of whiskey."

At least he had the grace to look sheepish about it.

"Well, go bring us up a pail of water," I said to Tom. "Seems like there's always supposed to be water and towels. Can you find the—"

"Eliza?"

I looked back at Kat. "Oh, Katarina, I'm sorry! There's just so much to think about and organize. What can I do for you?"

"It is starting again. I think I would feel better if I sat up." She writhed to her side and then pushed up to almost sitting. She pressed her lips together till they were ringed with white. Then it passed, and she started to cry—deep racking sobs.

"Oh, Katarina, the pain must be unbearable. Do you want laudanum? We have some. Let me get it for you."

"It is not the pain." She rolled her eyes toward the window. "It is the fear."

I thought of all the miscarriages she had gone through and of her kneeling among the graves under the oak. "Oh, Katarina, I can imagine," I said the words but really could not fathom her grief. "This *is* awfully frightening."

"No, you do not understand. I have never been so close before. It always ended early. Now I could go through all this and still... still fall from favor with God. Would he promise me all this and then take it away again? Let me gaze on the face of my living child and then close its eyes forever?"

Something hardened within me. She could not go on like this. It was not good for her or the baby. "You are going to stop this right now!" I wanted to slap her. Of course, she was afraid. But she had work to do. "I won't have it!"

I *wanted* to say, "See, Kat! This is exactly why I needed Chloë!" I bit my tongue.

~

Four hours passed and still no sign of Finn or Dr. Keidel. "Do you think Finn can't find him?" I paced the few feet from the bed to the window and back again. "I can hardly stand to think what circumstance might befall the boy."

"Please stop talking, Eliza." Kat slid to the edge of the bed. "Go downstairs with Tom and find some chore. It will do us both good. You will hear me if I need you. I can walk now. I will hold onto the bed and just walk from one post to the other."

I opened my mouth. "Absolutely not. It is out of the—"

"Do not argue with me. I will be perfectly all right." She stood. "Just help me with my gown. And Arno. Send the dog up. His silence is a great comfort."

Katarina

The door cracked open, and Arno stuck his nose through to nudge it the rest of the way. He came to stand next to me, and I laid my hand on his broad head. "You are the comfort of my life now, *Schatzi*. Until I become the comfort for *dieses Baby*—if all comes to pass as it should. For now, you keep me company, *ja?*"

He looked at me with those great soulful eyes. He was still a young dog. Not much over four years old, but he had never been frivolous. Günter had done most of his training, but I was the one Arno had chosen—to defend, to give solace. He was so protective of me that Günter had to send him from the room when we made love. Once he encountered a girl we had just hired to work in the kitchen, and he pinned her to the wall with his barking until we shushed him. We had to provide the girl with a cup of wine to calm her. And there was the time I fell from a stepladder. When I screamed, he took the ladder in his teeth and thrashed it side to side, snarling as though it were the culprit. My Arno. I knew he would stay by me until this was over, but I wondered what his reaction would be should the child survive and I did not.

No daring the Fates. I censored myself. Right now, I would move from bedpost to bedpost and gaze out the window to distract myself with the new wildflowers in the field, the flight of swallows, the shadow sliding down the wall as the day progressed.

And breathe slowly when the contractions came on. "*Slowly.*" I said aloud, cautioning myself not to hold my breath and bear down against the pain. I did not need some girl who had not yet seen twenty years spouting orders at me as though she was an authority. I did not want Tom Bailey asking moment to moment if I was all right. Arno and I and Dr. Keidel, if he ever got here, could manage this birthing episode quite well. "Can't we?" I bent to stroke Arno's ears, but pain gripped me as if my midsection was caught in a vice. Holding onto the post, I only hoped I had not dabbled in the overconfidence Master Finn so often did.

I had heard one should gauge the time between pains. Having no timepiece, I thought to count aloud the duration of each contraction and record it on paper. Shuffling to the bedside table, I found a pencil and a scrap I had saved. If I marked only in pencil, perhaps the paper could be reused at a later date. I was prepared. I walked to and fro holding only lightly to the bed foot rail. Turning away from the window, I took small steps to the door and back. Yes, I could handle this—most of it anyway—until the doctor came. He would be along soon. Finn could be trusted to bring him. Eliza and Tom were downstairs should I need them. And I paced.

Arno kept up with me for a while till he groaned and lay down near the door. I counted my footsteps between each contraction and scribbled down the small numbers separated by a slash.

Eliza knocked on the door. "Katarina? Are you all right? You must let me come in for a moment. Just to check on you."

A contraction kept me from answering.

"Katarina?"

"Yes, yes, I am fine. You go on now." I found myself breathless after the last pain but still managed to begin my marching as soon as it was over. I wanted to ask if the doctor was on his way, but obviously, Eliza could not know. I staggered to the window and searched the road, hoping for the plume of dust from his carriage.

Nothing. The shadows on the barn deepened and fell long across the fields. Another contraction seized me. My moan became keen, desperate even to my own ears. This time, I crawled into bed and clutched the spindles. I lost count of the seconds between contractions. Arno came to his feet, laid his chin on the cover, and placed one paw on my arm. I wanted to console him, wanted to sit up and try to stand to walk again, but I was swept by a wave of pain that forced a mewling sound from me.

When I could breathe again, I saw that the door had opened. Arno had pawed it ajar and left me here alone. *Turncoat.*

Eliza was in the room. Issuing orders to Tom as though she knew what she was doing. Then there seemed to be a different tenor, a third or fourth contributor to the fog of voices. I recognized a small wiry woman with a strangely asymmetrical face. Frau Meyer bustled through the door ahead of Finn.

Her voice broke through the haze. She spoke in German. At last, my mother tongue, firm in its familiar cadence. "*Frau* Lange, listen to me. You will not push now. You are not ready. Dr. Keidel cannot come. He tends four children—diphtheria. I am midwife come to help you. Do you labor long?"

What kind of question was that? It seemed hours and hours. I looked out the window to see dusk light fading through the oak leaves. I nodded.

Eliza stepped to the end of the bed. "Since morning."

With that, Frau Meyer ushered Tom and Finn from the room, as well as Arno who must have returned.

"*Nein!*" I raised up on one elbow. "*Lass Sie den Hund bleiben.*"

"What did she say about the dog?" It was Eliza again.

"She wants that animal," said the midwife, "but it is outrageous to have a dog in attendance to a birth. Why is the beast allowed in the house in the first place?"

"Let him stay!" Eliza seemed on the edge of hysteria. "He can do no harm. She needs him."

"But we will be a while yet. She is not long in labor."

I thought Frau Meyer's comment a hasty assessment. She was not the one being bent double with these pains.

Leaving Arno with me, Eliza closed the door behind her.

I dropped my hand to his head. "He belongs here with me."

Eliza

Several hours had passed and I had returned to see about Kat. "What's wrong?" I asked. "What's the matter with her?"

"She is sleeping. For now, it is good." Frau Meyer began lining up a host of utensils—scissors, a tub of lard, a stethoscope, laudanum vial. "You have basin, I see, towels. Fold them, *ja*?"

"Yes, of course. Hot water? Do you need it? I've always heard—"

"*Ja.* Bring it. Have you tea? A cup would be appreciated after the ride out here."

With that, she sat herself in the rocker near the window, leaned back, and appeared to drift off into sleep. So much for the midwife.

"I'll be back up in a moment," I said. As I closed the door behind me, I heard Kat begin to moan. I hurried down the steps and into the kitchen to start some water to boil. "So, you know this woman Meyer?" I asked Tom who was slipping on gloves to escape to the field or the barn or anywhere but here. "She helped your wife through childbirth?"

"Yes, Frau Meyer is competent. Quite competent. You just have to get past the uncompromisin' nature of the woman. Best to do what she says. *Exactly* what she says, and we'll all be fine as Dick's hatband."

"If it's tea she wants, then tea she'll get. I'm not sure if she wants me to be of help or get out of her way."

"There'll be no doubt in your mind once you're through the door. Good luck to ya. Come on then, Finn." And off they went, smiling with the relief of being released from expectation.

I climbed the stairs and stepped into the hallway to listen at Kat's door. It was quiet enough. I hated to come in on a scene of great distress. Just the same, I tapped before pushing open the door a crack. "All well?"

"Have you brought the tea?"

"Why, yes," I said as I stepped through the door and set the tea on the nightstand. "How is she?"

"*Gut.* A short contraction while you were gone. She sleeps between."

"Her water broke, you know. Did she tell you?"

Frau Meyer sat up straighter in the chair. "*Nein.* When was this?"

"Oh, hours ago."

"How many hours?"

"It was after breakfast. She came in from the barn complaining of the pain. And then it happened. So before 8 o'clock, but not much before. I know birth comes shortly after that."

"It must come soon, the birth."

"She's miscarried several times before. You knew that though, didn't you?"

"*Ja.* Not easy for her these years. A surprise, this one?" She cocked her eyebrow at this.

"Well, I could hardly speak to that. Her husband—"

"Gone to war I have heard."

"Yes," I said. "Is there anything I can help you with?" Diverting her questioning to something pertinent to the situation might not be easy. "I'll be happy to—"

Kat moaned. Her eyes flew open, and she grabbed the spindles. Her hips pushed down against the bedding. The moan became a cry that made me want to turn and run from the room.

"*Hör auf*! Blow. Blow until I tell you stop." Frau Meyer moved to the bedside and rested her hands on Kat's belly to test the strength of the contraction, I supposed.

The breaths that Kat produced, though she seemed to try with all her might to imitate the midwife's example, came out in the high-pitched cry I'd heard some birds make. And then she sighed and fell back against the headboard.

"I check her now," Frau Meyer said to me. "Hold her hand. Speak to her when she fights. She *vill* fight me."

Like a sleepwalker, I followed her instructions as Tom had said—*to the letter.* "Katarina, it's me, Eliza. You're going to have this baby soon. Isn't that wonderful? Isn't—"

She wrenched herself away from me, crying out in German to be left alone.

"Hold her," came the order from the midwife. She was sliding her lard-coated hand into Kat. "Ah!" she said. "Face up." She straightened briefly. "I turn. It will be easier for you," she said to Kat, but locked gazes with me and nodded.

Not entirely sure of the significance of "face up," I clutched Kat's wrists.

One hand on Kat's belly and the other inside her, Frau Meyer focused on the wall behind the bed, apparently searching for something only she knew of. Then, almost as a surprise move, she shoved against Kat's womb, rolling it as though it were a large melon. Crying out, Kat thrashed against the abuse and twisted away from us. But the midwife held the mound in position through the next few contractions. Then with a look of satisfaction on her face, she withdrew and straightened.

Another contraction began. Kat's whimpering escalated to a wail. Arno, quiet up to this point, gently took my arm in his teeth. I frowned at him, shook my head, and demanded that he release me. I tried to knee him away from the bedside, but he would not be dissuaded.

"Fine, then. If you must." So, the dog and I and the mother-to-be held onto one another while she cried out. A chain of creatures determined to see this child into our imperfect world.

Katarina

How many hours had passed? I wanted to ask, but the world had gone dark with bright flashes and pain, red behind my eyes. Voices demanded things I could not do. "Push!" But it was not me pushing; it was something beyond me. I called out, but an unyielding force redoubled its possession of my body and cared not one whit for the pain visited upon me.

"Push!"

I surrendered everything of myself to comply, my eyes open as someone had insisted. Then it was over. Such was the cessation of agony that I could only lean back and savor the peace of it.

In the subdued amber light from the lantern, the midwife lifted a blood-streaked, waxy-white infant and laid it across my belly. "You have a daughter."

I laid a tentative finger on the child. She frowned and blinked critically at me—a look I recognized as my mother's. "Ah," I said, "I know you well." Realizing all the while, I did not know her at all. She would be her own woman that a part of me would never understand.

"Oh, Katarina, a little girl." Eliza patted my shoulder. "You did it! Isn't she wonderful?"

Frau Meyer intervened. "She is small. Early. We get the fat on her, but I think she is fine." She forced a teaspoon of something between my lips. "Ergot," she explained. "Now the afterbirth."

It seemed simple enough. The afterbirth. But the midwife fretted over what I had produced and spent much time examining it. Then, as if labor had not been enough, she handed the baby to Eliza and turned back to besiege me, massaging my deflated belly with red-knuckled hands. I objected but was met with reprimand. I was vaguely aware of Eliza pacing the room, cooing to my child. I felt Arno's cold nose on my bare shoulder and wished he would remove this Hessian from the scene. I felt a burst of warm fluid escape from me. There, I thought, that must be it. Maybe she'll leave me alone now, and I fought to stay conscious.

There was a great rush of activity around me. Cotton, it felt like, being stuffed in me. I tried to fight, but I was so very tired. Would it hurt to close my eyes for a moment? Just a moment? Voices came at me, but I was sinking into the deep incomprehensible place where the lantern light and sound and anguish became oblivion.

Darkness etched the periphery of my vision until it overtook me, and I floated dreamlike in a shadowy world.

Eliza

The midwife cut the cord and tied it. Under her instruction, I took the baby, wrapped her tightly like a cocoon, and carried her from one side of the room to the other, humming some nameless melody. The infant studied me in wonder, her eyes a bleary blue. Kat seemed to have gone back to sleep, and I ignored the hurried doings near the bed. Cleanup, I imagined. But when I turned to speak to the midwife, I saw her face contorted in a frantic expression. And blood. Blood pooled on Kat's gown and soaked through the bedding and the towels. Like the slaughter of the piglet, only this was Katarina, the mother of this child for whom she had prayed and suffered countless losses.

Clutching the newborn, I felt faint and collapsed in the empty rocking chair. "What's wrong? My God, what is the matter? Is she dead?" The midwife responded in a torrent of German, too fast for me to comprehend. "I can't understand you! Tell me slow!"

"Hemorrhage. Get more towels."

"But the baby. She—"

"Put her in a drawer. Towels!" The midwife was twisting the towel she had into a roll and was pressing it into Kat. "And ergot. More ergot."

I opened the drawer to *der Schrank* and placed the child there. In the other drawer, I found fabric, perfectly stacked and set aside, probably intended for diapers next to a few small blankets Kat must have knitted. She had never told me. I grabbed the diapers and handed them to Frau Meyer, who without expression, continued to work quickly, alternating between massaging Kat's womb and checking the amount of blood absorbed into the cloth.

"Give her teaspoon more ergot."

"But she's sleeping. I can't make—"

"Not sleeping. Passed out. Pull bottom lip. Fill with ergot. Hold the mouth closed. It will absorb."

"Will she die?"

"Do not talk of death. Do not talk. Do what I tell you!"

It was another hour before Frau Meyer relaxed into the rocking chair, let her head fall back, and closed her eyes. "*Besser. Sie ist besser.*"

I breathed a great sigh of relief. "She'll be all right then? She's not going to die?"

"I have told you. We do not speak of death. I believe she will be good with much rest. I stay the night. You take the baby for now. Go."

"Shall I take these towels down? I'll wash them and hang them out."

"Go!"

I lifted the baby girl who had become restless and fussy and bounced her gently in my arms wondering if Tom knew better than I what to do with this baby. He was bound to. "I'm going," I said in as brisk a tone as I dared.

Arno blocked half of the doorway as he sprawled on the floor near Kat's bed. It would be better if he came downstairs with me, but despite my efforts to dislodge him, he refused. He did not bare his teeth at me but complained deep in his throat when I tried to urge him away.

"I understand," I said to him. "She belongs to you." I stroked his head and closed the door behind me.

Katarina

Light filtered through the window in thin slats, throwing dust motes into the air. Aching and stiff, I turned my face toward the far wall to see Frau Meyer slumped in the chair. Arno bumped my arm with his nose. The midwife's eyes opened as I tried to sit up but could not. I fell back against the pillow. Running my hands over the soft mound of my belly, I realized it was empty. Gone. How could I have thought otherwise? I was left an empty shell. Childless once again.

"*Ach*! You wake. *Gut*."

I waited for Frau Meyer to tell me they had taken the child, prepared it for the grave, but pulling back the sheets, she busied herself with examining me. Still, I lay there, silent, hardly caring whether I lived or died.

"*Gut*," she said again and replaced some of the cloths. "Now to eat a little something." Steering Arno out the door, she stepped through to call Eliza.

I tried to tell her I did not want to eat, but it seemed far too much effort. Moments later, I heard Eliza's voice coming from the stairway. "Is she awake? Is she better?"

I turned my face away. Being so young, she would never understand my grief.

"Katarina." Eliza pressed a bundle into my arm. "This little girl has been waiting to meet you."

Joy filled my heart beyond any gladness I had ever known. A child, a daughter. *After all these years. All these years. We have our baby. Oh, Günter, wait until you see her.*

CHAPTER 18

On May 23, 1860, Peter Bonn swore allegiance to the United States of America; he was granted citizenship. A few years thereafter he was forced to bear arms against his country. He was drafted into the Confederate army. His young wife with two small children stayed on the farm. Periodically he and a friend, Conrad Hahne, would desert and come home afoot to do field work. Those were treacherous days, for the Homeguard and the Haengerbande were equally to be feared by them. Peter disguised himself as a woman to work in the field.

– Ella A. Gold, "Peter Bonn", *Pioneers in God's Hills, Volume Two*, Gillespie County Historical Society

Eliza

May brought news of the war. Kat and I both wrote letters to our husbands, Kat adding baby Anna's name to her signature at the bottom of hers. We never knew, of course, if the letters reached them, but it seemed as though the act of putting pen to paper might somehow convey our thoughts across the miles, however lost the letters might be.

Taking advantage of the warm morning, I volunteered to do the wash. As I scrubbed diapers and baby clothes, a horseman approached and called out a few yards from our gate.

I glanced at the upstairs window and saw Kat holding the baby, peering down at us from behind the curtain. She stepped

away. Far out in the field, Tom and Finn turned toward us before darting deeper into the cornstalks. The morning sun blinded
me when I first looked up, but when I shielded my eyes, I saw
the butternut jacket and frayed trousers of a Confederate soldier.
He held his cap across his chest—a polite gesture. Without the
Henry in hand to intimidate him, I put little faith in polite gestures. The rifle was downstairs over the door and out of easy
reach. At least, I felt the slight heft of the pearl-handled derringer against my thigh, and Kat had the dead Secesh's Colt revolver in her room.

"Ma'am?" He was a southern boy and not German.

"May I help you?" I spread thick my own southern accent,
although my heart thundered in my chest. He was not much older
than I, and if I didn't have to shoot him, perhaps I could disarm
him in other ways.

"Name is John Cooper. May I step down?"

What could he want? Was it regarding the man we murdered
and heaved from the bluff? I glimpsed again at Kat's window. We
should have planned on a signal, some way to indicate danger. But
she could see the man, his uniform. She could at least train the
gunsight on this stranger, this youth, despite his engaging grin. I
stepped aside to give her a clear shot if need be.

I nodded and delivered a quick, coy smile. Distraction and
charm were the kindest weapons at hand. Never mind I was woe-
fully out of practice.

"It's been some months now, but I been sent from Camp Davis
to find one of our men who was out *recruiting*." At this word, he
stared down at his boots and cleared his throat. "Uh, recruiting in
this area. Wondered if you seen him."

"Why, we've seen no one, I am sure. Now if you'll excuse—"

"I'm required to ask that of whoever occupies the farm now."

"You are looking at who occupies this farm now."

He squinted out into the fields. "I'm also required to look

around. This place belongs to Günter Lange, Union sympathizer. Ain't that right?"

"My brother-in-law. Yes, but he was likely murdered at the Nueces."

"Not everybody was killed there. They did their share of killin', heard tell. Where's his wife? That her out in the cornfield?"

Thankful that Tom wore Katarina's bonnet and dress in disguise, I said, "Yes, but Frau Lange can barely talk since the loss of her husband. Gone quite mad, as a matter of fact, so I doubt she'd be of any help. She requires that young helper from town to get anything done at all." My accent got a little softer and sweeter. "*My* husband joined the Confederacy—truly loyal to our cause." I stepped toward the well. "Here now, you must be parched. Let me offer you some water."

He stared at me, taking in my information and, I noticed, taking in the cut of my blouse, tattered though it was. I hoped I wouldn't have to kill this boy, too. He seemed a nice fellow.

From inside the house the baby bawled, and then quickly shushed. It was too late, of course. Now the man was curious.

"Oh, I guess she went back to sleep," I said. "She does that sometimes. Just wakes up and screams for a minute and goes right back. Babies will do that. Do you have children?"

"No, ma'am." He laughed. "But you know, maybe one day in the unlikelihood I make it through this war."

I held up the ladle of water. "I will pray for you."

He shuffled uncomfortably. "Yes, ma'am."

"You can be assured I'll let you know if I see that man you're looking for. Can you describe him?"

"Guess you could say he'd had a hard case of the pox. Middle-aged, heavyset, and likely not to wear full uniform. Not that any of us can put one together anyhow. Pretty average. But you'd never miss that horse he was on. Looked like an Indian pony. Spotted all over."

"I bet the Comanches would love to get their hands on the likes of that. Let's hope they didn't do him in."

"Might've, of course, but I've been sent to ask around. Wouldn't bother me none if I never saw the man again. Me and him come to odds more than once."

"Is there anything else I can do for you?" I hooked the dipper on the well rim.

He peered out into the field again. "You say that's Lange's wife out there?"

My heart skipped a beat. "Yes. She has to do the harder labor since I had the baby." I strolled back toward the man's horse suggesting it might be time for him to move on.

He stopped. "And the other?"

"Oh, like I said, that's a neighbor boy come to help. We're mighty grateful for him. He's young but a hard worker."

He put his foot in the stirrup and stopped. "I thought you said the kid was from town."

"Well, *near* town. Oh, silly me, I was never good with distances. You probably can tell how many feet it is to the barn from here, or even *exactly* how many miles from here to town. What do you think? Is it closer to seven or eight? I just have no sense of miles at all." I gazed up at him with what I hoped was a vast appreciation of his talents.

He laughed. "Oh well, no ma'am. I ain't near that good."

"Oh, I bet you are. I've so enjoyed talking with a fellow Confederate, but if you'll excuse me, I better get back to work before that baby wakes up again. You know how they can be."

"No, ma'am." Smiling, he swung his leg over the saddle.

"We'll keep an eye out for that pony." I manufactured the smile of my Galveston days. "Thanks for stopping by, now."

He hesitated but tipped his cap and turned his horse away and headed back toward town.

I started to the washtub but sat in the dust instead, hung my head, and covered my eyes with my hands till my heart regulated its galloping beat.

Katarina

I watched her from the window and wondered if somehow she knew the young man who drew up at our gate. Perhaps she had met him in town on one of her trips to the post office. She was still pretty enough to tempt someone to call on her. It angered me that she might hold such secrets from me. And this rider was little more than a boy in a shabby Confederate uniform.

The rocking chair would have been more comfortable, but I needed to stand near the window to keep an eye on the proceedings. With Tom and Finn in the fields, I felt vulnerable. I had hoped to protect Eliza from this distance, but it became clear that she needed no protection. Regardless, I took no chances and retrieved the Secesh's revolver we kept in the nightstand. Unlike the derringer, it was effective at a distance. The baby fussed, and so with the gun tucked into the waistband of my skirt, I put her to nurse.

At last, the boy rode away, and Eliza finally made her way up the stairs with such sluggish steps I thought her ill.

"Who was *he*?" I could not keep the irritation out of my voice.

"John something. Sent out from Camp Davis to look for that man we disposed of. He saw Tom out in the field, and I told him it was you. I prayed he would not go out to confirm."

Regardless of Eliza's allure, I did not have the same confidence in her charms that she enjoyed. If there was any doubt in that rider's mind, he would bring a posse back here. "Did he say he might return?"

"I don't think he'll be back. The most important thing now is to protect Tom, don't you see?"

"True. I do see." I glanced down at the baby. Sound asleep and still against my breast, she lay with her lips pursed in a tiny, perfect rosebud. "Go out to tell Tom what happened. He saw the horseman ride up and will not come up until it is safe."

I watched her go, her skirt clutched in her fists and raised above her ankles. I saw Eliza and Tom come together deep in conversation, an implied intimacy in their postures, in their gestures. Some small bitter thread snaked its way into my thoughts, and I tried to push it aside.

~

Supper was late. Tom and Finn had stayed past dusk to finish the last work Tom would be able to do before returning to the coast.

"That rider coming around here puts you in danger, Tom," I said. "You must leave before dawn tomorrow if you are to remain safe. We can manage from now on." I turned to Eliza. "I am surprised Eliza has not insisted you leave already. That man's visit terrified us."

Studying their plates, Tom and Eliza both sat quietly until Eliza spoke in defense. "I dispatched the soldier and feel confident he'll not return. I've explained this to Tom so perhaps his departure need not be as imminent as you may—"

Finn interrupted. "If Da leaves tomorrow, I can do the rest of the work."

I recognized the hope for praise in his eyes.

He faced his father. "Can't I, Da?"

"There's much you can do, and it's well you intend it." He turned to Eliza. "You see that he does."

Finn straightened his shoulders. "I don't need no seeing to. I already been workin' and watchin' you." He set his fork down. "I guess I ain't so hungry anymore."

"Aw, put your big britches on, boy," Tom said. "Guess I forgot that you're coming up a fine young man. These ladies depend on ya. I know you'll do your best." He turned to Eliza as though he wanted to touch her. "I *will* get an early start tomorrow. Likely I'll not see you."

"We'll look for you late summer then." Eliza gave me a nervous glance. "Won't we, Katarina?" And smiled timidly—she had never been the least bit timid.

I nodded, a sharp bump of my chin. "Indeed. We are well set with the planting."

The baby fussed from her cradle, the one Tom had fashioned for her. I stood and gathered her to me. I needed to retire but could not bear to give them the luxury of privacy, though it seemed they did quite well as it was. Holding her, I immediately regretted my attitude. What would we have done without Tom? He risked his life to help us. I turned back to them and smiled as best I could. "I have not thanked you properly for all that you do, Tom. Since I will likely not see you in the morning, I shall leave biscuits and ham for you, so you will have them for your trip."

"Much obliged, Miss Katarina. I'll be seeing you come August."

"Come August then," I said. "If you will excuse me. *Gute Nacht.*" I went out into the warm evening and up the stairs. I stopped to listen to the whippoorwills—echoes and echoes tumbling across the hills. A lonesome cascade of voice. Why did I resent any gentle interaction between Tom and Eliza? Was I so bereft of affection that I was covetous of any between others? Yes, there might be some warmth between them. The loss of his wife must have been unbearable, and Eliza's youth a reminder of better times. I chastised myself. Oh, God. What if I were left to raise this child alone as Tom had been?

My little Anna liked to be swaddled and sung to as she was being fed. Had I been able to share this contentment with Günter, my life would have been complete at last. Though letters could never contain the tenderness this baby evoked, I imagined how he would dote on her, his formidable nature softened. For the first time in my life, I experienced the willingness to lay down my life for another. Still so tiny, she controlled every move I made. How remarkable—this power she already possessed. But she needed her father—his protection, his guidance. Each and every night, I fought the urge to *demand* God bring Günter home safely when all I could do was beg.

Even after Anna slept, I sat holding her for a while. But it was late, and I remembered my promise to leave Tom a meal. I placed her back in the drawer we reserved for her upstairs bed and stepped quietly through the door and out to the stairs.

Against the lantern light from the kitchen, Tom and Eliza stood as one shadow till they moved apart. Whispering her good-night, Eliza turned to start upstairs. I ducked back into my room before she saw me.

Eliza came up moments later, but I lay awake for hours, fuming over their duplicitous behavior. So. It *was* as I had thought. All those excuses I made in my head for them. At least, he was leaving. Apparently, just in time. Once again, the way he had risked his life to help us filtered through my accusations. I would make his supper for him to carry away from here, and good riddance. At least, until we needed him again. And maybe by then, they would have had a change of heart. Maybe by then, the war would be over, Wilhelm and Günter would be home again, and we could put all this behind us.

Before dawn the next morning, I roused myself. Tom, not up from the cabin, must still be sleeping, exhausted from his lustful night dreams no doubt. I would put together a sizeable food pack and leave it on the table for him to find when he got ready to leave.

Just as I finished, he stepped through the door and came to stand beside me. "I don't know what to say," he began.

I held up my hand to silence him. "No need to explain. We need-ed your help, and I understand how hard it must be for you to—"

"It ain't been hard for me, Miss Katarina, other than what this war has done to all of us. Y'all, you and Miss Eliza, have saved my boy and me, too. I want to tell you again how much I thank you for carin' for him and givin' him the love he lost when his ma...." His jaw tightened and he looked away.

"Oh, Tom." Tears stung my eyes. I cried so easily these days of early motherhood.

He took me in his arms. I understood then how Eliza must have felt in his gentle, loving embrace—its sorrow and tender consolation.

CHAPTER 19

The 1ˢᵗ Texas Cavalry...functioned admirably, despite confronting immense disadvantages...Overcoming these impediments, regimental commanders managed to organize, equip, and train a unit that performed at a consistently high level throughout the Civil War.
– Stanley S. McGowen, *Horse Sweat and Powder Smoke*

April 1864

Eliza

T he letters from Will were few. After his unit completed the prisoner exchange in Louisiana, there was a stretch of time in which I knew nothing of his location. All I could do was follow news of the Trans-Mississippi Department when Mamá sent copies of the *Houston Tri-Weekly Telegraph*. I had ceased worrying frantically from hour to hour. It seemed like the days went on forever, a long stream of work and worry for our own daily needs. But when Will's letters came, I took them to my room and savored them, sometimes waiting until the night hours when I knew if I cried after reading them, no one would have to witness or console me. The last one was dated April 1864.

My dearest wife—It still seems strange to call you my wife.
We have been apart more than we were ever together.
Deprived of your likeness, I have almost forgotten your
sweet face, but your dark eyes I see in my dreams at night

and remember their loving gazes. We are moving into
Louisiana along the Red River to defend against oncoming
Yankees (as you would happily call them). We stand between
them and Shreveport, which we must protect. I do not
intend to die trying, but if I must, it is a worthy cause. I
am yours, my darling girl and will always and ever be,
Your loving husband, Wilhelm

I spent the rest of the evening penning a letter to him, telling him about Finn and the antics of little Annie-pie, my nickname (much to Kat's annoyance) for the baby. I suggested that when he returned, we might make our own baby as a playmate for her. Meanwhile, I said, I longed for the day of his homecoming and asked him to imagine himself in my arms.

I told him I would ride into town the next day and deliver my letter to the post office. I added that Tom had come again last fall. Young Finn worked as hard as any man, but it was his father who saved us from starving by planting and bringing in our crops.

~

The April day was beautiful as spring days could be here. Bluebonnets ranged across the pasture lands. Creeks ran bright in the morning sun. As was our custom, Finn waited for me in a copse of oak on the outskirts while I collected the mail and completed our necessary trading.

A letter had come addressed to Frau Lange. Since I did not recognize the sender's name of Hans Schneider and hardly thinking of myself as "*frau*," I presumed the letter for Kat. Although I desperately had wanted to sneak it open and read it before we got back, I dared not.

Kat nodded knowingly when I handed it over that evening, but she let it sit there on the table. I finally spoke up. "My goodness,

Katarina, are you not going to read the letter? It might contain some exciting news."

"If you must know, I like to delay the pleasure of reading for the privacy of my room. Although Herr Schneider serves the Confederates, he may know something of Günter. You'll be the first to know at breakfast."

She stayed to do cleanup even when I volunteered to take care of the evening chores. Not until we were all ready to retire, did she start out the door and up the stairs to her room. I followed and said goodnight at her door, perturbed that I would have to wait until morning to hear any news.

Moments later, there was a gentle knock at my door.

And I *knew*. I knew it could only mean one thing. She had no other reason to come to my bedside after we had said goodnight—except to tell of some terrible news the letter contained. Not of Günter. She would not come to me if it were Günter. I wanted to rush from my bed and throw down the bar. As long as I denied entrance, nothing more could come of it.

But then she spoke. It was in her voice, already quiet and sympathetic. She needn't say another word. She could turn and go back to her bed and leave me with the truth conveyed in the timbre of her words. "Eliza, may I come in?"

I would not answer. Let her believe I had gone to sleep. I would not—

But she opened the door.

I turned away and covered my head with my pillow. "Go away."

"Eliza, I am so sorry." Her voice broke.

I felt the mattress shift as she sat beside me and the warmth of her hand as she touched my back.

"Do you want me to read the letter aloud or do you want me to leave it with you?"

"Go away. It's not true."

"It is here on the nightstand. I am close by if you need me."

She stood, and I heard the soft click of the door as she closed it. Her footsteps did not move away for a while. But finally, she left for her room, where her child waited.

It must have been past midnight when I sat against my pillow and picked up the letter.

Frau Lange, It grieves me to inform you your husband, Wilhelm Lange has died on the fields of Pleasant Hill, Louisiana. We, the men of his company, held him in great esteem. As his close friend, I hope to collect his personal effects if I am allowed to do so, but I am rushed to send you this sad epistle. We will never see his good face again, but it will soothe you to know he died a hero. He told us you so wanted him to fight for the honor of the Confederacy and—

I stopped reading. I hated the man for writing those last lines.

And I hated Kat for letting me read the words. It was the same as saying Will would have gladly died for me. And so he had.

Katarina

She had known the minute I stepped into her room with the letter in my hand. She would hate me. How could she not?

I paused outside her door, in case she called out, in case she screamed. For a time, there was nothing but quiet from her room, but then soft sobs filled the empty space of silence. Heartbreaking sobs, much like that of a child, despairing, wretched, helpless. I wanted to go to her, offer what little I could, but I knew she would refuse me. Arno whimpered, and I opened Eliza's door for him with the hope that he could give her what I could not.

She did not come down the next morning. I had not expected her to. Sitting quietly with Finn, I explained what had happened and that we might not see her for a few hours, even a day or two, nor would we anticipate anything from her for a while. "I will take up a biscuit and tea," I said, "and see if she will admit me. If not, I can leave it by her door, for I do not know what else I can do for her."

Finn sat as if he had been admonished to utter not a single word, then laid his hand on my shoulder before walking out the door.

Eliza

It was two days before I could make myself step outside my room. I had not combed my hair or bathed or changed my clothes. Arno, except for brief excursions, lay near me and finally accepted my pleas to move up onto the foot of the bed with me. My self-imposed isolation seemed to make perfect sense to the dog. Better than anyone except my husband, he offered quiet acceptance. Kat brought soup and bread and wine. She offered no remedy. There was none.

During the long hours, I wrote Mamá, telling her of Will's death. On the third day, I insisted on going into town to mail it. Kat objected, but I was adamant. "I have to get away," I said. "I have to leave these sad rooms. The ride will serve me well—a distraction." Finn was instructed to accompany me but to remain silent. I knew he could not, for the life of him, but his chatter could go unheeded like the chirping of sparrows.

The post office, always a hub of activity, was no different that day. When I collected our mail, there was a thick packet from Mamá, and I decided to read it before sending mine to her. I walked outside and sat on a nearby bench. She had included a page from *The Houston Tri-Weekly Telegraph*, which listed the fallen soldiers. Knowing what I would find, I still scanned the list, still hoping I had been misinformed or confused. But it was there, confirmed in black and white. And in that familiar hand, my mother's words begged me to come home where I belonged. Where

I had always belonged, where she could console me, where, despite this awful war, Chlöe could care for me. There was no reason to stay in the godforsaken hinterlands. Say the word, and she would send a driver.

Yes, home. Galveston. I took the letter I had written to Mamá, broke the seal and scribbled, *Mamá, I will come. I've been too long in this desolate place.*

When I returned from the post office, Finn sat waiting for me in the wagon, fearful, I imagined, of setting me off. "I don't know what to say, Miss Eliza."

I patted his arm. "So much the better, my young friend, so much the better." Not another word was spoken on the ride home, but Finn kept glancing at me from the corner of his eye as if he was aware of the change in me, a new firm set of my jaw.

That night at the supper table, I set down my napkin. "I've had a letter from Mamá. She insists I return home, and so I must. She will pay for a driver. Or I can hire a driver myself if need be. I still have my gold eagles. I am merely waiting for a return letter that will clarify what she has arranged. Perhaps Papa will even come to get me, and you can keep Legend and the buggy. I do not wish to quit you high and dry."

Kat stood so suddenly, the soup bowl slipped from her hand, dumped into her lap, and onto the floor. I tried to help her pick up the broken pieces, but she slapped my hands away and carried the shards to the washbasin where she let them shatter into smaller pieces. She stood facing away, refusing to acknowledge my statement.

There, I thought. There! I have said it, and I am satisfied it is the right thing. Of course, there might be friendships lost, but I must go home.

But another letter came from Mamá that dashed all my hopes.

I have eagerly anticipated your arrival, but alas, life in Galveston has taken a devastating turn. We have shortages of beef, fuel, clothing. Even flour and eggs have become gold. The last of our coffee is gone, and your father has refused me the twenty dollars to buy more. He just admitted that his business is failing. We must take what we can and escape to Houston. I cannot believe I must say that you are better off where you are. When the war is over, ma petite, we will rescue you. Until then, my darling. Until then.

How foolish of me to have hoped, to have clung to the idea of retreating to my adolescence. It is gone from me. This war will never let me escape. Now I must reinstate myself and ask for forgiveness for planning to desert them. And most of all, I must resign myself to this life.

When I broke down crying as I told Kat of my change in plans, she sneered. "And not a single thought for the welfare of your parents? I see you remain consistent in your affection for yourself."

I hoped one day Kat would apologize for that hurtful comment. I did not doubt that she, herself, maintained a high level of self-regard.

CHAPTER 20

One morning a rattle snake crawled across the pallet upon which Katherina Zammert had been sleeping. Katherina, then three years old, was ready to grasp the snake, when her father killed it with a stone.
– Esther Miller, *Pioneer Life in Fredericksburg,* in *Frontier Times*

Autumn 1864

Katarina

A capricious flirt, Anna may as well have been Eliza's child. At eighteen months, she tormented Arno who doted on her. She could scamper away on little chubby legs before I could catch her. I thought to have her likeness done, but did not have the money, so Eliza sketched a pen and ink while the toddlekin slept, for the child could not hold a pose even when given cookies to tempt her. She chased the chickens, and when Finn was milking, she begged to have Greta's milk squirted into her mouth. Finn happily obliged.

September remained hot. We sat out under the grape arbor early that Sunday evening, fanning our faces with our bonnets and watching Anna chase fireflies. We had cautioned her to stay within a distance where we could quickly run her down. We relied on Arno to corral her closer to us when we called. It was his nature, being from cow herding stock. He was vigilant to the point of being annoying, sometimes taking her arm in his mouth and steering her back within reach.

"Come on back now," Eliza called. "That's plenty far."

Her chin tilted up in defiance, the child turned and laughed before she tottered off even faster. I started to retrieve her, but Arno had already headed in her direction, so I sat to watch. Instead of gently leading her back, he butted her, knocking her off her feet. With her behind him, he turned again and began an outburst of snarls, feinting and lunging. We were all out of our seats, sprinting to him and the baby. Finn reached them first, snatching Anna and handing her off to me. It was then we saw the rattlesnake.

I seized my child, kicking and squalling, and dashed off to a safe distance. There was no controlling the dog. I had only seen him like this twice before—insensate with rage—when the intruder attacked Eliza and the time I fell from the ladder that he then thrashed to splinters. We screamed for Arno to leave the snake alone, but nothing would disengage him.

Arno had the rattler in his teeth, flinging it side to side, but repeatedly, the snake was able to strike his face and neck. At last, it hung limp, crushed in Arno's jaws. It was his, the spoils of victory, and he refused to relinquish it until at last, he whined briefly and set it down between his paws.

We led him into the kitchen, gave him water, and began the search for bites, not knowing what we could do for him. He was a hundred-pound dog, and maybe he could survive one bite, or even two, but there were several—his head, his neck, his shoulder, his leg.

The tremors did not begin until night came. And the panting. Anna patted him on his hip, saying over and over again, "Puppy, puppy, puppy." I could not stand it and insisted Finn take her upstairs, her bellowing every step on the way, crying out for the dog.

I sat alongside Arno on the floor, stroking his head. He never whimpered, not once. I begged Eliza to see to my child. I would not leave my companion, my guardian, my friend. *Could not.* Wanting to be left alone with him, I sent the others to bed and closed the door between the kitchen and parlor where Finn slept. I knew he would not intrude until I stepped from the room.

I took the cushion from a kitchen chair, slipped it under Arno's head, and lay beside him. His eyes were closed now, but I knew he was listening. "Remember," I whispered in the language he understood best, "when you were just a puppy and you kept falling in the postholes Günter dug? He had to rescue you time after time. You had the biggest feet of any pup I had ever seen." I talked on and on to him— "Remember, remember." And although I could not say the words, I thought of all those days he sat beside me among the small headstones up by the red oak, his head on my knee, waiting for me to cease my tears. Now he had saved my child.

The next morning, Finn took Arno's body in a cart to the small cemetery that held my unborn children and where Arno would rest. Some would ridicule our choice to bury a dog among our graves. But when the time came for us to join him, it was right that we spend the long days and nights together—the cold of winter and the heat of summer with nothing about but a breeze full of memories.

Eliza

Finn did not speak of Arno until a month later when he and I rode into town to check for mail and trade our extra honey. He drove the buggy and was silent for the longest time before he finally spoke. "I guess I better pen a letter to Da. I might need a little help with the spelling. My ma used to sit me down and make me tend to my letters and cipher some, and y'all have helped me a lot, but sometimes I can't hardly remember how. Always did turn 'em back to front. Anyways, Da ought not to come home to find Arno gone. I sure miss Arno. Don't ya wish there was a heaven for dogs?"

I hardly knew what to say to him. A lad of twelve now, he was changing and had left childhood behind. I remembered a conversation I had once had with my mother after my grand-mother died. Mémé and I had been close even though she lived in New Orleans. She came twice a year and doted on me. I was only five when she died, but the burial was engraved in my memory. She was placed in an above-ground tomb in the family cemetery where all the Pitots were laid and where I suspected my mother would demand to be entombed one day. After we returned to Galveston, I had tormented my mother with questions.

"I want Mémé."

"She has gone away, darling. To heaven."

"Where is heaven?"

"It is far above us. Above the clouds even, *ma petite*."

"No, she is where we left her. In New Orleans. I saw you put her there."

"But she did not stay. She has gone to heaven."

"She is in that little house. You go get her *now*."

Even to that day, part of my childhood resistance remained. How could there be a heaven? How could there be a God who would let my Will die and our country be torn apart?

"Miss Eliza?"

"Yes, Finn. I'm sorry. I am listening." I had no intention of imparting my doubts to him. He needed to believe, and I said, "I feel sure that if there is a heaven for people, there is one for dogs."

"There ain't no God, and there ain't no heaven." He clicked Legend into a trot.

"Oh, Finn, now you must believe." I took his hand that was white with tension and relaxed it on the rein. "Why, look all about us. The beauty of the trees and hills and skies. Of course, there must be."

"No, ma'am. If there was a God, He wouldn't have let them Comanches do what they done. My mama and little sister ain't in no heaven. They're somewheres I don't wanna think about."

I wanted to argue or console or offer forgetfulness, but I held no remedy. We sat silent for the rest of the journey into Fredericksburg. He waited just outside of town, and when I returned, I brought him penny candy we could ill afford. "We'll write to your da tonight." I said. "We must tell all our sad news— about Arno and Mr. Wilhelm, too. I'll help you. But let's end with something hopeful. Let's say how delighted we will be when your father comes walking down the road." Even I was aware of the false enthusiasm in my voice. There was no guarantee we would ever get to see that happy sight.

That night I lay with my window open to the cool evening, wondering how I might have consoled Finn when I could not comfort myself with a belief in heaven. Although the oak tree blocked the starlight, I knew the stars were there, brilliant, slowly spinning across our world. Where *did* we go when we die? It was common knowledge that our bodies returned to the stuff clay was made of, the stuff the hills were chiseled from. Maybe, beyond that, there was a place love remembered. I could say that flowers bloomed from us when we died. I believed that to be true. But I wanted to take a stand. Be emphatic. Say, "Why Finn, shadows are shaped of our spirits, the wind sings of us. You've seen the Milky Way and how it appears to be a dust of stars? Well, we become the dust of the Milky Way when we die, looking down on the ones we've left behind." *There*! That's what I would tell Finn had I solace to offer. But I had none to give. Perhaps one day I could. But truly, I wanted no more talk of death. Or heaven or God, for that matter. All I could think of was Will's grave unmarked except for a thin staked cross and his beautiful body damaged and lying under a mound of dirt already bloodied with a hopeless cause.

CHAPTER 21

...the wife of a soldier relates that food was not so scarce during the war, but that there was a great scarcity of money and clothing; in order to obtain clothing "she spun wool on halves for others, then sold part of her share to merchants in San Antonio."
– Frank W. Heintzen, *Fredericksburg, Texas During the Civil War and Reconstruction*

January 1865

Katarina

The war was nearly four years old. A war that was supposed to last the short time it took to put the Union back together. How vain, how presumptuous both sides. Abraham Lincoln was re-elected, even winning some Southern states. It was no wonder we were all tired. Not just the soldiers, though the soldiers suffered most. We were defeated, we were hungry and eager to be done. Those last few months, Atlanta burned, Savannah fell.

Christmas had come and gone, and once again we had made a sad attempt at celebration. Had it not been for Anna and Finn, Eliza and I would have gladly seen it go the way of any other date. The day itself was cold and still, the only bright sign a red smear of color—a cardinal in flight. We sang songs with voices that trembled, and we prayed and prayed that the war would end. It no longer mattered which side won.

Less of an irritant than she used to be, Eliza had lost her youth.

While she once drove me mad with her foolishness, of late I missed those hours of folly and idiocy. I supposed if I were to be honest, I would have to admit that her adolescence had made me the superior one, the voice of reason, the stalwart matron. The war left me merely the elder of two despairing women.

~

Two weeks into the new year, I warmed myself over the rabbit stew that bubbled on the stove. Little Anna played at my feet, happily dismembering a sock doll I made for her. I should have scolded her, but this destructive play busied her and kept her out of my hair so I could get supper. Finn and Eliza worked in the barn.

The knock on the door startled me. Without Arno, the solicitation was both a surprise and a threat. I took down the Henry and pulled Anna behind me. I called through the door, "*Was möchten Sie?*"

"I have a letter to deliver to Frau Lange from Tom Bailey. I was directed here."

In my hurry, I fumbled with the door latch but hoped I had composed myself when I set down the rifle and faced the stranger. "Yes, yes. You may come in." Looking over his shoulder, I checked to see that no one traveled with him. "I am afraid I am overly cautious. Please, sit. I can see you must be bone-weary."

I offered to take his coat even though I suspected the seams housed vermin, but he shook his head and said, "It will take a while for me to warm. Believe I better wear it a while longer."

"Will you have some tea?" I could not take my eyes from the brown envelope I saw tucked into his belt.

At that moment, Eliza and Finn burst through the door. A gust of cold swirled about them blowing scraps of Anna's doll across the floor.

"What does he want?" Eliza had lost her penchant for coquettish behavior since Wilhelm's death and Tom's long absence. Not bothering to remove her coat, she stood with her hands on her hips.

"He has a letter from Tom." I pulled out the kitchen chair. "Sit." Turning to Finn, I patted the chair next to Eliza. The letter could be more important to him than to either of us. I poured the visitor a cup of blackberry tea and offered one of the morning's biscuits.

His fingers, gloved in loose knitted wool, trembled as he lifted his drink with both hands. "My thanks." He set the cup down. "Tom was well when I left him. We caught the tail end of the Red River Campaign down in Louisiana, but that was the only gunfire we saw except for firing at Union gunboats over on the Brazos." He gave a tentative smile toward Eliza.

I rapped my knuckles on the table. "The letter, if you please, Herr—"

"Becker. I have forgot my manners. Ernst Becker." He pulled the envelope from his waistband. "He wrote it in English. I would be happy to translate it for you if I had not lost my spectacles down on the Brazos."

Eliza reached across me to intercept it. "I assure you we are capable of reading and writing in English as well as German."

"Perhaps Finn would like to open his father's letter." I laid my hand on hers.

"Of course...of course." Smiling in recovery, she offered it to Finn.

"I never had a letter before." He turned it from back to front and back again.

"You take your time." Once Eliza refrained from monopolizing the letter, she moved to an elaborately generous mode. "We can help if you run across a troublesome word." She patted his hand that still rested on the unopened envelope. "Just ask."

I took Anna onto my lap and fed her a biscuit and jelly while Finn, his forehead furrowed and lips silently manipulating the syllables, read the letter from his father.

After some minutes, he set the page down on the table. "Well, good then."

We waited, and then I finally asked. "What did he say exactly?"

"That he expects he could get home soon."

Eliza broke in. "Did he say when?"

"Well, he wasn't real clear about that, but—"

She snapped the letter from where it lay between them and took it into a corner by the fireplace to read. As if in private. As if the words belonged only to her.

"Eliza!" I put Anna on the empty chair and stood. "Eliza!"

Her shoulders hunched, she turned her back to me and finished reading. Her face flushed and her eyes bright with the beginning of tears, she said, "His company has been ordered to Hempstead not far from Houston. It's a shorter walk, he said." Her eyes dropped to the page. "'We are about done here,' he says. 'Done with it all. I am a'coming home soon.'"

"He fought in Louisiana. Did he ask? Had he heard anything about Günter?"

"He says that he heard a bunch of Union boys were taken to the prison at Camp Ford outside Tyler. Günter might have been one of those. That's all that—"

"Tyler? Where is this Tyler? Far?" I wanted to snatch Eliza bald. How could she leave that information out until I asked directly of Günter?

Herr Becker cut in. "Pretty far east Texas from what I hear of it. Couldn't say the miles. Just a long piece to walk."

So now I am told Günter might be captured and held at a Confederate prison in a town I never heard of. Stepping forward, I backed her against the wall and pinned her there with my eyes, fierce as I could make them. Careful not to tear the paper, I pried her fingers away. Still letting my eyes bore into hers, I said, "Finn, if you do not mind, I would like to go over the letter as well. But only with your permission."

He nodded.

"If you will excuse me then, Herr Becker. Before you go, I am sure Finn would be happy to rub down your horse and give it some grain to tide it over. You were very kind to deliver the letter to us. As you can see, it is much coveted." I turned to face down Eliza one last time and took the letter nearer the fireplace so that I could sit and read and think about what the news might mean.

Eliza came to my room later that night. "I'm sorry, Katarina. Forgive me. I hardly know what's the matter with me these days. I should not have taken the letter so abruptly. I—"

"What is it between you and Tom?"

"Why, nothing more than concern for a friend." She turned, her hand on the doorknob. "He's your friend, too. There's just so little to hope for now. You have word, at least, that Günter may be out of the fighting even if he's imprisoned. That must give you some kind of relief." She stepped through the door and closed it behind her.

Perhaps she was right. Günter might be safer there than on the battlefield. No other letters had come from him, and I did not know if he ever received mine. It was possible he still did not know of the birth of our child.

Eliza

Sometimes I didn't recognize myself anymore. My behavior downstairs reminded me of my petulant comportment as a child. I must restore the esteem I had once, at least with Finn. Now he had seen me at my worst, and it confused him. But even though I had embarrassed myself beyond redemption, joy flooded me as I imagined Tom coming home soon.

Although he lacked Will's sophistication, Tom's humility and kindness and protectiveness held him dear to me. Determined to rise above my own possessiveness, I vowed not to engage in any such petty competitions with Kat again. As soon as this damnable war was done and Mamá and Papa returned to Galveston, I'd find a way back home even if I had to beg Tom come with me.

I set about the next day to find a time to apologize to Finn. I sat watching him as he worked with Legend.

"Legend don't get to trot into town since Da brought in that old nag. If you don't keep him up the way a horse like him should be, you're gonna have a fat, lazy critter on your hands instead of a fine, sleek animal. He won't be able to outrun any Secesh or Indians or nobody else neither."

"Either, Finn."

"Huh?"

"Nothing. I am quite sure you are right. Thank heavens we have your expertise."

"My what?"

"Your know-how." I smiled at him and went to stand beside him as he slipped a bit of apple to the horse and let Legend rest a minute.

Touching his shoulder, I said, "Will you forgive me my poor manners regarding your father's letter? I'm afraid I was too anxious to hear his news and disregarded your feelings in my enthusiasm. I acted quite abominably."

"Why, Miss Eliza, I get excited sometimes, too. You ain't never yelled at me, and I ain't gonna yell at you. I know you wanted to read the letter for yourself in case he mentioned something special just for you."

"Oh, he would hardly single me out for any news." I thought to turn away, having made my apology and aware of the unnerving direction of conversation.

"I thought he might. I mean if you asked me." He gave me a knowing look. "I seen some things."

"Finn Bailey! I am quite sure I have no idea what you are talking about." Had he witnessed our embrace the night before Tom left? Though platonic, I supposed it could be misconstrued. Even in the brisk air of the afternoon, I felt my face flush with discomposure. "I appreciate your forgiveness of my behavior, and I do promise to spend more time working with Legend." I excused myself.

How could Finn jump to such outlandish conclusions when it had not yet been a year since Will had died. I had just been impatient to see Tom's letter. Finn had misunderstood my eagerness, plain and simple.

~

Winter eased on by us, and with the spring came the heartbeat of expectation. Surely, the waiting was almost over. Please God. Tom had sent another message with a Fredericksburg soldier. This time we did not fight over it. With an eye on Kat, I smiled demurely and handed the note to Finn. When he looked up, his eyes were bright with tears. He stretched out his hand with the note in it. "It's short," he said. "Said to look for him any day."

Another week went by. It was mid-March and we needed Tom badly to help with the tilling. But it was more than that. We all knew it was much more. He was our anchor—the embodiment of our safety and survival. Proof that we would endure this war.

One afternoon he came marching down the road openly and in broad daylight, disregarding the danger of being reported. How could he be so confident? I held back and let Finn trot out to meet his father, but Kat did not.

At Finn's shout, Kat turned from her work, grabbed her skirt and Annie-pie's hand, and hurried to greet him before he even got to the gate. She did not embrace him but clutched his arm briefly as she walked with him back to the house. Although Annie-pie could not have remembered Tom, she mimicked the celebration of the others, grabbing his leg and holding on so he had to hobble along the road. Kat admonished her, but Tom and Finn both laughed. Tom lifted her and carried her for the rest of the way.

I stood, shielding my eyes from the afternoon sun and perhaps concealing tears. With Annie-pie on his shoulders, Kat on his arm, and Finn carrying his musket, Tom came through the gate smiling. I saw the brief flash of want in his eyes when he came to stand before me.

"Tom." My voice broke then. I swiped at the tears. "Oh, Tom, you *have* made it home."

"Aye, I have." And with the others still attached, he reached with his free arm to run his thumb across the last tear that managed to get loose down my cheek. "'Twas a sad letter I received from my boy. 'Tis a heartbreak to lose your mate."

He had misread the tears. Perhaps I did not understand them myself. I was happier than I had been in a long time.

Katarina

We all remained at the table that night. Anna crawled into my lap and sat brightly for a while before beginning to suck her thumb and laying her head back against my shoulder. While we listened to Tom tell what he knew of the war, Eliza—subdued enough to make me suspicious—kept her eyes lowered to her folded hands. I could not even say why, except that it was very unlike her to be so restrained.

"They let us go," Tom continued. "Sent us on home, in a manner of speaking. Said they couldn't feed us. Said nobody'd be trackin' us down if we took a hankerin' to stroll off the premises. Never saw battle but that one at Mansura. Ugly, this whole business of war. We did our share of damage, but so did they. A bloody battle I was lucky to walk away from. We couldn't hold the Yankees, but we slowed them down some. Then it was back to Hempstead and with nothing going on there, they handed us our walking papers." He laughed a little. "And I been walkin' for nine days, but my step got livelier when I crossed the Pedernales."

Although Tom talked as much as he had in the past, now his jaw clenched some when he spoke. Once lyrical, his brogue seemed a tight sequence of syllables. I glanced at Eliza to try to see if she noticed the difference. Her dark eyes revealed nothing. They seemed to absorb light and prevent thoughts from escape. She was so very quiet.

We all sat for a brief time without speaking. So much to wonder and question. If Tom had changed, I could hardly imagine how Günter might be different. War altered men. I knew that. Except for the early years, Günter had never been a very demonstrative man. And although we had yearned for a child, would this one be difficult for him to accept when he had not been here to hope and pray with me day in and day out that she could really come to be? Would I have changed enough for him to forget why he married me? These years had aged me. Worn me. I wanted to search my mirror, wipe away the new lines that had formed.

Gazing into the fire, I was lost in my thoughts and jumped when Tom stood and rubbed his hands together like he was preparing for a chore.

"I thought all the way back here about the things that needed doing," he said. "Your crops need to go in the ground, and there's repairs to be done. And I'll be rebuilding my own place. 'Tis a proper mess."

"Anything I say will sound like an excuse to keep you here," I said. "Stay in the cabin. We need your help, and you need a roof over your head. This bitter war has made us dear friends when we may have been too independent of each other in peacetime. Do not rush to get back to your own place."

He smiled, but it was a weary effort. He could rebuild the house, but would it be a home without his wife and daughter? Finn might be off and gone in a few years. Would Tom even want to stay without a family?

"You are tired, and it all seems too much to bear," I said. "At least, let us pamper you a few days. And by the grace of God, my man will come walking down that road soon. Did you hear of any likelihood of that?"

He shifted in his seat. "Well now, Katarina. 'Twould be a foolish man to predict the future, but I would pray for it, and maybe the good Lord will see to answerin' your prayers right shortly."

"The one thing I know for sure, Tom Bailey. You must rest. Stay here tonight. Finn may be too excited to sleep, but I daresay you are not. The cabin is yours for as long as you like." I laid my hand on his and turned to Eliza. "Are you coming up, Eliza?"

She made only the smallest intake of breath, like her heart had skipped a beat. She stood and excused herself before the rest of us.

Tom offered to carry Anna up for me, but I declined. "She is a small child for her age, and a feather to carry. But *Danke*. Sleep well. It is good to have you home, Tom."

"'Tis a fine thing to be here."

I closed the door gently behind me and waited a few moments. Tom spoke in a quiet, reverent voice. "I know it cannot be so, but when I came down the road to the house, I thought for a minute I heard that ol' dog bark. I'll be missin' his bearded face. Arno was a good one."

I took the stairs quickly before the tears could blind me.

CHAPTER 22

Comanches again swarmed near Fredericksburg and the vicinity of Austin.
– T. R. Fehrenbach, *Comanches, The Destruction of a People*

Katarina

Spring was the loveliest time of the year. Wildflowers covered our hillsides even on the rocky knob of our small graveyard, and I went there often that spring, leaving Anna with Eliza at naptime. Although I took the revolver with me, it was peace I sought that afternoon. Eliza was coming up the hill to find me. Perhaps I had stayed later than I should.

Although there had been no suggestion of rain, it seemed thunder rumbled, and I searched the skies for storm clouds. Instead, a reverberation of hooves sent a shudder of dread climbing from my heart to my throat. I saw Eliza freeze and look about her, then turn to sprint back to the house, her skirt clutched above her knees, her hair falling loose. Comanches rode upon us. In the midst of that realization, I thought her pretty in her flight and knew the Indians would see her delicate as a deer in her attempt to escape. Lovely prey.

On that spotted pony that had once belonged to the Secesh, a Comanche caught her. Reaching down, he scooped her up like some rag doll and held her there in one arm. A shot came from the house, and the heathen flinched. Digging his heels into his mount, he rode past the others and was gone.

I cocked my gun but felt worthless, knowing if I interfered, they would take me too. I had no way to get to the house, to my baby. No way to do anything but provide the heathens another victim. Flattened among the grave markers, I imagined myself one of the bodies that already lay sleeplike in the ground. Only God's intervention would keep my form from becoming another grave before the night was over. I closed my eyes and prayed Tom and Finn could protect my child and themselves within our stone house. Finn had become a good marksman, but they were up against over a dozen attackers.

Smoke poured from the barn, the animals driven out. My Greta and her calf, bawling, going to their knees as though begging for their lives, were shot full of arrows in the yard. The old horse that Tom had brought was led out then let go. Laughing and hooting like drunken children, the Comanches slaughtered the chickens and rummaged through our tools for the knives, picks, and saws. Others kept up a steady barrage against the house. Tom shot only a few.

Maybe an hour had gone by, and I knew they would tire of those bloody games and set fire to the roof. Finn would be converted to their pagan ways, making him a willing, even enthusiastic murderer like themselves. I had heard of it happening time after time. They would take Anna like they had Cynthia Ann Parker and give her to some squaw who would mother her until she herself became a squaw bearing some primitive's child. Or if she cried, oh God, if she cried, they would smash her head against a tree trunk.

Unless they murdered them all. And then without one regret, I would turn my revolver on myself.

Eliza

My ribs felt fractured as he crushed me to him and carried me some distance before slinging me across the withers of the horse.

The breath knocked from me, I could not scream nor would it have served any purpose. Nothing would dissuade the savage. It was him. The intimate funk of his odor—pungent, familiar. His skin—greased with paint and sweat. The black charcoal of his war paint smeared across my arm.

I tried to calm my panic, tried to reassure myself that he had never shown the cruelty I had heard Comanches capable of. He had terrified me but never drawn blood. When he could have just as easily tortured, raped, and murdered me, he had accepted my gift of the music box and the long length of hair I severed from my own head. He let me ride away when I delivered that scoundrel's spotted pony to his herd. Had he misconstrued my behavior as a welcome to further advances?

But this time he was taking me away, as though he had planned it for some time.

After we had ridden for miles, he propped me astride against him, and we continued at a hard pace. The heat of him, his breath against my cheek, and the rhythmic thrust of his body against mine held a dark intimacy that overwhelmed me, horrified me.

I saw no hope, no remote chance that I could survive. The jarring beat of the horse's gait punished me, aggravating some vague injury in my side. My only hope was to will myself an observer, remote and insensate. Like slow immersion in an icy pond, I became numb to pain and fear as though immobilized in a heavy opium state. I saw but no longer felt.

Until I saw the blood. It streamed down the side of his leggings before puddling and coagulating into his moccasin. I could not determine how badly wounded he was. Or how long until his strength might diminish.

We crossed a river, broad but shallow, its limestone bed glowing white in the moonlight. Trees fell away to a prairie filled with spangled light as though the world revolved among stars until we plunged into the trees again and into darkness.

Near dawn, we stopped near a creek. He dragged me with him as he dismounted and set me propped against a boulder. He cut a strip of leather from his breechcloth and tied it at his groin. I turned away. My skirt was stiff with his blood, but I curled my blistered legs under the shredded fabric and folded my arms to me. I had lost a shoe. Having no knowledge of why we stopped, I stared into the small fire he built, I supposed, to smoke the mosquitos that swarmed around us. He studied me as though waiting for me to provoke him to some action.

He wore two eagle feathers in his hair. Angular and chiseled, his face was greased red on one side and painted green marked with black bands on the other. Whether sweat or paint, his skin glowed brilliant in the firelight. His eyebrows were shaved. His arms, banded with leather and silver, were powerful and tattooed. Smooth. So very smooth. Odd geometric designs covered his skin. I remembered that from before. The smell of him, of course, the animal musk, primitive and sexual. Exotically beautiful like a poisonous snake. Coleridge's poem flashed through my mind—

And all should cry, Beware! Beware!
His flashing eyes, his floating hair!
Weave a circle round him thrice,
And close your eyes with holy dread,
For he on honey-dew hath fed,
And drunk the milk of Paradise.

I hugged my knees to me and laid my forehead on my arms. Better not watch him or appear to look for an escape. There *was* no escape. Unless he bled to death, and that would take some time. I tried not to think, but my stomach knotted with fear of what might have happened at the homestead. Katarina had been at the graveyard. Maybe she stayed hidden, but the rest—oh God, the rest.

And if I survived the mutilations, no one would want me back, not even Will if he had lived. I would be a freak in a circus sideshow.

The quiet dawn began to fill with birdsong. I ventured a glance. He was so still. In the pale light, I could see he slept. Or appeared to sleep. As his fingers relaxed, the palm opened, releasing his grip on the knife he had used to cut the leather. He had started to bleed again, and I wondered how much it might weaken him. Lacking the strength to overpower him, I was left with one option—swipe the knife across my own jugular before he could stop me.

I leaned forward onto my knees but changed my mind. That position, a predatory one, would result in—I wasn't going to think of the outcome. The Comanche was weakened, not stupid. I had to rely on his one vulnerability—the loss of blood, to give me a small advantage for getting my hands on the knife. Over the length of a half-hour, I stayed in a seated position and scooted inches at a time closer and closer to him. Each time I stopped and waited, my head on my arms as though I too were sleeping.

At last, I sat almost shoulder to shoulder with him. Snaking my fingers under the point, I lifted the end of the knife to stand it on its handle just outside his upraised palm. Holding my breath, I eased the knife away from his hand. Almost there. Almost there—

He seized my wrist and twisted it to the breaking point. I had known it could happen. Expected it to happen. But I could not help crying out as the knife dropped from my hand, and he pushed my arm above my head and pinned me to the dirt. I dared look into the eyes of the man who would end my life. I would never forget what I saw there—the brief flame of something beyond hatred, deep and feral. I knew at that moment I had romanticized him even in my wretched terror. I had thought because he had not abused me, that he might not, that the blood loss would render him pitiable. That he might forgive my white skin. But in that quick moment, I knew that I was his animal to be had. To be petted if he wanted, to be mauled, mutilated, and toyed with. To be destroyed when he tired of me.

My free hand clawed at the sand around me searching for the knife. It spun in the grit, but I found its handle and drove the blade into his neck. He lurched back in pain and surprise. I rolled out of his reach, scrambled to my feet, and stumbled away. He came to one knee but staggered. He yanked the knife out and threw it to the ground.

Running like I had never run in my life, I flung myself on the pony. Clinging to his mane, I pushed him to a hard gallop. Anywhere. I had no idea where I was going. The pony made a few attempts to turn back, but I kept a tight fist on the reins and prayed for some sign that I was sending the horse toward Fredericksburg.

~

Slowing to a trot and finally to an exhausted walk, I followed the late morning sun toward the east. We crossed what I hoped was the Llano River. I continually looked over my shoulder toward the west. Behind me lay nothing but a thin film of my own dust sifting up and fields and fields of flowers they called Indian Blankets and Indian Paintbrush. Indian, *Indian!* Everything bore their name. They owned this land. We were the interlopers.

My back throbbed from riding, but I was afraid if I dismounted, I might never get back on. If I could find the San Saba Road, surely, I would come across someone who could help me, but there was no one in sight. We were traveling slowly now. Riding hard, my captor had covered all those same miles in the hours from dusk till dawn, but I could manage only a fraction of the distance *if* I were even traveling toward home.

Midday, moving fast, a rider came up out of the east. If I angled crosswise through the scrub brush and called, he might see me. I dug my heels into the pony and moved into a gallop to cut the rider off. He was only a half-mile away, but it seemed so very far.

It took only moments for him to notice me, and he came on—a slow trot at first and then a dead run. I recognized Legend before I did his rider—Tom. Oh God, it was Tom.

He swung off Legend and pulled me down to him. We stood there for a long time, until I was finally able to control my sobbing and the words he whispered in my ear began to make sense. Until I was finally able to ask about the others. He carried me to Legend and set me up. Leading the spotted pony off a short distance, he put the Henry to its head and fired. Legend startled, but held ground, his ears rigid to the sound, his nostrils flared with recognition.

Tom mounted, scabbarded the rifle, pulled me to him. Gripping his arm, I rested back against his chest and closed my eyes. I may have dozed on the way home, but I was conscious of only one thought—hold on, hold on.

Katarina

I saw them coming. A slow, careful pace as if Legend carried something fragile. We were all about broken, but only God knew what that heathen had done to Eliza. They stopped at the gate, and Tom lifted her down the way you would a delicate bird. I rushed to meet them and searched Tom's eyes for some evidence of what had befallen her. Despite the concern in his eyes, I could see that perhaps she had been saved from the worst. Blood stained her dress from the bodice to the skirt, but it was not completely torn from her.

"Oh, Eliza, oh Eliza." I gathered her into my arms.

"I'm all right, Katarina. I am all right." She looked straight into my eyes. "I think I killed him." And then she slumped to my shoulder and wept.

With my arm around her waist, I led her up the stairs to her bedroom. "You lie down now. Can you sleep?" I asked as I removed her ragged clothes and pulled the coverlet over her. She said nothing, but hugged the pillow, brought her knees to her chest like a child might, and seemed to lose consciousness. I slipped quietly from the room leaving her to what I hoped would be sweet oblivion and not the nightmares of the past day and night.

Before going down to speak with Tom, I peeked in on baby Anna who napped peacefully on my bed. Her white-blond hair streamed about her. I peeled away a strand of it sticking to her cheek. Her pink little mouth pursed as though she were nursing as she slept. Such innocence. Such faith that her world was safe. Such blessed ignorance.

In the kitchen, Tom sat at the table with Finn who fidgeted with cleaning the pistol that he had cleaned twice earlier. Tom held his palms together as if in prayer. "'Tis a brutal test life puts us through. Livin's hard enough but facin' down the devil—" He stopped talking.

I sat down next to him and cupped my hands over his. "Do you think she is really all right?" I gave him a meaningful look.

Finn put down the gun. "Don't think I don't know what you're talking about—mincin' around the truth of what he did. You mean, did he rape her. He didn't cut off her breasts or scalp her, but there's other things he coulda done to her." He stood up, knocking his chair backward. "Things that don't show, things I hear women never get over."

Tom jumped to his feet and put his arm around him. Finn shrugged it off but looked at his father with such despair that I saw the lie forming on Tom's lips before his words were ever spoken. "She told me all about it on the way back home, Finn. He roughed her up, but that's all. Scared her. But she's going to be fine. She needs rest is all."

Maybe it was not a lie, after all, but I could simply not fathom an Indian abduction without the things Finn spoke of. Even if Eliza denied them. Knowing her, she *would* deny them. Deny the shame until her dying day knowing no man would ever want her if he knew the truth. Perhaps we would never know. Well, let her keep her pride, her secrets. I could not say that I would not do the same.

"Work will free the mind," I said. "Always has for me and it will for you. The barn needs a new roof, the burnt walls replaced. No time for lamenting what we cannot change. I must tend Eliza and Anna. I will be out to help when I can." With numb compliance, they nodded, put on their hats, and went out to the charred structure.

~

It was the next morning before I heard Eliza stir in the room next to mine. I drew her water and brought her the rose soap we had made from honeycomb.

"Let me help you," I said to her. "You do not have to talk about any of it if you prefer. Lean back against my arm, and I will wash your hair. Let me care for you this one time. There," I said, "just so." I gently brushed away the twigs and sand that had caught in long auburn locks. "There."

Her mouth trembled, but she gained control. "Thank you, Katarina." She reached up to touch my cheek. "Thank you."

After she had bathed and put on a fresh nightgown, she took up her hand mirror and brushed through her hair. "Guess I'm lucky to still have this." She held out a long lock. "Will you braid it for me?"

I settled behind her and parted her hair for the braids. The questions I promised not to ask were burning in my mind. But I had promised. "We were lucky, you know. Here at the house. The Comanches started with the barn."

"Thank God they did not get Legend."

"Legend was well hidden, but they got the old mare Tom brought home. They tortured Greta and her calf before they slaughtered them. They beheaded the chickens and giggled like children as the hens floundered around the barnyard. Someone must have seen the smoke from the barn and summoned the Homeguard. If not, what would have become of us? The Comanches took what

they could and disappeared with few losses. Tom immediately set out to find you while Krauskopf's men stayed to help us
squelch the flames."

"It was the same one, you know," Eliza said. "The one who
came before. Do you remember the music box that I paid a gold
eagle for? With the silly little bird that popped out and sang?"
She looked up at me waiting for recognition. "And I think he
was the same one who saw and followed me when I let free
that spotted pony. Maybe I was some kind of trophy. He had
enough chances to kill me but didn't. Except maybe this time he
would have when I fought back. If I hadn't gotten away." She
turned to face me, her braid uncoiling and falling loose about
her shoulders. "He was already wounded and had lost a good
amount of blood. But I stabbed him, Katarina. If I didn't kill
him, he'll find me, and this time he'll waste no time on me. I
don't know if I can live with that fear. And the fear for you all."
She gripped my arms.

I did not want her to see my face. I turned her back around
to braid the plait that had come undone. "We will be all right,
Eliza. The war will be over soon, and our men will be able to
come back to guard the frontier. We will rid ourselves of the
Comanches. It is hard now, but it cannot last. Have faith." I
remembered the girl Eliza had been when she came to us four
years before. She was never meant for this life. I did not know
what to say to her. What could anyone say? I squeezed her
shoulder. "Have faith."

"Faith?" Her dark eyes blazed in the reflection of her handheld
mirror. "I hope he bleeds to death and rots on the ground he falls
on. That is my faith. That is my prayer every night for the rest of
my life. I hope I killed him."

Despite the vehemence in her words, the tightly woven hatred,
I could still detect loose threads of doubt. She could never be sure
if he were still alive and coming for her.

Eliza

Every afternoon that week, I practiced my accuracy with the Henry until Kat admonished me for wasting the copper casings that housed the bullets. But I could not afford to be complacent. How long would the Comanche wait before he found me alone? Until some early morning when I went to the well? Or a bright sunny day as I worked in the garden?

Every night I watched out my window. I mistrusted the call of the coyotes, the gobble of wild turkeys. Sometimes I fell asleep at the windowsill, my head in the crook of my arm and the Henry propped against the wall near the window. Some nights I took the rifle and put dark objects in the sights, imagining the cool steel of the trigger pulling, pulling until it jolted with the discharge. Each night of that April, the new moon waxed. Each night, its light swelled brighter as it climbed at midnight above the horizon, casting long silhouettes across the garden stakes, the smokehouse, and the live oak. The Comanche moon.

Until finally, the breeze that had distorted oak tree shadows against the barn wall calmed. Silence lay on the hills. I could feel him—a brief intuition, a malignant presence just beyond the garden below the oak. He didn't sneak, he didn't hunch though I knew he was wounded. He stood tall. A quiet specter. Motionless. Had I not been waiting for him, I would never have seen him. Certainly never heard him. I would not call for help.

I lifted the Henry, placed the barrel on the windowsill, and searched for my target until he came into the sights. He must have been demented to pursue me like this. He had had every opportunity to kill me and yet he had not. Well, I was not going to give him one more chance to rethink his decision.

Vengeance is mine, sayeth the Lord.

That night it was mine.

I fired. He slumped, but I fired again.

Kat rushed through my door. *"Mein Gott! Was ist das?"*

"It's done, Katarina. This country has made me a murderer."

Within moments, Tom, who had stayed late to work, was there, followed by Finn. Tom stared at me as though he didn't know who I was. What he saw was me all right. Through the smoke of the rifle still wafting about me, he saw the *real* me. And I began to cry.

Tom took the rifle from my hands and looked outside. "Stay here. I'll go take a look. You don't know if you killed him. Not for sure. It only makes it harder if I have to protect you as well as myself."

"I don't need protecting," I said. "Not anymore."

"Let him take care of the rest, Eliza. We will go down-stairs to wait and—"

"No, I'll watch from the window," I said. "He's there at the live oak just beyond the garden. You'll find him."

Tom turned to his son. "Finn, I'll be needin' your help, boy."

Baby Anna's voice moved from a complaint to a demand. *"Mutti! Mutti!"*

Katarina scooted the chair next to the window and set me down. "You can stay right here. I'll be back with tea as soon as I get Anna settled." She went to the door, turned, and admonished me with a pointed finger. "You wait right there. Hear me?"

"How could I not?" I said but looked to the window knowing I would not sit there and wait for Tom to eventually report back. I had to see for myself—the outcome of my retaliation.

As soon as I heard her close the door to her room, I slung a shawl over my nightgown and slipped down the stairs, barefoot in my haste. I would remember every detail of that night—the call of the whippoorwill, the dew just forming on the grass beneath my feet.

Finn stood back in the shadows but said nothing when he saw me running toward them. Tom bent over the figure sprawled against the oak tree. I lay my hand on his shoulder, and he jumped. "Eliza! I told you to stay in the house!"

"Do you think I could not look upon his face? See the monster who would commit unspeakable acts, who would single me out to dismember, mutilate—" I gasped.

In one rough gesture, Tom had turned the Comanche over, and I stared into the face of my offender—softened in the moonlight, the bright pigments of his war paint blanched. His lips were full and youthful, no longer a grimace. He was nude to the waist, his black hair flung about him like a Spanish fan, his arms bangled with silver and slung wide as though expecting an embrace—a peculiar grace.

I touched where I had shot him, not far from his heart. In a whisper, I asked Tom, "Are you sure he's dead? He still feels warm." I laid my palm flat on the Indian's chest before pulling it away bloodied—like the red handprints I had seen pressed on Comanche ponies. "His name is Isatai," I said. "He told me once, but I had forgotten until now. Isn't it funny how the mind works? After I have killed him, I remember his name—Isatai."

Tom stood and turned away from me.

"What will you do with him?" I asked.

"Find a soft bit of ground to bury him in, I guess. Close to the creek." Tom looked down toward the trees that followed Wolf Creek.

"Don't tell me where. I won't go looking. But disguise it well."

The moon rose higher in the spring night, and I watched the shadows of leaves fall across the Comanche's face. A brave. That's what they were called. I think he must have been mad, but perhaps that intensity was what defined the race. I thought I would still be afraid of him, but I wasn't. I leaned forward and rested my cheek against his chest to listen against all probability for a heartbeat. *Nothing.* Tom pulled me away and wiped my face.

Finn stepped forward to look over my shoulder. "He's a son-of-a-bitch. But if he hadn't dragged you off, them other heathens woulda got you."

CHAPTER 23

In the meantime the war went on. Battle after battle was fought and the Confederacy finally broke down.
– Wm Paul Burrier, Sr., Ed. *August Siemering's The Germans in Texas during the Civil War*

May 1865

Katarina

If the rumors were true, the war was over. Men were drifting home, a few having deserted some time before. Well-armed, Tom took Legend to town twice weekly for any information that fed the rumors. My husband had not come home, he had not written, and I had no knowledge that he would. Our lives were run by speculation.

Tom and Finn did the best they could. They plowed, walking behind the white-muzzled, scrawny mule for which Eliza relinquished two of her gold eagles saying she would never put Legend to the plow. Better Legend than Tom, I thought, remembering the past years when Tom in my bonnet and dress, pushed a hand plow ahead of him. I said nothing.

We could milk again. Eliza gave up the last of her coins for a cow. "There," she said to us, her hands widespread and empty. "I wish I had more to offer."

That year, we got a full crop planted. It was a busy time, and I hoped to bury my fears in work. I always had, packing thoughts like so much silage under the daily chores of cooking and gardening and cleaning. Mindless repetition. Yet worries always surfaced again. Why had I not heard from Günter? If he were alive, surely, he could have sent word.

Not long after Lee surrendered, I sat with Eliza on the bench under the grape arbor. She sighed deeply. "I thought I'd care more that the South lost," she said. "I believed the damn war would make a difference. But all it has done is diminish us. Strip us of the lives we knew. Even Galveston, which used to be the jewel of culture and commerce on the coast of Texas, is deserted."

I laid my hand on her shoulder and tried to portray a sympathy for her I did not feel. Except for the loss of Wilhelm. Except for that. Eliza paid for her Southern sentiments with the death of her husband. Although we Germans had not been long in this country, we could have told them. We *tried* to tell them, but it would not do to remind anyone now.

~

On the first week in June, Tom rode in from town at a brisk trot. "A letter!" he called. I met him at the gate, and he handed the envelope over to me before dismounting. I did not wait for privacy but stood there in the rising dust and tore it open. I could feel everyone's eyes on me as I read its three sentences.

My dear—coming home. Hope to find a ride. Will walk if I must. Günter

There was no date on the grimy scrap that served as stationery, no indication of the distance he would have to travel. But I read the determination in the familiar scrawl. I turned, clutching the letter to my breast. "My husband is coming home." I watched Eliza bow her head and cover her eyes.

Every day after that became a vigil. Any dust on the road, any rare passerby sent us to the gate. Now that it was relatively safe for me to take the buggy into town, I went, praying that Günter had made it that far. Or that someone knew of him. My pace back to the house was slower than the sharp trot into Fredericksburg.

Men *were* coming home. I listened to the reports in Fredericksburg. Union men and Confederates alike—lice-ridden, with trouser legs pinned to their hips, weakened with dysentery. And there were stories, tales no one wanted to hear. But if the men walked this far west, they must be home. There was little beyond these hills.

On these trips, I imagined finding Günter on the road. I would know him from the moment he came into view, recognizing his stride, the proud way he had always carried himself.

That was not the way it happened at all.

~

That spring into early summer, we took to trading our honey to neighbors in the surrounding communities. Like a common peddler, I hitched the mule to the wagon and with the Henry by my side, traveled to offer jars of honey for a skein of wool or a laying hen or a precious yard of pretty cotton fabric for Anna a dress. It was against my nature, the idle conversation it required, or worse, the tales of loss. Better suited to the task was Eliza. Still fearful of Comanches, she refused, begging instead to tend little Anna and spend the day pulling weeds or making cheese in exchange.

The part I did not mind was the quiet of traveling. It was not silence, but it demanded nothing of me. No child, however endearing, to pull at my skirt, begging for something sweet or to be toted about. No list of chores I carried around in my head—that never-ending list. I found the creak of the wagon, the occasional complaint of the mule surprisingly soothing. The trees overhead, the flowers in the fields, and the buffer of distance brought a peace to me that I could never find in the household.

It was the last stop at Frau Müller's that I became a victim of my own frailties. After achieving a profitable day, I felt particularly generous giving another jar of honey in exchange for an extra set of knitting needles. One day I would teach Anna to follow my knits and purls.

As I was leaving, the oldest child brought it out—a whining, squirming pup bigger than a hand-fed piglet. "The mama is wearing out feeding them. Getting right snappy with them." She offered it up to me with a foxy little grin on her face.

"They grow into fine hunters and guards," added Frau Müller who could not conceal her desire to have one less pup to put up with. "Why, before the war, they brought a pretty penny. You want to take her now? She will serve you faithful."

I shook my head even as the child pushed the brindle young Dane into my lap. I remembered the dogs the Müller's touted four or five years ago. It was no wonder they had to get rid of these pups. They would eat them out of house and home.

That pup could serve no good for another year or two. It would be underfoot and another mouth to feed. Anna would want it in her bed, and there would be rather large accidents to clean up judging from the size of the mutt, and it could in no way compare to the companion and protector Arno had been. Why, it would be an insult to his memory if I were to bring home this—

But then the *verdammter Hund* stopped her whining and wiggling. She stared straight up into my eyes, unlikely behavior for so young a dog, and gave one quick wag of her tail. She held my gaze and wagged again. Although barely able to fit in my lap, she pushed her nose up under my elbow and settled in. Speechless, I nodded to Frau Müller, clucked the mule forward, and drove off at a fast clip. *Du bist reingelegt worden.* "Hoodwinked!" I said aloud in English.

I was expected by mid-afternoon. I had been delayed only once before, but I could see I would not get home at the intended time. When I left the Müller farm, the sky to the southwest blackened. Thunder clouds bunched on the horizon, and by the time I reached the tree line of the road, the day had deepened to dusk. No wind pushed through directly, but there was a restlessness about the air, a stirring, an energy that flitted briefly among the leaves and then quieted. The mule, generally insensitive to the weather, shied at a sharp momentary rustle of undergrowth.

The first drops fell. Just a few, but they marked the mule's haunches in great coin-sized dollops. He moved into a startled trot until his hide was completely covered, but then the rain and wind began in earnest. The pup finally looked up in mild surprise at the disruption in its sleep. I pulled up less than a mile from the house to wait until I could see ahead. The silence I had so enjoyed had given way to cacophony.

I tied the reins in a knot, collected the puppy, and scrambled under the tarpaulin in the bed of the wagon. The racket was awful, but it kept us out of the brunt of the weather until the rain lessened and I felt the wagon move forward, pulled by the mule intent on getting home.

The mule was so eager to get to the barn that I doubted I could have stopped him any sooner. I hoped Finn would rub down the cantankerous critter and give him a flake of hay for his work, however ornery he had been in achieving it. I bent under my hat and hurried to the porch where everyone waited.

I set down the pup and stared up into the eyes of someone I had known once. So out of the ordinary was his presence that I could not reckon his identity. But familiar. So familiar.

"Do you not know me, Fräulein?"

Eliza

Earlier that afternoon, just before the rain, a straggler arrived at the gate. Bearded and frail, he looked like all of the returning soldiers I had seen, men shabby and unshaven, limping down the dusty road. But there *was* something in the way he stood expectantly and waited there for someone to usher him into the yard. *Something.* I started to call for Tom, but when the man removed his hat, I saw. I thought I saw— "Can I help you?" I took Anna's hand and walked slowly toward the gate. I cocked my head and squinted to better study the face that had once been familiar. Not three feet away from him, I finally dared speak his name. "Günter?"

Anna shrank behind me as I gripped his shoulders. "Dirty man," she said.

"Oh, no, child, he's—"

He faltered then and reached for the gate post to steady himself.

Shouting for Tom, I stepped under his shoulder for support and slid my arm around him. We hobbled together to the porch chairs as Tom came 'round from the garden as the wind began and then the thunder.

"It's Günter," I called, fearing Tom's reaction to the stranger. "Günter Lange!" as if he wouldn't know.

Leaning on the arms of the chair, Günter sat heavily. "My wife?"

"She'll be back soon, I promise. Oh my, she will be so happy to see you. We all are, aren't we? We've waited and waited and then finally hardly knew you." Immediately regretting my inference that he looked beyond recognition, I tried to gloss over my apparent shock. "It's been so long." Heavens, what do you say to a half-starved prisoner of war who has just walked over God knows how many miles? "You sit here, Günter. You sit right here, and I'm going to bring you something to drink. Tom? Finn? Talk to him. Tell him how glad we are to see him. Keep him company for a minute?"

Tom produced an indulgent smile. "'Twill be my pleasure, indeed. Run on, now. I'll see to my friend."

With Anna clinging to my skirt and chattering her objections to the man, I rushed to the kitchen.

"Now, darling," I said. "He's just traveled a very long way and got a little dirty, but he is very nice. You'll see. Your mama will explain everything. And she will be back quite soon."

As I brewed the tea, and then the last bit of coffee we had, I tried to ignore the knot that rose in my throat. I leaned my forehead against the wall, taking time to collect myself and trying to be glad for Kat. Tears burned for the few moments I imagined it could have been Will, whole and eager to take me in his arms, standing at that gate. Oh, it *could* have been. But it wasn't.

With a tray laden with a cup of coffee, a cup of tea, a cup of wine, and the last of yesterday's Sunday cake, I set my mouth in what I hoped was a smile and placed the tray before Günter and said, "I didn't know which you wanted so I brought them all. Oh, Günter! It is so good to have you home!"

We passed the time watching the rain, trying not to appear alarmed that Kat had not gotten home yet. "Sometimes she gets to talking and forgets the time," I said.

Tom rolled his eyes, and Finn couldn't suppress a snicker.

"Well, *sometimes*!" I stood and walked to the end of the porch to look down the road. "I bet she waited out the storm at the Müllers."

Then as the rain faded to a mist, that old mule honked a greeting as they hurried around the last turn in the road. We watched as Katarina trudged through the mud to the house. Hunched over some bundle she carried in her arms, she never looked up until she reached the porch. Günter started to rise to meet her but failed. When their eyes met, she seemed to lose her balance. She's going to fall, I thought and moved to catch her, but she pushed me gently aside and as if in a sleep walk, went to stand before him.

Tom touched my shoulder and nudged his chin toward the door to the house. Finn took Anna by the hand, who despite being knocked over by the puppy, squealed with delight, and we stepped to the kitchen.

I stood a moment to watch—a voyeur trying to experience a scene I would never, never know.

Katarina knelt before Günter, locked her arms around his knees, and laid her cheek against the faded blue uniform.

CHAPTER 24

After the Civil War closed, and her husband returned home, there followed the trying days of reconstruction…
– Esther Miller, *Pioneer Life in Fredericksburg,* in *Frontier Times*

Katarina

What do you do for returning soldiers? You cry happy tears for them, bathe them, feed them, you bandage and console them. But none of that would prevent the series of missteps and misunderstandings that followed.

The day Günter returned, Tom and I supported him up the stairs to our bedroom while Eliza distracted Anna downstairs. I cared for him much the way I had for Eliza after the Comanche attack. Tom and Finn hauled the hip bath and buckets of hot water to our bedroom so that Günter might bathe in quiet privacy. He refused to be shaved at first, but I insisted. "The lice, *mein Liebster,* the lice." I swept up the remnants of his beard and haircut quickly and discarded them out the window. I knelt beside him and gently sponged his bruised skin, his bleeding feet, his emaciated cheek. We spoke very little. I kissed the hollows between his shoulders that had once been muscled and firm.

I helped him from the tub, slipped his nightshirt over his head, and led him to the rocking chair for his supper. I wanted to lift the ladle of stew to his lips and feed him, but he took the spoon from my hand with a shaky grip and gulped down the meal. He seemed too tired to speak, so I kept my silence.

He let me pull the coverlet over him as I settled him into bed, his weight a bare indentation in the mattress. I sat on the floor beside him and stroked his cheek. "I have sad news of Wilhelm, Günter. The saddest news, and I am so sorry to tell you, but—"

"He has died at Pleasant Hill. At Camp Ford, I was told. I have done my grieving." He tightened his fist in the bedsheet, but I heard him sob just once, so very quietly before he closed his eyes. He slept but pulled me to him as I slipped in beside him.

From Eliza's room, I could hear Anna calling for me and objecting to being dressed for bed. "Hush, now," said Eliza. "This evening is very special, and you can sleep with me." Then Eliza's soft voice sang a lullaby. It was French. Leave it to Eliza to sing a French lullaby, but the fussing stopped, and the night grew quiet. In that moment, I forgave Eliza every petty annoyance she had ever levied on me and yielded to the comfort of her singing. That night I must sleep alone with my husband.

Günter woke once in the night and cried aloud, but I comforted him in the whispered language of our homeland and put my arms around him the way you would a frightened child.

The morrow came, and although the sun filtered light through the oak, Günter slept on. Below I heard Anna's high-pitched demands to see me. I dressed quickly and hurried down to bring coffee and biscuits back up for my husband. *My husband.* The man who had protected me, set the rules, and orchestrated the pace of everyday living. Dominated my life.

I set his breakfast on the bedside table and stroked his back. I could not remember a day we had taken our morning meal in bed. Ever. He turned and looked about him before his eyes settled on me.

"Katarina," he said, soft disbelief in his voice—the first time he spoke my name since coming home.

I kissed his cheek. "Have your breakfast, and then there is someone I want you to meet."

I had told Anna of her father who had gone to war—her

father who was handsome and brave, a hero who would some-day take her for pony rides and carry her on his shoulders. She had touched his face on the only likeness I had of him and called him *Papi*. But I could not make her believe that this stranger was the father I had described in those sweet stories. She would not let him near her.

For nearly three years I had waited, yearned for his return. For this stranger. He *was* a stranger to me. Certainly to our child. He was a puzzle piece that no longer fit.

Eliza

As the weeks went on, I saw it—the tension between Katarina and Günter generated by Annie-pie's jealousy of any attempt at affec-tion between her parents. Used to sleeping with Kat, she provided a human wedge between them at night. I heard the conflict at bed-time when Kat put Anna in her own little bed.

Of an evening, Tom and I sat in the kitchen and listened as the ruckus began upstairs at bedtime. "I may not ever marry again and have children," I said as we smiled at each other and shook our heads.

"'Tis a proper challenge. This one more ballyhoo than most. Each one's got a claim on Katarina they're not likely to be generous with."

"That is exactly my point," I said. "Does Katarina have no claim to herself?"

"Give the matter time. 'Twill work itself out."

As if he knew. As if he were an expert in such matters.

His voice took on a serious tone. "Soon Günter will no longer be needin' us, and my boy and I must change our way of goin'. I fear we're a hindrance to their privacy." He came to his feet and paced to the fireplace and back.

At the determination in his voice, I insisted, "Y'all are no im-position. To the contrary. Günter is not ready to resume *all* the duties of the farm. Not by a long shot. He needs you and Finn. And will be happy for you to stay on in the cabin."

"He needs his homeplace back. I can help out, but it's a likely thing he sees me as a rival of sorts."

"Oh, my, no! Tom. He'll get over that. Why—"

"Look at it from his way. His little daughter still thinks I am fine, almost a father to her. His wife has needed my help and shows me great kindness. Even you—"

"Even I, what?"

He blushed then. "Well, you've—"

"Needed you?" I stepped closer to him.

"Now, Miss Eliza, you're doing it again."

"*Miss* Eliza, indeed." I grinned at him. "Doing what, exactly?"

"Temptin' me."

I stood close enough to encourage a kiss if he'd been inclined. And by the looks of things, he was very inclined. I lifted my chin a little to dare him.

The doorknob rattled as Finn carried in the puppy. "She was scratching at the bedroom door. Probably wantin' to climb into the crib with little Anna. Caught her just in time. She'd better sleep—"

Tom shoved his hands in his pockets, and I turned away to gather the last of the dishes.

"I was gonna say, she'd better sleep in the barn." Finn hesitated then opened the door and set her outside.

Tom raised his voice for Finn to hear. "I was just telling Eliza that we should head back over to our old cabin. What with Günter home, he'll be wantin' his place back to himself. With the comfortable weather, we'll make a bed under the stars. By the time the first cool wind blows, we'll have a roof over our heads and a warm fire in the hearth."

Finn sat down hard on the kitchen chair. "I'm not ready. Not yet."

"Neither am I, if anyone's asking," I said. Tom infuriated me sometimes. He made up his mind without the least consideration of others and announced it as a proclamation.

He turned to me. "We'll be back to help with the heavy work till Günter has got his full strength. Anyway, it's time we got to puttin' our own home back in order."

"Günter might need you more than you know." I slapped the dishcloth across a plate and stacked it on the shelf. It made more noise than I intended. "You don't know everything, Tom Bailey."

"I know how a man feels, Eliza."

"And I know how a woman feels!"

"Do ya, now?"

I stripped my apron off and with a brisk goodnight to Finn, went out the door. I turned when I heard the door close behind me. Tom caught me against him before I made the first stairstep.

He spoke against my ear, his voice husky. "Walk with me."

I glanced up at Kat and Günter's room. The lights were off, and all was quiet. I took his arm, and we moved through the night down to the cabin. When we reached the door, he lifted me, my skirt skimming my thighs, his arms against my skin, and took me inside.

He turned to me and began at my neckline to pursue the long line of buttons down the front of my dress pausing at each with a look as though asking permission. I closed my eyes and tilted back, offering myself gladly, believing this was right, believing nothing mattered but the two of us.

Outside the breeze hurried among the oak leaves and hushed other night sounds. It muted the past and quieted memories of other lovers. We did not speak. We did not need words to say that we both begged for the return of that life-confirming passion, the heat and desire that made us believe we could be human again.

CHAPTER 25

We can't form our children on our own concepts; we must take them and love them as God gives them to us. Raise them the best we can, and leave them free to develop.
– Johann Wolfgang von Goethe, *Hermann and Dorothea*

Katarina

Autumn was in the air, the crisp, quiet days waiting for the first frost. Four months had gone by, and I still caught Günter watching our daughter with a look of skepticism. I knew why—he searched for a semblance of himself in her. Although I had read somewhere that the firstborn most often favored the father, Anna was nothing like him. She bore my likeness and had already adopted some of my traits. Eliza happily pointed them out—the hands on my hips, the bossy manners. They were emphatic postures, not bossy ones, I insisted, but even I could recognize the similarities. Of Günter—there was nothing.

That the war had physically debilitated him was obvious to everyone, but perhaps only I was aware of a deep anger that seemed to fester beneath his frailty.

Even with Tom and Finn coming almost daily to help, farming so exhausted Günter that he failed to participate in family life. He studied me as if to love me again, to reacquaint himself, and perhaps to discover a fondness for Anna.

The child did nothing to encourage her father's affection. She adored Finn. She idolized Tom. But she eyed Günter with suspicion and objected to his sharing my bed. Like Finn, she called him "Mister" if she addressed him at all. She swatted away his rare attempts to touch her. And heaven help him if he tried to correct her behavior, no matter how badly she deserved it. I asked him to let me do the discipline for the time being, and for the most part, he agreed, but one evening when she was already grumpy and should have been put to bed, he could resist no longer.

When denied another cookie, Anna threw herself to the floor and demonstrated what Eliza called a wall-eyed hissy fit. Since I considered Eliza a tantrum expert, I nodded in agreement.

Günter, however, was not amused with the colloquialism and promptly snapped Anna up under his arm and carried her like a piglet out the door and up the stairs. Under her breath, Eliza said, "Uh oh" as she stepped out of the way. For the moment, the child, shocked into silence, gave up her screeching. I hurried after them but feared the damage had already been done.

Günter turned to me. "I *vill not* have zis behavior in my house!" His American accent, which he had worked so diligently to master, failed him entirely.

I peered around him to see our little Anna curled on the bed, her lower lip a petite shelf. "She is not but two years old, Günter!" I tried to step past him, but he blocked my way.

"She is nearly three! Love is not without discipline, my wife." And then in a softer voice, "Misbehavior, if allowed, will make her unlovable." He turned to her. "You must understand, *kleines Mädchen*—little girl—you must be polite and say thank you for a cookie, not squeal and demand more." He reached to pat her, but she shrank from him. "Leave her then to study the error of her ways." He escorted me out the door and down the stairs with more influence than I appreciated. As soon as the door closed behind us, the howling began.

Near tears myself, I tried to explain. "She is a baby, Günter! And she is afraid of you. She hardly knows you at all, and you are being far too rough with her!" I turned to go back up the stairs to her, but he refused to let me pass.

"We will sit and have some tea and wait for the screaming to abate. There will be no more catering to a spoilt child." He marched me by the elbow into the kitchen and sat me in a chair.

Eliza raised her brows as she, Tom, and Finn who had stayed for supper, removed themselves to the parlor.

At that moment, I hated him. He had suffered much at war and found family life not at all as he remembered, but I would not allow this stone-hearted treatment of my baby. As soon as I could, I would console her. Just as soon as she quietened. Meanwhile, we sat and glared at each other and listened to the caterwauling from above.

Then it was quiet.

"There! Are you satisfied? She has stopped. I am going to see to her." My lip trembled, and I felt quite sure Günter reckoned my behavior as petulant as our child's. I hardly cared. All I wanted was to gather her in my arms and kiss away the teardrops on her cheeks.

"Wait a bit longer. We must not be quite so quick to forgive."

It would be an even longer time until I could forgive *him*, but I sat with my hands in my lap and glowered at him. I watched the clock. Finally, he grunted, which I chose to interpret as permission. I stood, adjusted my bodice, tugged my sleeves into place, and walked stiffly for the door, all the while plotting revenge—a disguised but nonetheless satisfying reprisal.

I stepped softly lest she be sleeping. Praying she would slumber the night through, I planned to slip her nightgown over her head and tuck her under the covers of her own little bed.

She was not there. Not under the bed. Nor in Eliza's room. Surely, she had hidden herself somewhere—in *der Schrank*, behind the rocker. I called gently. No answer, no sniffling. I almost cried out for Arno. He would have found her. He would never have allowed this. *He* would have been with her every moment.

And then I was filled with rage. *Günter. He* let this happen. He *made* this happen. I stumbled down the steps and into the kitchen. "She is gone! She is run off! And you, Günter! *You* have caused it." I pressed my lips into a grim line and levied an accusing glare at my husband. "I shall never forgive you."

I turned to Tom. "Find her, Tom! She loves *you*."

When I looked back at Günter, I saw the injury I had rendered but could not repent of it. It *was* his fault. All that ran through my mind were the very real dangers—Comanches, coyotes, any number of deadly snakes.

Tom laid a hand on my shoulder. "I know you're frettin', but let's all be workin' together to find our little girl." He paused and corrected himself. "*Your* little girl. I'll be glad to help, of course."

I grabbed the lantern and shoved past them to the door. "By the time you men get around to deciding who is going to take charge, there is much to harm my child."

Eliza blocked my way. "Let them go, Katarina. You and I must wait here in case little Anna wanders back home. She can't have gone far. Trust the men."

I shrugged away from her but unwillingly saw the reason in her words. "Go then! *Beeilung!*"

The hurt still in his eyes, Günter took the lantern from me and rushed out, followed by Tom.

Crying after them, I called, "The chicken house! Check the chicken house!"

The light of the lantern wavered in the dark, and Günter's voice mumbled—"*Ja, ja. Natürlich,*" his resentment unambiguous. He would have known to look there. I did not need to manage him. I had given him little regard as Anna's father, but his reluctance to claim her had read plain on his face since the day he arrived. Young as she was, Anna sensed it and was not willing to be dominated by someone she hardly knew. I had underestimated the distrust between my husband and my daughter—my two strangers.

I closed the door and tried to sit, perhaps to knit or repair Günter's torn shirt. "*Es ist nicht gut*, Eliza." I flung the sewing to the floor. "I cannot bear it."

She took my hands in hers. "Then we will walk around the front of the house. We will see her if she comes running back afraid of the dark."

We stepped into the evening. "She is never afraid," I said. "The silly child. You can put the fear of God in most children when it comes to the things that lurk in the night, but not Anna. Not that naughty girl! Perhaps this will teach that willful child!" Glancing out into the shadows, even the silhouettes of familiar buildings seemed like menacing forms, and I was filled again with horror. "Oh, I did not mean that. I did not! I only want her to see the possibility of danger in the night. I only want her home safe."

Eliza put her arm around my waist. "I know, Katarina. I know."

"No, you have no idea. You never will until you are a mother."

She withdrew her arm and turned to face the dark. "It will not do to behave so."

Once again, I had admonished someone trying to console me. "*Nein*, you are right. I beg your forgiveness."

"It's Günter's forgiveness you need. You were cruel to him."

This I chose to ignore. "If Arno were here. He could find her. He would never let her venture out into the countryside. He—"

"The dog is not here, my friend, but your husband is. I may not be a mother, but I had a husband who I loved dearly. And I have lost him. So do not tell me I cannot understand anguish. I understand it too well."

An inkling of guilt pricked through the blame I wanted to foist on someone else. My child wandered in the night. Was she crying out for me? Did she stumble and fall over some unseen obstacle? I twisted my fingers together until they hurt. I turned and paced the other direction before turning again. Then I heard the men coming back through the yard.

Günter's face, awash with relief in the lantern light, carried Anna. I ran to them, my hands reaching to take her from him. She sat up pertly in the crook of his arm. "Hello, Mama! I slept with the puppy. Mister found me."

I crushed her to me, and through my sobs said, "*Gott sei Dank.* Thank God!"

"If anyone's to be thanked, 'twas *Günter* what found the child," Tom said under his breath.

Eliza took his arm and pulled him away.

"She...Anna was in the barn." My husband's voice softened when he said her name, although I hardly allowed myself to acknowledge the significance until later.

She was home safe. I wanted to scold her for terrifying me, but the relief was too great. We would speak of it later. Saying not another word, I carried her up the stairs, laid her in our bed, and curled around her until she fell asleep. I must make amends to Günter. Between leaving to find her and returning with her, he seemed a different man. I could not discern the cause, but there was repentance in his eyes.

There should be repentance in my heart.

He had not come up, and so I patted Anna's back until I was sure she would not wake and took the stairs down to speak with my husband. When I entered the room, Tom and Eliza hastily excused themselves and stepped out into the evening.

Günter sat at the table twisting hemp together for rope. He did not look up at me. "I hear hemp rope is preferred for a hanging. Does not stretch much. Shall I twist you an extra length to string me up?"

"Oh, Günter, I regret my words to you. They were heartless. Anna is your baby, too, and I have persisted in demanding you love her as much as I do. It is understandable to be less tolerant with a stranger, and she *is* a stranger to you, is she not?" I stepped forward wanting to touch him, to show my remorse.

"I must confess." He continued to examine the rope, tugging on it, testing the fiber strength. "I did feel a stranger to her. Anna resembles you, but I saw nothing of me in her until tonight. She slept in the hay pile of the barn, hugging that puppy by the neck. I am still surprised the thing tolerated it. She sucked the back of her hand at the crook of the wrist. It will leave a little callus." He rubbed a spot on his own wrist. "It brought to mind a story of my childhood my mother recounted to me numerous times. I was older than Anna, but not by much. When denied a favorite toy, I grabbed it anyway and ran to hide. Later, Papa found me asleep clutching the family dog and sucking my wrist. Laughable that such silly gestures can be passed from father to child, but there she was—my baby, sucking on her wrist as I did as a child."

So. He never fully believed until that night that he had fathered Anna.

Without speaking, he rose and came around to me. He took me in his arms and held me to him. He did not exactly ask forgiveness, as I had not, but I felt for the first time in years that he was mine again.

CHAPTER 26

At the end of the Civil War, with it's population reduced by at least fifty percent, Galveston looked like the war-ravaged city that it was... It did not remain in that condition for long, however, as former residents made their way back to the island and newcomers arrived in the city on each train and steamer.
– Merri Jane Scheibe, Galveston's First Reconstruction, 1865-1874, Master's Thesis, University of Houston

Summer of 1866

Eliza

A year had come and gone since the war was over. I watched changes taking place as Günter reestablished himself as head of the household. As well he should, but I was increasingly edged to the periphery. I wanted my own home. If Tom and I did not become husband and wife, I would become a burden to Kat and Günter—a maiden aunt, a spinster, a thornback.

Letters came from Mamá. She wrote that they had returned to Galveston, as I must as well.

I read aloud to Kat.

The Union has removed the blockade and reestablished the custom house. A Catholic college is underway and your father's business is back and thriving, so there is no need for you to remain on the desolate frontier.

I have been indisposed lately with lumbago and an
unexplained weakness. Is it too much to ask to see my
only child before I am called before the great dark angel?
(I rolled my eyes). *Upon hearing from you, your father*
will set out to bring you home where you belong. You
will be happy to know that Chloë remains with us as we
have promised her an ungodly amount to retain her.

Thinking Kat would be amused at the extravagance of rhetoric, I caught her eye, but she stood abruptly and turned away. Her eyes luminous with tears, she said, "And Tom's reaction to your leaving for an extended time? I thought you might marry."

"Oh, I admit I miss my family, but I have not agreed to return even though Mamá has asked me often enough to make me feel guilty. It is very likely she is not nearly as ill as she portrays. And Tom? He has not asked me, Katarina. I have mentioned receiving my mother's letter, but he has not offered any comments regarding it. If only he would propose marriage, that would be the end of it. In any case, I need him to step forward if he wants me."

"He does not have the audacity of that young German boy you married. Having lost much, he must be overly cautious if for no other reason than to protect himself. Unlike Wilhelm, he will not sweep you off your feet and carry you to parts unknown before you have a chance to consider the gravity of your decision. Perhaps he fears the luxury of Galveston will seduce you, or he does not trust the old adage that 'absence doth make the heart grow fonder.'"

Memories of my family—the effusiveness of my mother, a trait I once eschewed but now seemed so endearing, and the well-meaning protectiveness of my father—brought tears to my eyes. Our Galveston home itself, the floor-to-ceiling windows, the way light fell across the polished cypress floors. The music room. And although we were on a city street, the gardens of bougainvillea and gardenias and oleanders offered an oasis in the city even in winter—even, I imagined, in the recovery from the war. Despite it all, I wanted my home to be here with Tom.

The next afternoon I prepared to take Legend for a quick trip to Tom's place. I explained to Kat that I finally must force a conversation with him.

"I am relieved," she said. "I thought perhaps you might run away without a promise to return. He loves you, you know."

I smiled. "He's slow to make those affirmations."

"Better ardent action than a mouthful of words."

"Passionate displays don't always reflect genuine feeling. And the Irish have not been known for their reticence."

Kat grinned. "You have made a point, but if I were you, I would have no doubts. Not from what I have seen."

~

I walked up the hill to the spot where Tom would be working on his new house. He had moved the site to a higher knoll that was farther from the creek's water. It gave a better view of sunsets he'd said, and he could get good water from a well he'd already dug. He had hauled the limestone from nearby quarries but had been so diligent in helping during Günter's recovery that he had only finished the first part of his own home.

We stood looking at the work he had done on the house. A small stone building stood not six feet away from the front door.

"So, now you've got a stone outhouse with peepholes?" I nudged him with my elbow and indicated the small rectangular slots in its rock walls.

"The Germans have a word for it, but I can't ever remember what it is. Closest I can come to it is a safe house. Those holes are so you can stick your rifle barrel through in case of attack." A hard look came into his eyes. "I'm gonna be prepared next time."

"Are you never tempted to leave? Find someplace a little closer to civilization. Closer to Galveston maybe?"

"Nope. I need the hills and the solitude, I guess. Anytime I begin thinking about a softer life near those towns on the coast, I wonder if I want to die of yellow fever. Better a Comanche arrow, if you ask me."

I shuddered. "Why, Mamá and Papa have lived along the Gulf most of their lives, and they're just fine." I touched his arm. The light of the setting sun fragmented across the hills, as scattered as my thoughts. "Oh, I'm carrying on about nothing. This is a glorious site."

He must have felt me tense for he turned and held me at arm's length to look into my eyes. "What's wrong? There's something wrong."

"Oh, it's just Mamá. I've told you she's been writing, talking about how well Galveston is recovering from the war."

"So, she'll be wantin' you back then."

"Oh, you know mothers. It's hard for them to let go."

"And I'm supposin' it'd be troubling for a girl to refuse her family."

I couldn't answer. I didn't know myself. I had spent five years here. Five years! What would it mean to go back home and be treated like a child again? For one brief moment, I longed for the luxury. Such a respite might come at a price, but I missed my family and would love to see them once more—perhaps one last time if Tom and I married.

"Of course, I miss them, it's just —"

"Well." Tom stuffed his hands in his pockets and looked out toward the hills. "You should go on then." His words held a final sound. A decisive declaration.

"But I don't have to. Not if—" I waited for him to ask me then. To say, *Don't go. Stay and be my wife.*

But the words were never spoken.

After waiting so long as to be embarrassing, I finally said, "It's going to be lovely, Tom, your home here on the hillside. Beautiful, truly." I smiled up at him, but the moment was gone. What had I said that silenced him?

Then I remembered the few nights I had shared with him, the secret, poignant, desperate nights. Could he not trust me to remember those? Could I believe he had forgotten them?

I turned and walked away to say goodbye to Finn. Oh, Finn would break my heart.

Blame and a glaze of tears flashed in his eyes as he shrugged off my embrace after I told him of my decision. His voice cracked. "I thought—"

"I know, but my mamá needs me back home. Just for a while, you see and—"

The look he threw at me made it clear that he was a child no longer and would not be so easily pacified.

"I'll miss you, Finn," I said.

He turned to walk away but stopped, rushed back, and grabbed me, his fuzzy young beard mixed with tears against my neck. He ran then, without another glance.

Mamá's letters kept coming. Finally, I sent her my answer.

~

On the sixth of October, the letter arrived. Papa would set out the fifteenth, and I was to be ready. He would take a brief stop in Fredericksburg to rest the horses before we started back to Galveston, but there would be no opportunity to linger. Surely, there would not be much to pack, Mamá wrote. *It will be a matter of starting over. I have approached a dressmaker and chosen the fabrics. Oh darling, to see you again!"*

I began to set aside the few things I had brought with me—my wedding ring, which I had put away sometime after Will died.

Books I would leave for Kat and Finn. My best dress was hardly fit for travel but would have to do, though Mamá would be appalled. I thought about the music box that had long ago disappeared with the Comanche—its silly little bird, a trinket really. I had been a child, but it had meant the world to me then. So little to show for these years. Except for these people I had come to love.

Günter and Kat sat in the parlor and stared up at me as I told them that Papa would be arriving within a few days. Günter spoke first. "I will be sad to see you go, Eliza, but I will understand if you choose to remain with your family. I can also understand why Tom may be hesitant to formally declare himself until he is quite certain you will wholeheartedly return."

"I hope he will come to say goodbye, at least. Tomorrow, perhaps." I kept my voice steady as though I were sure he would arrive to kiss me passionately and demand my promise to return to him. Then I saw a glance between Günter and Kat that seemed to deny that possibility. I wanted to ask exactly what they knew that I did not, but instead, I said, "The time will fly. And admit it, you might relish having your home back for just your little family."

"After what we have been through together?" Kat stood and turned her back to me as though she truly believed I would never return. "The war years? Those desperate times? How could—"

Laying my cheek on her shoulder, I wrapped my arms around her and leaned against her. "Forgive me," I whispered. "It breaks my heart to leave you, even for a few months, but Mamá needs me. She writes she is not well."

"You are taking far more than your few possessions, you know."

I nodded and turned away, my eyes to the floor.

~

A storm came that night, brief and vicious, the lightning soul-shaking and blinding. I stood at the window watching the shadows writhe

against the barn, the oak shuddering and then glowing as ball lightning snaked along its branches.

In the exchange of gloom and radiance as the storm faded,
I imagined the Comanche as he had waited for me on that night
a year ago. Terrors existed here. But if you hushed the warning
whispers, if you closed your eyes to the dangers that lurked in the
hills or even in your own home on nights when the moon was full,
if you disregarded the rattle of death in the heat of a summer afternoon, then…oh then, that watercolor sunset could soothe your
fears and nestle into your memories with a serenity never found in
the bustle of a city.

Katarina

What more could I ask of Eliza now? She had stayed by me those
years of the war. Driven me crazy. Saved me. This life was not
what she would have chosen had she not been so infatuated with
that beautiful boy—Wilhelm. I, too, had traipsed after a young,
good-looking man. How could I criticize? Oh, but I hated to see
her go. Finally, after all these five years, she had become a sister
to me, maddening and darling.

It was ten o'clock that morning when the dog set up a fero-
cious ruckus announcing the arrival of the carriage. And quite a
carriage it was, complete with a driver in livery. Eliza put her hand
over her heart and turned to look at me. "It's Papa, isn't it?" Her
eyes shone with regret. Almost panic.

I thought she might change her mind at that point, but she
stepped out onto the porch and walked with outstretched arms to
greet her father just descending from the coach. His gaze passed
over her at first as if he searched for *his* daughter—until recognition lighted his eyes. And he flinched.

He held her to him as he scanned the area. "Not as bad as
I feared, but you must be desperate to come home." His voice

reflected a Northern upbringing, clipped and nasal. When we were introduced, he grimaced when he shook my rough hands, took in my sunburned face, my work dress. That I spoke very practiced, excellent English seemed to surprise him.

"A pleasure, sir," I said, "you must join us for tea."

"Why, yes, you must, Papa. We sweeten with honey from our own bees," Eliza's voice lifted for the first time.

Clearly driven more by curiosity than etiquette, her father allowed me to escort him to the parlor. Brusque and constrained, his entire conversation revolved around cursed reconstructionists and heathen Comanches. He directed his man to hitch Legend to the back of their carriage. "Paid a small fortune for that horse," he said. "I refuse to leave him behind. He's got a good many years left in him."

Eliza excused herself and returned carrying her carpetbag and a parasol I had rarely seen. "I believe I'm ready," she said, but obviously she could find nothing more to say and wanted to run.

Despite my fears of never seeing her again, I wanted to keep us both from crying. "We will be right here when you get back. Maybe you can bring me a pretty piece of fabric to make Anna and me a dress to match? Just if you think about it."

She bent her head and nodded—a frantic gesture.

And then it was over.

Eliza hugged Anna to her, but the child stared in solemn distrust at the stranger and returned to hide behind my skirt. "Where is 'Liza going? When is she coming back? Why is that man taking her away?"

"Don't come out," Eliza said to me as she leaned forward to offer her cheek. It was a throaty whisper. "I don't think I can bear it."

And she was gone. As Legend moved into a trot behind the carriage, he called back once—the only real sound of goodbye.

CHAPTER 27

During the Civil War Union officers feared yellow fever more than Rebel bullets. Two years after the war in 1867, while Texas remained under Union control, the state endured the deadliest yellow fever season in its history.
– Penny Clark, *Yellow Fever,* Texas State Historical Association, Handbook of Texas Online

1867

Eliza

Mamá met us at the front gate. She gripped my arms, then took my face in her hands before sobbing openly and calling for Chloë to help. Once home, I was cosseted. Papa remarked after the first few weeks that Mamá would flat out ruin me, but she exclaimed that "restoration" was not spoiling.

I allowed it all, succumbed to the pampering—luxuriating in the hot baths and creams and buffing of my skin. Chloë set about with an intensity I had seldom seen. "These nasty calluses, Miss Eliza. We gonna do somethin' about dem. And yo hair! Ain't you put a brush to it the whole time you was gone?"

At last, Mamá deemed the repair complete. Despite her "weak spells," she set about planning *soirees*. Girls with whom I had been schooled plagued me with questions. "Is it true you shot a Comanche? That's what your mama told us. And all those

Bavarians! Why, those people don't even speak English. How did you ever survive?"

How could I answer them? They would never understand. I barely comprehended my own experiences. You just summon the courage, I wanted to say to them. But it would have been water off a duck's back to those delicate flowers of the monied class.

At one of Mamá's "evenings," one gentleman, dignified and less solicitous than some of the younger men, seemed to offer a sense of humor and certain steadiness. "This must be quite a change from the frontier," he said. "To come back here after four years—"

"Five."

"Pardon?"

"Five years. I was there five years."

"Ah, yes. Well then, was it a challenge?"

"Quite. But so was the war. For everyone. Why do you ask?"

"Oh, I suppose everyone is curious as to why it has taken so long for you to come back. I am not critical, you understand. I am merely curious as to your reasoning. I, among many, hope you will stay." He bowed slightly as the quartet began to play. "Would you dance?"

I took his arm as we stepped out onto the floor.

He was an accomplished dancer—able to speak eloquently while he glided about the floor. Glancing down at me, he said, "I admire you, you know. Most women, ladies, I guess you might say, would have never agreed to follow even the most devilishly handsome man into those Comanche territories."

Was he mocking me? I stopped dancing and leaned back to study his eyes. "Yes, I was foolish, but it made a woman of me. One I never would have amounted to in these confines of society."

"Challenges present themselves in the 'confines of society,' as well, my dear." Smiling down at me, he picked up the step again and whispered into my ear. "Tasks that can accomplish much."

"Are you throwing down the gauntlet?" I felt a glimmer of the coquette I used to be. I laughed and would not tell him that nothing would make me happier than to return to that frontier, Comanche territory, the hinterlands. Competent not coiffured. Callused not coddled.

~

And then a Mr. T.C. Frost invited Papa to discuss a business operation in San Antonio, and when Mamá declined due to the lumbago, I insisted I go in her stead. "It'll do me good to have a change of scenery."

I thought Chloë would be happy to accompany me, but she complained about the long carriage ride. When I promised her a bonus, however, she put aside any qualms and fussed instead with plans for my wardrobe. "You never know who you might be introduced to, and you better shore up your advantages. Maybe this here Mister Frost ain't married. Maybe he got rich friends. Ain't got but a month's time to get you ready."

A month gave me enough time to beseech Tom to meet me there. Less than half a year had passed, but he would think me changed if he relied on looks alone. I must convince him that nothing that mattered had altered. I intended to give up this Galveston life.

Having written the letter over twice marking out phrases that seemed like pleading, I folded it into the envelope and pressed my seal onto the flap. My hand trembled as I released it into Chloë's hand to post.

Tom's letter came on the second week. Yes, San Antonio, the Menger Hotel dining room. June first. Six in the evening.

Pressing the letter against my heart, I made my plans. Chiding myself for falling back on age-old feminine wiles, I allowed Chloë to "shore up my advantages," but I intended to pack my own bags to return to Fredericksburg with Tom. In them would be the embroidered cotton and silk fabric I bought for Katarina and little Anna.

~

From my hotel room window, I viewed the plaza—its dilapidated buildings and sad remnants of Texas battles. But this old town was where I would join the man I wanted to spend the rest of my life with now. He would be waiting for me. I even imagined a quick wedding and Kat's face when we arrived, husband and wife, at her door. Even if Tom's house was not quite finished, I would be there to help—Tom and Finn and I together.

Even though its yellow fabric had come at a dear price, I had my dress made into a simple, tailored frock. But fussing like a mother around the bride on her wedding day, Chloë brought out the one elaborate costume I had taken to satisfy Papa if I were summoned one evening to meet his business partners. "You sho' will look fine, missy. All coifed and delicate."

"This is a quiet supper with a dear friend, not a gala. I'll wear the yellow dress."

"What you mean?" She stood back with her hands on her hips. "Don't you want that old friend you been talkin' about to see the change in you from that time you come home a regular ragamuffin? Why, he be plumb dumbfounded gettin' to have supper with the likes of you."

"My sweet old Chloë, I am not as much changed from the ragamuffin as you might think. The yellow dress, if you please."

She whisked away the elegant gown. And with snippy little comments, fastened all the buttons up the back of my simpler costume.

I stood facing the mirror and saw a grown woman, no longer the southern belle of my adolescence. I understood my fears and recognized my strengths. I knew what I wanted.

Muttering all the while, Chloë handed me my hat, small and unadorned. I tied it at my throat, nodded to myself in the mirror, and headed to the door. I would not be coy and make him wait.

Having practiced the walk to the dining room a few times, I knew it would take me exactly two minutes, but my heart pounded while I watched clock hands turn to two minutes before six.

Chloë picked up her reticule and made to follow.

"No, not this time," I said. "It will be just Mr. Bailey and me."

"Yo daddy gonna fire me if I let you go meet a man without a proper chaperone."

I snapped on my gloves. "I, my dear Chloë, am twenty-two years old and a widow. My father has far less control over me than he surmises. I'll be in the dining room, so you quit your fussin'." I heard her huff as I closed the door behind me and began the walk down the stairs.

I paused at the entrance to the dining room and searched the guests. Tom stood hat in hand, turning it 'round and 'round by the brim. His shirt was brand new, his shoes polished. With an obviously fresh haircut, a slight nick in the cleft of his chin, he turned to me with that smile I remembered so well. I had to look away for a moment.

Taking a deep breath, I walked toward him, praying my lips did not quiver, or if they did, just enough to reveal what this moment meant to me. "Tom." I stretched out my hands even though I wanted to rush into his arms.

Stunned for a moment, his eyes went to my mouth, my hair, my corseted waist before he remembered to pull out the chair for me. He held it but lingered behind me longer than polite. The faint scent of tobacco, the rough-cut wool of his jacket against my back, the nearness of him. My breath caught.

I stood before he could make it back around to the other side of the table. "Let's walk instead, shall we?" I said. "It's such a lovely day."

He nodded with relief as if sitting would only make him restless. The noise of the town lessened as we crossed the bridge on St. Mary's Street and strolled along the riverbank.

"Well, my goodness." I said, "How have you been? And Finn and Annie-pie and the Kat?"

He smiled at this, but kept walking, meting out quiet, one-word answers.

He's not going to ask me, I thought. It's all going to be up to me. "Tom." I stopped and turned to him, touching his shoulder to keep him from walking on. "Tom!"

He stood there, his hands in his pockets. His gray eyes so solemn and sad he could not meet mine.

I stepped in close to him and kissed his cheek, lingering longer than proper. "It's me, Tom. Why, don't you know me? It's not like you to be so reticent. Heavens, I'd hoped we could—"

"Start where we left off?" The irony in his smile said more than I wanted to comprehend.

"Well, yes, why not? I had to go back to Galveston to see my parents and—"

"Recover from life out in the hills? Not that I blame you. Not one little bit. Life out there gave *me* a chance for a better life away from Ireland, but for you—"

"For me? I thought it might have been for me that you were building your house. For us. Why I *told* you I'd be back. But it had been five years since I'd been home, and my mother needed me. Surely you can understand that." Tears burned behind my eyes. I would not cry. *I would not.* "I long for the solitude of the country. I long for— There's nothing for me in Galveston. I cannot live like that bunch of aging debutantes who have no idea what it takes to survive."

"*If* you survive." He held out his arm for me and covered my hand with his own. "Let's start back. Someone will be askin' for you." He smiled down at me. "We had some times, didn't we?" Taking my hands and turning them over, he said, "These hands, my darlin' girl, are so smooth, so soft." He kissed the upturned palms. "I'll not be the one to rough them up. After a while, you'd come to hate that life."

"Rough hands, sunburned brow—is that what makes you believe a woman is capable? No, Tom! I know what I'm getting into. I—"

He cut me off with a kiss that I would remember for the rest of my life; it was filled with memories of the nights we shared, the hardships and laughter, the short few years we had known each other when we were both so lost.

"I'll not sacrifice another wife or child to the Comanche country," he said. His voice broke. "I'll not do it. I do not doubt *you*. It's me that cannot take the loss." He held my face in his calloused hands for a long moment before he turned and walked away.

I stood there watching, waiting for him to turn back around and say he'd been a fool and had changed his mind. But he turned the corner and was gone.

Katarina

I eagerly awaited Tom's return from San Antonio. Eliza had written me that she would be meeting him there. Had, in fact, packed all she would need in the trunk she told her father was filled with necessary gowns required for elegant evenings in the old city. If Tom said that he wanted her to come back to Fredericksburg, she would never look back toward the city of Galveston.

But when days went by and the young couple had not shown up at our door, I took the wagon out to Tom's place. He heard me arrive but ignored me and continued with his task of wood-splitting. It was not until I touched his arm that he turned to me.

Unshaven and unkempt, he stared at me with dull eyes. "If you've come to ask about the San Antonio trip, you can save your breath. 'Twas a waste of my time." He lifted the ax and delivered a powerful blow, splintering the weathered oak stump.

"What on earth, Tom? You put down that ax and speak to me in a calm manner."

"Nothing to speak about. She's not suited to this life."

"Whatever do you mean? She wrote me more than once about her intention to return. And of late had only waited for encouragement from you. She was packed to join you. What happened to change her mind? Did she explain?"

"Wasn't words that told the story, Katarina. You should have seen her. I'd forgotten how small she was. She reminded me of those china dolls I heard tell of. She couldn't make do out here, not with those delicate hands, that pretty little dress."

"Oh, wait now. Do not assume there is no strength beneath beauty." I studied him a minute more. "It cannot be you really think she is unequal to the task. You know she is. Eliza spent the war years becoming equal to the task. It is *you. You* are the one willing to live a lifetime of regret to escape tragedy. Life is full of tragedy, and it is short. Tom, you go get her!"

He took up his ax again and set the wedge. "I still got crops to harvest. I need to—"

"Da?" Finn who had stood within listening distance came forward. "You told me that she *couldn't* come, that she'd changed her mind. That's not the story I'm hearing now."

"Well, if she came it would be the same story—the same story as your ma and little Eileen. Think you could go through that again? If you're askin' me, I'll not do it."

"So, it'll be you that can't take the chance. Would that be right? And you've no interest in askin' what I might have to say on the subject? I've seen the girl, a woman now, I'm well aware. I knew her when you were gone—when all the men but a wiry tyke like me were off at war. I am here to tell ya, I'd put her up against a Comanche any day. You seen it yourself."

Tom colored at that last remark but picked up the ax and let it slam into the oak log.

"Anyway, she loves us." Finn stood almost even with his father and leveled his eyes at him. "She left for a little while, but I knew she was coming back. Well, she was till you went and broke her heart. Go get her, Da. One of these days, I'm gonna up and leave you. You're gonna need that woman to protect you!"

Smiling, I spoke before turning to go. "Listen to your son, Tom. I think he got that courage and wisdom somewhere."

~

It was a week later when Finn rode up to the house, and my young dog set up a welcoming barrage. Gangly and awkward, still not having come into her own, she galloped out to meet him.

"Any news?" I called from the porch.

"'Tis a fine day when a man comes to his senses." Smiling, Finn stepped down from his horse.

"So, at last, he has gone to get her? It has taken him a week to get up the gumption to go claim her?"

"Yes, ma'am, but he left this morning, soon as it was daylight."

~

But that was the summer of 1867.

Our letters must have crossed in the mail. Eliza had not received mine. Hers was no more than a note.

My dearest Katarina,

By now you must know Tom and I have gone our separate ways. I do feel betrayed. I thought he knew me. Perhaps, one day he will regain belief in me. But I belabor the issue. Regardless, my life is changing irrevocably once again. Yellow fever is assaulting our fair city. Despite Mamá's objection, I volunteer at St.

Mary's Hospital that has more patients than the nuns
can care for. I see now that I should have never left
you all, but now that I have, I am committed to helping
fight this plague. Like the Comanches, this scourge
takes many lives, and it, too, is a brutal death.
    Kiss my darling Annie-pie for me.
                I remain your devoted sister by marriage,
                        Eliza

In the fine penmanship that would define so many of my hours, memories of Eliza would be held together by those few ink lines pressed into parchment.

~

One month later, I wept as I sat under the grape arbor reading in disbelief, the letter from Eliza's mother. She informed me that yellow fever had taken the only sister I would ever have. We faced such difficult times together, survived them, and kept most of them secreted between us. Only she and I would know the truth of those years when our husbands were gone, and our survival depended on each other.

MARY BRYAN STAFFORD

is the author of two previous novels, *A Wasp in the Fig Tree* and *The Last Whippoorwill*. She is also published many times in *The Texas Poetry Calendar* and in the anthology, *Women Write about the Southwest*, winner of the Willa award. She lives with her husband in the Texas Hill Country.

CPSIA information can be obtained
at www.ICGtesting.com
Printed in the USA
JSHW022020181222
35128JS00001B/4